THE FIRST LASER BEAM
CAUGHT THEM UNAWARE

The second laser hit was a high-energy pulse deliberately aimed at the bridge's observation port. It cracked the impact-resistant plastic as easily as a hammer smashes an egg; the air pressure inside the bridge blew the port open. The six men and women became six exploding bodies spewing blood. There was not even time to scream.

Commander Hazard grasped the console's edge with both white-knuckled hands. "You killed six kids," he said, his voice so low that he barely heard it himself. It was not a whisper but a growl. Buckbee's lips moved slightly in what might have been a smile, but his eyes remained cold. "We had to prove that we mean business, Hazard. Now surrender your station or we'll blow you all to hell."

Tor Books by Ben Bova

BEN BOVA

BATTLE STATION

A TOM DOHERTY ASSOCIATES BOOK

BATTLE STATION

Copyright © 1987 by Ben Bova

First printing: October 1987

A TOR Book

Published by Tom Doherty Associates, Inc.
49 West 24 Street
New York, N.Y. 10010

Cover art by Alan Gutierrez

ISBN: 0-812-53202-3
CAN. ED.: 0-812-53203-1

Printed in the United States of America

0 9 8 7 6 5 4 3 2 1

ACKNOWLEDGMENTS

To Mike Gamble, from both of us.

CONTENTS

Foreword

Nobody wants to militarize space, but . . .

The fact is that the military was in space long before anyone else.

The first man-made objects to soar past the Earth's thin shell of atmosphere and enter the pristine domain of space were Nazi Germany's V-2 rockets, in 1944.

World War II ended in the twin mushroom clouds of Hiroshima and Nagasaki. It did not take much imagination to realize that a nuclear weapon riding atop a long-range rocket made a formidable weapon —perhaps the "ultimate" weapon.

But by June of 1947 an eminent team of American scientists led by Dr. Vannevar Bush, of MIT, advised the U.S. government that it would be impossible to build rockets big enough and accurate enough to serve as long-range nuclear-armed missiles.

"I think we can leave that out of our thinking," said the redoubtable Dr. Bush. "In my opinion, such a thing is impossible for many years."

But three months *earlier*, the Soviet government authorized formation of a state commission to examine the feasibility of long-range ballistic missiles. Joseph Stalin told his Kremlin aides that a nuclear-armed missile "could be an effective straitjacket for that noisy shopkeeper, Truman. We must go ahead with it, comrades! The problem of the creation of transcontinental rockets is of extreme importance to us."

By 1949 the Soviets detonated their first atomic bomb. By 1957 they sent the world's first artificial satellite into orbit, announcing to the world that Soviet rockets were large enough and accurate enough to drop a hydrogen bomb on any city in the world.

The military was in space.

Yes, the scientists followed with unmanned spacecraft that eventually explored all the worlds of the solar system, out to Uranus. (And in 1989 *Voyager II* will fly past Neptune, cameras clicking.)

Yes, the first man to set foot on the Moon was a civilian. So was the last man. The ten in between were U.S. Air Force and Navy fliers serving with NASA.

And while we were sending men to the Moon and machines beyond the edge of the solar system, while the United States was developing the space shuttle and the Soviets put a succession of space stations into low orbit around the Earth (two of them are up there now), the military was using the "high ground" of space for its own purposes: communicatons, surveillance, weather observation, navigation, geodesy.

In 1967 the United States and the Soviet Union, together with sixty-one other nations, signed the Outer Space Treaty, which, among other things, bans nuclear weapons from space and guarantees that the Moon will not be used for military purposes.

But weapons have flown in space. The Soviets tested an orbital bombardment system before the ink was dry on the 1967 treaty. And they have developed an operational antisatellite weapon capable of destroying satellites in orbits as high as twelve hundred miles.

Both nations have worked on space-based defenses against that "ultimate" weapon, the hydrogen-bomb-carrying intercontinental ballistic missile (ICBM). The American Strategic Defense Initiative program has received enormous publicity, and has been the center of a raging controversy ever since President Reagan startled the world with his "Star Wars" speech in March 1983. Soviet work in strategic defenses has been much quieter, but equally intense.

Why fortify heaven? Why extend human aggression into space?

You might as well ask, Why have navies? Why have armed fleets steaming in the world's oceans?

Every major nation on Earth maintains a navy to protect its seacoasts and its maritime commerce from enemies, real and potential. Navies and war fleets have been with us for so many millennia that we never hear people say, "Let's keep the oceans free of weaponry! Don't militarize the seas!"

In fact, sometimes it is comforting to know that there are "good guys" out there on the high seas, willing and able to help or protect you if you need it. In a world of hijackers, pirates, and natural emergencies such as hurricanes, disciplined naval personnel can be the difference between life and death.

So it will be with space. If my vision of the future is correct (and it's a vision I share with many men and women, both science fiction people and "mundanes"), much of the human race's next generation of commerce and wealth will be space-based. Where your purse is, there your thieves will be also—small-time thieves such as pirates, and bigger thieves, too. The kind of people who can steal a country probably will not blanch at stealing whole worlds. Or trying to.

Even if you believe that the only legitimate purpose for a nation's armed forces is to protect the nation against attack, it must be admitted that *every square inch of land in the world is open to attack from space.*

ICBMs soar above the atmosphere and dive down on their targets from space.

The military is in space to stay. The question is, Can the competing nations of Earth learn to cooperate enough in this new environment of space so that their military forces can work together to prevent aggression on Earth? Satellites orbit around the whole world; they can be used to protect every nation against attack by any nation or any subnational group.

The answer to that question will determine whether or not the twenty-first century is an era of peace. If it is not, perhaps there is not much of a future for the human race, after all.

But I am an optimist, as those of you who read my collection *Prometheans* know full well. I see the military cooperating in space, evolving into an International Peacekeeping Force that will play the role of an honest cop in orbit and prevent the nations of the world from destroying one another.

The sixteen stories and articles in this book deal with the prospects of war and peace in orbit, together with other glimpses of possible futures. Most of them treat directly with the military aspects of space. Others are devoted to allied facets of the human race's expansion into the solar system.

The nonfiction articles are based on the latest factual information available at the time of their writing, interpreted through my own experiences and opinions. The fiction shows what mere facts cannot: how tomorrow's technology will affect individual human lives.

The great strength of science fiction is that it can show the *human* future, it can deal with the emotions that tomorrow's changes will stir. But without a solid basis in factual science and technology, fiction about the future becomes fantasy and loses its power to prepare us for the real world that awaits us with the next dawn.

In the sixteen works assembled here you will see:

• How an International Peacekeeping Force might actually work—even when betrayed from within.

• How energy projectors firing pinpoint beams of light may spell doom for the "ultimate" weapon.

• How baseball may become a tool of international diplomacy.

• How a new method of generating electrical power could cut your electricity bill in half—and supply the power for space-borne energy beam weapons.

• How computers may one day replace politicians.

• How telephones may become small enough to be implanted in your skull.

• How benign extraterrestrials may have already influenced human history.

• How space stations in orbit will include zero-gravity hospitals—and honeymoon hotels.

Nobody wants the military in space. But they will be there. They are already there. If we are wise, we will see to it that they serve to protect the peace and defend the human race against attack.

As Franklin D. Roosevelt wrote, "The only limits to our realization of tomorrow will be our doubts of today."

—Ben Bova
West Hartford, Conn.
March 1987

Battle Station ═══════════════════

"Where do you get your crazy ideas?"

Every science fiction writer has heard that question, over and over again. Sometimes the questioner is kind enough to leave out the word "crazy." But the question still is asked whenever I give a lecture to any audience that includes people who do not regularly read science fiction.

Some science fiction writers, bored by that same old question (and sometimes miffed at the implications behind that word "crazy"), have taken to answering: "Schenectady!" There's even a mythology about it that claims that members of the Science Fiction Writers of America subscribe to the Crazy Idea Service of Schenectady, New York, and receive in the mail one crazy idea each month—wrapped in plain brown paper, of course.

Yet the question deserves an answer. People are obviously fascinated with the process of creativity. Nearly everybody has a deep curiosity about how a writer comes up with the ideas that generate fresh stories.

For most of the stories and novels I have written over the years, the ideation period is so long and complex that I could not begin to explain—even to myself—where the ideas originally came from.

With "Battle Station," happily, I can trace the evolution of the story from original idea to final draft.

"Battle Station" has its roots in actual scientific research and technological development. In the mid-1960s I was employed at the research laboratory where the first high-power laser was invented. I helped to arrange the first briefing in the Pentagon to inform the Department of Defense that lasers of virtually any power desired could now be developed. That was the first step on the road to what is now called the Strategic Defense Initiative.

My 1976 novel *Millennium* examined, as only science fiction can, the human and social consequences of using lasers in satellites to defend against nuclear missiles. By 1983 the real world had caught up to the idea and President Reagan initiated the "Star Wars" program. In 1984 I published a nonfiction book on the subject, *Assured Survival.* In 1986 a second edition of that book, retitled *Star Peace* and published by Tor Books, brought the swiftly developing story up to date.

Meanwhile, from the mid-1960s to this present day, thinkers such as Maxwell W. Hunter II have been studying the problems and possibilities of an orbital defense system. While most academic critics (and consequently, most of the media) have simply declared such a defense system impossible, undesirable, and too expensive, Max Hunter has spent his time examining how such a system might work, and what it might mean for the world political situation.

I am indebted to Max Hunter for sharing his ideas with me; particularly for the concept of "active armor." I have done violence to his ideas, I know, shaping them to the needs of the story. Such is the way of fiction.

Another concept that is important to this story came from the often-stormy letters column of *Analog* magazine more than twenty years ago. Before the first astronauts and cosmonauts went into space, the readers of *Analog* debated, vigorously, who would make the best candidates for duty aboard orbiting space stations. One of the ideas they kicked around was that submariners— men accustomed to cramped quarters, high tensions, and long periods away from home base—would be ideal for crewing a military space station.

So I "built" a space battle station that controls laser-armed satellites, and placed at its helm Commander J. W. Hazard, U.S. Navy (ret.), a former submarine skipper.

I gave him an international crew, in keeping with the conclusions I arrived at in *Star Peace: Assured Survival*, that the new technology of strategic defense satellites will lead to an International Peacekeeping Force (IPF)—a global police power dedicated to preventing war.

Once these ideas were in place, the natural thing was to test them. Suppose someone tried to subvert the IPF and seize the satellite system for his own nefarious purposes? Okay, make that not merely a political problem, but a personal problem for the story's protagonist: Hazard's son is part of a cabal to overthrow the IPF and set up a world dictatorship.

Now I had a story. All I had to do was start writing and allow the characters to "do their thing."

The *ideas* were the easiest part of the task. As you can see, the ideas were all around me, for more than twenty years. There are millions of good ideas floating through the air all the time. Every day of your life brings a fresh supply of ideas. Every person you know is a walking novel. Every news event contains a dozen ideas for stories.

The really difficult part is turning those ideas into good stories. To bring together the ideas and the characters and let them weave a story—that is the real work of the writer. Very few people ask about that, yet that is the actual process of creativity. It's not tough to find straw. Spinning straw into gold—*that's* the great magical trick!

_____

We should avoid a dependence on satellites for
wartime purposes that is out of proportion to our
ability to protect them. If we make ourselves
dependent upon vulnerable spacecraft for military support, we will have built an Achilles heel
into our forces.

—Dr. Ashton Carter, MIT
April 1984

The key issue then becomes, is our defense capa-
ble of defending itself . . .?
—Maxwell W. Hunter II
Lockheed Missiles and Space Co., Inc.
February 26, 1979

The first laser beam caught them unaware, slicing
through the station's thin aluminum skin exactly
where the main power trunk and air lines fed into the
bridge.

A sputtering fizz of sparks, a moment of heart-
wrenching darkness, and then the emergency dims
came on. The electronics consoles switched to their
internal batteries with barely a microsecond's hesitation, but the air fans sighed to a stop and fell
silent. The four men and two women on duty in the
bridge had about a second to realize they were under
attack. Enough time for the breath to catch in your
throat, for the sudden terror to hollow out your
guts.

The second laser hit was a high-energy pulse deliberately aimed at the bridge's observation port. It
cracked the impact-resistant plastic as easily as a
hammer smashes an egg; the air pressure inside the
bridge blew the port open. The six men and women
became six exploding bodies spewing blood. There
was not even time enough to scream.

The station was named *Hunter*, although only a

handful of its crew knew why. It was not one of the missile-killing satellites, nor one of the sensor-laden observation birds. It was a command-and-control station, manned by a crew of twenty, orbiting some one thousand kilometers high, below the densest radiation zone of the inner Van Allen belt. It circled the Earth in about 105 minutes. By design, the station was not hardened against laser attack. The attackers knew this perfectly well.

Commander Hazard was almost asleep when the bridge was destroyed. He had just finished his daily inspection of the battle station. Satisfied that the youngsters of his crew were reasonably sharp, he had returned to his coffin-sized personal cabin and wormed out of his sweaty fatigues. He was angry with himself.

Two months aboard the station and he still felt the nausea and unease of space adaptation syndrome. It was like the captain of an ocean vessel having seasickness all the time. Hazard fumed inwardly as he stuck another timed-release medication plaster on his neck, slightly behind his left ear. The old one had fallen off. Not that they did much good. His neck was faintly spotted with the rings left by the medication patches. Still his stomach felt fluttery, his palms slippery with perspiration.

Clinging grimly to a handgrip, he pushed his weightless body from the mirrored sink to the mesh sleep cocoon fastened against the opposite wall of his cubicle. He zipped himself into the bag and slipped the terry-cloth restraint across his forehead. Hazard was a bulky, dour man with iron-gray hair still cropped Academy close, a weather-beaten squarish face built around a thrusting spadelike nose, a thin slash of a mouth that seldom smiled, and eyes the color of a stormy sea. Those eyes seemed suspicious of everyone and everything, probing, inquisitory. A closer look showed that they were weary, disappointed with the world and the people in it. Disappointed most of all with himself.

He was just dozing off when the emergency klaxon started hooting. For a disoriented moment he thought he was back in a submarine and something had gone wrong with a dive. He felt his arms pinned by the mesh sleeping bag, as if he had been bound by unknown enemies. He almost panicked as he heard hatches slamming automatically and the terrifying wailing of the alarms. The communications unit on the wall added its urgent shrill to the clamor.

The comm unit's piercing whistle snapped him to full awareness. He stopped struggling against the mesh and unzipped it with a single swift motion, slipping out of the head restraint at the same time.

Hazard slapped at the wall comm's switch. "Commander here," he snapped. "Report."

"Varshni, sir. CIC. The bridge is out. Apparently destroyed."

"Destroyed?"

"All life-support functions down. Air pressure zero. No communications," replied the Indian in a rush. His slightly singsong Oxford accent was trembling with fear. "It exploded, sir. They are all dead in there."

Hazard felt the old terror clutching at his heart, the physical weakness, the giddiness of sudden fear. Forcing his voice to remain steady, he commanded, "Full alert status. Ask Mr. Feeney and Miss Yang to meet me at the CIC at once. I'll be down there in sixty seconds or less."

The *Hunter* was one of nine orbiting battle stations that made up the command-and-control function of the newly created International Peacekeeping Force's strategic defense network. In lower orbits, 135 unmanned ABM satellites armed with multimegawatt lasers and hypervelocity missiles crisscrossed the Earth's surface. In theory, these satellites could destroy thousands of ballistic missiles within five minutes of their launch, no matter where on Earth they rose from.

In theory, each battle station controlled fifteen of the ABM satellites, but never the same fifteen for very long. The battle station's higher orbits were deliberately picked so that the unmanned satellites passed through their field of view as they hurried by in their lower orbits. At the insistence of the fearful politicians of a hundred nations, no ABM satellites were under the permanent control of any one particular battle station.

In theory, each battle station patrolled one ninth of the Earth's surface as it circled the globe. The sworn duty of its carefully chosen international crew was to make certain that any missiles launched from that part of the Earth would be swiftly and efficiently destroyed.

In theory.

The IPF was new, untried except for computerized simulations and war games. It had been created in the wake of the Middle East Holocaust, when the superpowers finally realized that there were people willing to use nuclear weapons. It had taken the destruction of four ancient cities and more than 3 million lives before the superpowers stepped in and forced peace on the belligerents. To make certain that nuclear devastation would never threaten humankind again, the International Peacekeeping Force was created. The Peacekeepers had the power and the authority to prevent a nuclear strike from reaching its targets. Their authority extended completely across the Earth, even to the superpowers themselves.

In theory.

Pulling aside the privacy curtain of his cubicle,

Hazard launched himself down the narrow passageway with a push of his meaty hands against the cool
metal of the bulkheads. His stomach lurched at the
sudden motion and he squeezed his eyes shut for a
moment.

The Combat Information Center was buried deep
in the middle of the station, protected by four levels of
living and working areas plus the station's storage
magazines for water, food, air, fuel for the maneuvering thrusters, power generators, and other equipment.

Hazard fought down the queasy fluttering of his
stomach as he glided along the passageway toward the
CIC. At least he did not suffer the claustrophobia that
affected some of the station's younger crew members.
To a man who had spent most of his career aboard
nuclear submarines, the station was roomy, almost
luxurious.

He had to yank open four airtight hatches along the
short way. Each clanged shut automatically behind
him.

At last Hazard floated into the dimly lit combat
center. It was a tiny, womblike circular chamber, its
walls studded with display screens that glowed a
sickly green in the otherwise darkened compartment.
No desks or chairs in zero gravity; the CIC's work
surfaces were chest-high consoles, most of them covered with keyboards.

Varshni and the Norwegian woman, Stromsen,
were on duty. The little Indian, slim and dark, was
wide-eyed with anxiety. His face shone with perspiration and his fatigues were dark at the armpits and
between his shoulders. In the greenish glow from the
display screens he looked positively ill. Stromsen
looked tense, her strong jaw clenched, her ice-blue
eyes fastened on Hazard, waiting for him to tell her
what to do.

"What happened?" Hazard demanded.

"It simply blew out," said Varshni. "I had just spoken with Michaels and D'Argencour when . . . when . . ." His voice choked off.

"The screens went blank." Stromsen pointed to the status displays. "Everything suddenly zeroed out."

She was controlling herself carefully, Hazard saw, every nerve taut to the point of snapping.

"The rest of the station?" Hazard asked.

She gestured again toward the displays. "No other damage."

"Everybody on full alert?"

"Yes, sir."

Lieutenant Feeney ducked through the hatch, his eyes immediately drawn to the row of burning red malfunction lights where the bridge displays should have been.

"Mother of Mercy, what's happened?"

Before anyone could reply, Susan Yang, the chief communications officer, pushed through the hatch and almost bumped into Feeney. She saw the displays and immediately concluded, "We're under attack!"

"That is impossible!" Varshni blurted.

Hazard studied their faces for a swift moment. They all knew what had happened; only Yang had the guts to say it aloud. She seemed cool and in control of herself. Oriental inscrutability? Hazard wondered. He knew she was third-generation Californian. Feeney's pinched, narrow-eyed face failed to hide the fear that they all felt, but the Irishman held himself well and returned Hazard's gaze without a tremor.

The only sound in the CIC was the hum of the electrical equipment and the soft sighing of the air fans. Hazard felt uncomfortably warm with the five of them crowding the cramped little chamber. Perspiration trickled down his ribs. They were all staring at him, waiting for him to tell them what must be done, to bring order out of the numbing fear and uncertainty that swirled around them. Four youngsters from four different nations, wearing the blue-gray fatigues of the IPF, with colored patches denoting their technical specialties on their left shoulders and the flag of their national origin on their right shoulders.

Hazard said, "We'll have to control the station from here. Mr. Feeney, you are now my Number One; Michaels was on duty in the bridge. Mr. Varshni, get a damage-control party to the bridge. Full suits."

"No one's left alive in there," Varshni whispered.

"Yes, but their bodies must be recovered. We owe them that. And their families." He glanced toward Yang. "And we've got to determine what caused the blowout."

Varshni's face twisted unhappily at the thought of the mangled bodies.

"I want a status report from each section of the station," Hazard went on, knowing that activity was the key to maintaining discipline. "Start with . . ."

A beeping sound made all five of them turn toward the communications console. Its orange demand light blinked for attention in time with the angry beeps. Hazard reached for a handgrip to steady himself as he swung toward the comm console. He noted how easily the youngsters handled themselves in zero gee. For him it still took a conscious, gut-wrenching effort.

Stromsen touched the keyboard with a slender finger. A man's unsmiling face appeared on the screen: light brown hair clipped as close as Hazard's gray, lips pressed together in an uncompromising line. He wore the blue-gray of the IPF with a commander's silver star on his collar.

"This is Buckbee, commander of station *Graham*. I want to speak to Commander Hazard."

Sliding in front of the screen, Hazard grasped the console's edge with both white-knuckled hands. He knew Buckbee only by reputation, a former U.S. Air

Force colonel, from the Space Command until it had been disbanded, but before that he had put in a dozen years with SAC.

"This is Hazard."

Buckbee's lips moved slightly in what might have been a smile, but his eyes remained cold. "Hazard, you've just lost your bridge."

"And six lives."

Unmoved, Buckbee continued as if reading from a prepared script, "We offer you a chance to save the lives of the rest of your crew. Surrender the *Hunter* to us."

"Us?"

Buckbee nodded, a small economical movement. "We will bring order and greatness out of this farce called the IPF."

A wave of loathing so intense that it almost made him vomit swept through Hazard. He realized that he had known all along, with a certainty that had not needed conscious verification, that his bridge had been destroyed by deliberate attack, not by accident.

"You killed six kids," he said, his voice so low that he barely heard it himself. It was not a whisper but a growl.

"We had to prove that we mean business, Hazard. Now surrender your station or we'll blow you all to hell. Any further deaths will be on your head, not ours."

Jonathan Wilson Hazard, captain, U.S. Navy (ret.). Marital status: divorced. Two children: Jonathan, Jr., twenty-six; Virginia Elizabeth, twenty. Served twenty-eight years in U.S. Navy, mostly in submarines. Commanded fleet ballistic-missile submarines *Ohio*, *Corpus Christi*, and *Utah*. Later served as technical advisor to Joint Chiefs of Staff and as naval liaison to NATO headquarters in Brussels. Retired from Navy after hostage crisis in Brussels. Joined International Peacekeeping Force and appointed commander of orbital battle station *Hunter*.

"I can't just hand this station over to a face on a screen," Hazard replied, stalling, desperately trying to think his way through the situation. "I don't know what you're up to, what your intentions are, who you really are."

"You're in no position to bargain, Hazard," said Buckbee, his voice flat and hard. "We want control of your station. Either you give it to us or we'll eliminate you completely."

"Who the hell is 'we'?"

"That doesn't matter."

"The hell it doesn't! I want to know who you are and what you're up to."

Buckbee frowned. His eyes shifted away slightly, as if looking to someone standing out of range of the video camera.

"We don't have time to go into that now," he said at last.

Hazard recognized the crack in Buckbee's armor. It was not much, but he pressed it. "Well, you goddamned well better make time, mister. I'm not handing this station over to you or anybody else until I know what in hell is going on."

Turning to Feeney, he ordered, "Sound general quarters. ABM satellites on full automatic. Miss Yang, contact IPF headquarters and give them a full report of our situation."

"We'll destroy your station before those idiots in Geneva can decide what to do!" Buckbee snapped.

"Maybe," said Hazard. "But that'll take time, won't it? And we won't go down easy, I guarantee you. Maybe we'll take you down with us."

Buckbee's face went white with fury. His eyes glared angrily.

"Listen," Hazard said more reasonably, "you can't expect me to just turn this station over to a face on a screen. Six of my people have been killed. I want to know why, and who's behind all this. I won't deal until I know who I'm dealing with and what your intentions are."

Buckbee growled, "You've just signed the death warrant for yourself and your entire crew."

The comm screen went blank.

For a moment Hazard hung weightlessly before the dead screen, struggling to keep the fear inside him from showing. Putting a hand out to the edge of the console to steady himself, he turned slowly to his young officers. Their eyes were riveted on him, waiting for him to tell them what to do, waiting for him to decide between life and death.

Quietly, but with steel in his voice, Hazard commanded, "I said general quarters, Mr. Feeney. Now!"

Feeney flinched as if suddenly awakened from a dream. He pushed himself to the command console, unlatched the red cover over the "general quarters" button, and banged it eagerly with his fist. The action sent him recoiling upward and he had to put up a hand against the overhead to push himself back down to the deck. The alarm light began blinking red and they could hear its hooting even through the airtight hatches outside the CIC.

"Geneva, Miss Yang," Hazard said sternly, over the howl of the alarm. "Feeney, see that the crew is at their battle stations. I want the satellites under our control on full automatic, prepared to shoot down anything that moves if it isn't in our precleared data bank. And Mr. Varshni, has that damage-control party gotten under way yet?"

The two young men rushed toward the hatch, bumping each other in their eagerness to follow their commander's orders. Hazard almost smiled at the Laurel-and-Hardy aspect of it. Lieutenant Yang pushed herself to the comm console and anchored her softboots on the Velcro strip fastened to the deck there.

"Miss Stromsen, you are the duty officer. I am depending on you to keep me informed of the status of all systems."

"Yes, sir!"

Keep them busy, Hazard told himself. Make them concentrate on doing their jobs and they won't have time to be frightened.

"Encountering interference, sir," reported Yang, her eyes on the comm displays. "Switching to emergency frequency."

Jamming, thought Hazard.

"Main comm antenna overheating," Stromsen said. She glanced down at her console keyboard, then up at the displays again. "I think they're attacking the antennas with lasers, sir. Main antenna out. Secondaries . . ." She shrugged and gestured toward the baleful red lights strung across her keyboard. "They're all out, sir."

"Set up a laser link," Hazard commanded. "They can't jam that. We've got to let Geneva know what's happening."

"Sir," said Yang, "Geneva will not be within our horizon for another forty-three minutes."

"Try signaling the commsats. Topmost priority."

"Yes, sir."

Got to let Geneva know, Hazard repeated to himself. If anybody can help us, they can. If Buckbee's pals haven't put one of their own people into the comm center down there. Or staged a coup. Or already knocked out the commsats. They've been planning this for a long time. They've got it all timed down to the microsecond.

He remembered the dinner, a month earlier, the night before he left to take command of the *Hunter*. I've known about it since then, Hazard said to himself. Known about it but didn't want to believe it. Known about it and done nothing. Buckbee was right. I killed those six kids. I should have seen that the bastards would strike without warning.

It had been in the equatorial city of Belém, where the Brazilians had set up their space launching facility. The IPF was obligated to spread its launches among all its space-capable member nations, so Hazard had been ordered to assemble his crew at Belém for their lift into orbit.

The night before they left, Hazard had been invited to dinner by an old Navy acquaintance who had already put in three months of orbital duty with the Peacekeepers and was on Earthside leave.

His name was Cardillo. Hazard had known him, somewhat distantly, as a fellow submariner, commander of attack boats rather than the missile carriers Hazard himself had captained. Vincent Cardillo had a reputation for being a hard nose who ran an efficient boat, if not a particularly happy one. He had never been really close to Hazard: their chemistries were too different. But this specific sweltering evening in a poorly air-conditioned restaurant in downtown Belém, Cardillo acted as if they shared some old fraternal secret between them.

Hazard had worn his IPF summerweight uniform: pale blue with gold insignia bordered by space black. Cardillo came in casual civilian slacks and a beautifully tailored Italian silk jacket. Through drinks and the first part of the dinner their conversation was light, inconsequential. Mostly reminiscences by two gray-haired submariners about men they had known, women they had chased, sea tales that grew with each retelling. But then:

"Damn shame," Cardillo muttered, halfway through his entrée of grilled eel.

The restaurant, one of the hundreds that had sprung up in Belém since the Brazilians had made the city their major spaceport, was on the waterfront. Outside the floor-to-ceiling windows, the muddy Pará River widened into the huge bay that eventually fed into the Atlantic. Hazard had spent his last day on Earth touring around the tropical jungle on a riverboat. The makeshift shanties that stood on stilts along the twisting mud-brown creeks were giving way to industrial parks and cinderblock housing developments. Air-conditioning was transforming the region from rubber plantations to computerized information services. The smell of cement dust blotted out the fragrance of tropical flowers. Bulldozers clattered in raw clearings slashed from the forest where stark steel frameworks of new buildings rose above the jungle growth. Children who had splashed naked in the brown jungle streams were being rounded up and sent to air-conditioned schools.

"What's a shame?" Hazard asked. "Seems to me these people are starting to do all right for the first time in their lives. The space business is making a lot of jobs around here."

Cardillo took a forkful of eel from his plate. It never got to his mouth.

"I don't mean them, Johnny. I mean us. It's a damn shame about us."

Hazard had never liked being called "Johnny." His family had addressed him as "Jon." His Navy associates knew him as "Hazard" and nothing else. A few very close friends used "J.W."

"What do you mean?" he asked. His own plate was

already wiped clean. The fish and its dark spicy sauce had been marvelous. So had the crisp-crusted bread.

"Don't you feel nervous about this whole IPF thing?" Cardillo asked, trying to look earnest. "I mean, I can see Washington deciding to put boomers like your boats in mothballs, and the silo missiles, too. But the attack subs? Decommission our conventional weapons systems? Leave us disarmed?"

Hazard had not been in command of a missile submarine in more than three years. He had been allowed, even encouraged, to resign his commission after the hostage mess in Brussels.

"If you're not in favor of what the American government is doing, then why did you agree to serve in the Peacekeepers?"

Cardillo shrugged and smiled slightly. It was not a pleasant smile. He had a thin, almost triangular face with a low, creased brow tapering down to a pointed chin. His once-dark hair, now peppered with gray, was thick and wavy. He had allowed it to grow down to his collar. His deep-brown eyes were always narrowed, crafty, focused so intently he seemed to be trying to penetrate through you. There was no joy in his face, even though he was smiling; no pleasure. It was the smile of a gambler, a con artist, a used-car salesman.

"Well," he said slowly, putting his fork back down on the plate and leaning back in his chair, "you know the old saying, 'If you can't beat 'em, join 'em.'"

Hazard nodded, although he felt puzzled. He groped for Cardillo's meaning. "Yeah, I guess playing space cadet up there will be better than rusting away on the beach."

"Playing?" Cardillo's dark brows rose slightly. "We're not playing, Johnny. We're in this for keeps."

"I didn't mean to imply that I don't take my duty to the IPF seriously," Hazard answered.

For an instant Cardillo seemed stunned with surprise. Then he threw his head back and burst into laughter. "Jesus Christ, Johnny," he gasped. "You're so straight-arrow it's hysterical."

Hazard frowned but said nothing. Cardillo guffawed and banged the table with one hand. Some of the diners glanced their way. They seemed to be mostly Americans or Europeans, a few Asians. Some Brazilians, too, Hazard noticed as he waited for Cardillo's amusement to subside. Probably from the capital or Rio.

"Let me in on the joke," Hazard said at last.

Cardillo wiped at his eyes. Then, leaning forward across the table, his grin fading into an intense, penetrating stare, he whispered harshly, "I already told you, Johnny. If we can't avoid being members of the IPF—if Washington's so fucking weak that we've got to disband practically all our defenses—then what we've got to do is take over the Peacekeepers ourselves."

"Take over the Peacekeepers?" Hazard felt stunned at the thought of it.

"Damn right! Men like you and me, Johnny. It's our duty to our country."

"Our country," Hazard reminded him, "has decided to join the International Peacekeeping Force and has encouraged its military officers to obtain commissions in it."

Cardillo shook his head. "That's our stupid goddamn government, Johnny. Not the country. Not the people who really want to *defend* America instead of selling her out to a bunch of fucking foreigners."

"That government," Hazard reminded him, "won a big majority last November."

Cardillo made a sour face. "Ahh, the people. What the fuck do they know?"

Hazard said nothing.

"I'm telling you, Johnny, the only way to do it is to take over the IPF."

"That's crazy."

"You mean if and when the time comes, you won't go along with us?"

"I mean," Hazard said, forcing his voice to remain calm, "that I took an oath to be loyal to the IPF. So did you."

"Yeah, yeah, sure. And what about the oath we took way back when—the one to preserve and protect the United States of America?"

"The United States of America *wants* us to serve in the Peacekeepers," Hazard insisted.

Cardillo shook his head again, mournfully. Not a trace of anger. Not even disappointment. As if he had expected this reaction from Hazard. His expression was that of a salesman who could not convince his stubborn customer of the bargain he was offering.

"Your son doesn't feel the same way you do," Cardillo said.

Hazard immediately clamped down on the rush of emotions that surged through him. Instead of reaching across the table and dragging Cardillo to his feet and punching in his smirking face, Hazard forced a thin smile and kept his fists clenched on his lap.

"Jon Jr. is a grown man. He has the right to make his own decisions."

"He's serving under me, you know." Cardillo's eyes searched Hazard's face intently, probing for weakness.

"Yes," Hazard said tightly. "He told me."

Which was an outright lie.

"Missiles approaching, sir!"

Stromsen's tense warning snapped Hazard out of his reverie. He riveted his attention to the main CIC display screen. Six angry red dots were worming their way from the periphery of the screen toward the center, which marked the location of the *Hunter*.

"Now we'll see if the ABM satellites are working or not," Hazard muttered.

"Links with the ABM sats are still good, sir," Yang reported from her station, a shoulder's width away from Stromsen. "The integral antennas weren't knocked out when they hit the comm dishes."

Hazard gave her a nod of acknowledgment. The two young women could not have looked more different: Yang was small, wiry, dark, her straight black hair cut like a military helmet; Stromsen was willowy yet broad in the beam and deep in the bosom, as blonde as butter.

"Lasers on 324 and 325 firing," the Norwegian reported.

Hazard saw the display lights. On the main screen the six red dots flickered orange momentarily, then winked out altogether.

Stromsen pecked at her keyboard. Alphanumerics sprang up on a side screen. "Got them all while they were still in first-stage burn. They'll never reach us." She smiled with relief. "They're tumbling into the atmosphere. Burn-up within seven minutes."

Hazard allowed himself a small grin. "Don't break out the champagne yet. That's just their first salvo. They're testing to see if we actually have control of the lasers."

It's all a question of time, Hazard knew. But how much time? What are they planning? How long before they start slicing us up with laser beams? We don't have the shielding to protect against lasers. The stupid politicians wouldn't allow us to armor these stations. We're like a sitting duck up here.

"What are they trying to accomplish, sir?" asked Yang. "Why are they doing this?"

"They want to take over the whole defense network.

They want to seize control of the entire IPF."

"That's impossible!" Stromsen blurted.

"The Russians won't allow them to do that," Yang said. "The Chinese and the other members of the IPF will stop them."

"Maybe," said Hazard. "Maybe." He felt a slight hint of nausea ripple in his stomach. Reaching up, he touched the slippery plastic of the medicine patch behind his ear.

"Do you think they could succeed?" Stromsen asked.

"What's important is, do *they* think they can succeed? There are still hundreds of ballistic missiles on Earth. Thousands of hydrogen warheads. Buckbee and his cohorts apparently believe that if they can take control of a portion of the ABM network, they can threaten a nuclear strike against the nations that don't go along with them."

"But the other nations will strike back and order their people in the IPF not to intercept their strikes," said Yang.

"It will be nuclear war," Stromsen said. "Just as if the IPF never existed."

"Worse," Yang pointed out, "because first there'll be a shoot-out on each one of these battle stations."

"That's madness!" said Stromsen.

"That's what we've got to prevent," Hazard said grimly.

An orange light began to blink on the comm console. Yang snapped her attention to it. "Incoming message from the *Graham*, sir."

Hazard nodded. "Put it on the main screen."

Cardillo's crafty features appeared on the screen. He should have been still on leave back on Earth, but instead he was smiling crookedly at Hazard.

"Well, Johnny, I guess by now you've figured out that we mean business."

"And so do we. Give it up, Vince. It's not going to work."

With a small shake of his head Cardillo answered, "It's already working, Johnny boy. Two of the Russian battle stations are with us. So's the *Wood.* The Chinks and Indians are holding out but the European station is going along with us."

Hazard said, "So you've got six of the nine stations."

"So far."

"Then you don't really need *Hunter.* You can leave us alone."

Pursing his lips for a moment, Cardillo replied, "I'm afraid it doesn't work that way, Johnny. We want *Hunter.* We can't afford to have you rolling around like a loose cannon. You're either with us or against us."

"I'm not with you," Hazard said flatly.

Cardillo sighed theatrically. "John, there are twenty other officers and crew on your station . . ."

"Fourteen now," Hazard corrected.

"Don't you think you ought to give them a chance to make a decision about their own lives?"

Despite himself, Hazard broke into a malicious grin. "Am I hearing you straight, Vince? You're asking the commander of a vessel to take a *vote*?"

Grinning back at him, Cardillo admitted, "I guess that was kind of dumb. But you do have their lives in your hands, Johnny."

"We're not knuckling under, Vince. And you've got twenty-some lives aboard the *Graham*, you know. Including your own. Better think about that."

"We already have, Johnny. One of those lives is Jonathan Hazard, Jr. He's right here on the bridge with me. A fine officer, Johnny. You should be proud of him."

A hostage, Hazard realized. They're using Jon Jr. as a hostage.

"Do you want to talk with him?" Cardillo asked.

Hazard nodded.

Cardillo slid out of view and a younger man's face appeared on the screen. Jon Jr. looked tense, strained. This isn't any easier for him than it is for me, Hazard thought. He studied his son's face. Youthful, clear-eyed, a square-jawed honest face. Hazard was startled to realize that he had seen that face before, in his own Academy graduation photo.

"How are you, son?"

"I'm fine, Dad. And you?"

"Are we really on opposite sides of this?"

Jon Jr.'s eyes flicked away for a moment, then turned back to look squarely at his father's. "I'm afraid so, Dad."

"But why?" Hazard felt genuinely bewildered that his son did not see things the way he did.

"The IPF is dangerous," Jon Jr. said. "It's the first step toward a world government. The Third World nations want to bleed the industrialized nations dry. They want to grab all our wealth for themselves. The first step is to disarm us, under the pretense of preventing nuclear war. Then, once we're disarmed, they're going to take over everything—using the IPF as *their* armed forces."

"That's what they've told you," Hazard said.

"That's what I know, Dad. It's true. I know it is."

"And your answer is to take over the IPF and use it as *your* armed forces to control the rest of the world, is that it?"

"Better us than them."

Hazard shook his head. "They're using you, son. Cardillo and Buckbee and the rest of those maniacs; you're in with a bunch of would-be Napoleons."

Jon Jr. smiled pityingly at his father. "I knew you'd say something like that."

Hazard put up a beefy hand. "I don't want to argue with you, son. But I can't go along with you."

"You're going to force us to attack your station."

"I'll fight back."

His son's smile turned sardonic. "Like you did in Brussels?"

Hazard felt it like a punch in his gut. He grunted with the pain of it. Wordlessly he reached out and clicked off the comm screen.

Brussels.

They had thought it was just another one of those endless Easter Sunday demonstrations. A peace march. The Greens, the Nuclear Winter freaks, the Neutralists, peaceniks of one stripe or another. Swarms of little old ladies in their Easter frocks, limping old war veterans, kids of all ages. Teenagers, lots of them. In blue jeans and denim jackets. Young women in shorts and tight T-shirts.

The guards in front of NATO's headquarters complex took no particular note of the older youths and women mixed in with the teens. They failed to detect the hard, calculating eyes and the snub-nosed guns and grenades hidden under jackets and sweaters.

Suddenly the peaceful parade dissolved into a mass of screaming wild people. The guards were cut down mercilessly and the cadre of terrorists fought their way into the main building of NATO headquarters. They forced dozens of peaceful marchers to go in with them, as shields and hostages.

Captain J. W. Hazard, USN, was not on duty that Sunday, but he was in his office nevertheless, attending to some paperwork that he wanted out of the way before the start of business on Monday morning.

Unarmed, he was swiftly captured by the terrorists, beaten bloody for the fun of it, and then locked in a toilet. When the terrorists realized that he was the highest-ranking officer in the building, Hazard was dragged out and commanded to open the security vault where the most sensitive NATO documents were stored.

Hazard refused. The terrorists began shooting hostages. After the second murder Hazard opened the vault for them. Top-secret battle plans, maps showing locations of nuclear weapons, and hundreds of other documents were taken by the terrorists and never found, even after an American-led strike force retook the building in a bloody battle that killed all but four of the hostages.

Hazard stood before the blank comm screen for a moment, his softbooted feet not quite touching the deck, his mind racing.

They've even figured that angle, he said to himself. They know I caved in at Brussels and they expect me to cave in here. Some sonofabitch has grabbed my psych records and come to the conclusion that I'll react the same way now as I did then. Some sonofabitch. And they got my son to stick the knife in me.

The sound of the hatch clattering open stirred Hazard. Feeney floated through the hatch and grabbed an overhead handgrip.

"The crew's at battle stations, sir," he said, slightly breathless. "Standing by for further orders."

It struck Hazard that only a few minutes had passed since he himself had entered the CIC.

"Very good, Mr. Feeney," he said. "With the bridge out, we're going to have to control the station from here. Feeney, take the con. Miss Stromsen, how much time before we can make direct contact with Geneva?"

"Forty minutes, sir," she sang out, then corrected, "Actually, thirty-nine fifty."

Feeney was worming his softboots against the Velcro strip in front of the propulsion-and-control console.

"Take her down, Mr. Feeney."

The Irishman's eyes widened with surprise. "Down, sir?"

Hazard made himself smile. "Down. To the altitude of the ABM satellites. Now."

"Yes, sir." Feeney began carefully pecking out commands on the keyboard before him.

"I'm not just reacting like an old submariner," Hazard reassured his young officers. "I want to get us to a lower altitude so we won't be such a good target for so many of their lasers. Shrink our horizon. We're a sitting duck up here."

Yang grinned back at him. "I didn't think you expected to outmaneuver a laser beam, sir."

"No, but we can take ourselves out of range of most of their satellites."

Most, Hazard knew, but not all.

"Miss Stromsen, will you set up a simulation for me? I want to know how many unfriendly satellites can attack us at various altitudes, and what their positions would be compared to our own. I want a solution that tells me where we'll be safest."

"Right away, sir," Stromsen said. "What minimum altitude shall I plug in?"

"Go right down to the deck," Hazard said. "Low enough to boil the paint off."

"The station isn't built for reentry into the atmosphere, sir!"

"I know. But see how low we can get."

The old submariner's instinct: run silent, run deep. So the bastards think I'll fold up, just like I did at Brussels, Hazard fumed inwardly. Two big differences, Cardillo and friends. Two *very* big differences. In Brussels the hostages were civilians, not military men and women. And in Brussels I didn't have any weapons to fight back with.

He knew the micropuffs of thrust from the maneuvering rockets were hardly strong enough to be felt, yet Hazard's stomach lurched and heaved suddenly.

"We have retro burn," Feeney said. "Altitude decreasing."

My damned stomach's more sensitive than his instruments, Hazard grumbled to himself.

"Incoming message from *Graham*, sir," said Yang.

"Ignore it."

"Sir," Yang said, turning slightly toward him, "I've been thinking about the minimum altitude we can achieve. Although the station is not equipped for atmospheric reentry, we do carry the four emergency evacuation spacecraft and they *do* have heat shields."

"Are you suggesting we abandon the station?"

"Oh, no, sir! But perhaps we could move the spacecraft to a position where they would be between us and the atmosphere. Let their heat shields protect us—sort of like riding a surfboard."

Feeney laughed. "Trust a California girl to come up with a solution like that!"

"It might be a workable idea," Hazard said. "I'll keep it in mind."

"We're being illuminated by a laser beam," Stromsen said tensely. "Low power—so far."

"They're tracking us."

Hazard ordered, "Yang, take over the simulation problem. Stromsen, give me a wide radar sweep. I want to see if they're moving any of their ABM satellites to counter our maneuver."

"I have been sweeping, sir. No satellite activity yet."

Hazard grunted. Yet. She knows that all they have

to do is maneuver a few of their satellites to higher orbits and they'll have us in their sights.

To Yang he called, "Any response from the commsats?"

"No, sir," she replied immediately. "Either their laser receptors are not functioning or the satellites themselves are inoperative."

They couldn't have knocked out the commsats altogether, Hazard told himself. How would they communicate with one another? Cardillo claims the *Wood* and two of the Soviet stations are on their side. And the Europeans. He put a finger to his lips unconsciously, trying to remember Cardillo's exact words. *The Europeans are going along with us.* That's what he said. Maybe they're not actively involved in this. Maybe they're playing a wait-and-see game.

Either way, we're alone. They've got four, maybe five, out of the nine battle stations. We can't contact the Chinese or Indians. We don't know which Russian satellite hasn't joined in with them. It'll be more than a half hour before we can contact Geneva, and even then what the hell can they do?

Alone. Well, it won't be for the first time. Submariners are accustomed to being on their own.

"Sir," Yang reported, "the *Wood* is still trying to reach us. Very urgent, they're saying."

"Tell them I'm not available but you will record their message and personally give it to me." Turning to the Norwegian lieutenant, "Miss Stromsen, I want all crew members in their pressure suits. And levels one and two of the station are to be abandoned. No one above level three except the damage-control team. We're going to take some hits and I want everyone protected as much as possible."

She nodded and glanced at the others. All three of them looked tense, but not afraid. The fear was there, of course, underneath. But they were in control of themselves. Their eyes were clear, their hands steady.

"Should I have the air pumped out of levels one and two—after they're cleared of personnel?"

"No," Hazard said. "Let them outgas when they're hit. Might fool the bastards into thinking they're doing more damage than they really are."

Feeney smiled weakly. "Sounds like the boxer who threatened to bleed all over his opponent."

Hazard glared at him. Stromsen took up the headset from her console and began issuing orders into the pin-sized microphone.

"The computer simulation is finished, sir," said Yang.

"Put it on my screen here."

He studied the graphics for a moment, sensing Feeney peering over his shoulder. Their safest altitude was the lowest, where only six ABM satellites could "see" them. The fifteen laser-armed satellites under their own control would surround them like a cavalry escort.

"There it is, Mr. Feeney. Plug that into your navigation program. That's where we want to be."

"Aye, sir."

The CIC shuddered. The screens dimmed for a moment, then came back to their full brightness.

"We've been hit!" Stromsen called out.

"Where? How bad?"

"Just aft of the main power generator. Outer hull ruptured. Storage area eight—medical, dental, and food-supplement supplies."

"So they got the Band-Aids and vitamin pills," Yang joked shakily.

"But they're going after the power generator," said Hazard. "Any casualties?"

"No, sir," reported Stromsen. "No personnel stationed there during general quarters."

He grasped Feeney's thin shoulder. "Turn us over,

man. Get that generator away from their beams!"

Feeney nodded hurriedly and flicked his stubby fingers across his keyboard. Hazard knew it was all in his imagination, but his stomach rolled sickeningly as the station rotated.

Hanging grimly to a handgrip, he said, "I want each of you to get into your pressure suits, starting with you, Miss Stromsen. Yang, take over her console until she . . ."

The chamber shook again. Another hit.

"Can't we strike back at them?" Stromsen cried.

Hazard asked, "How many satellites are firing at us?"

She glanced at her display screens. "It seems to be only one—so far."

"Hit it."

Her lips curled slightly in a Valkyrie's smile. She tapped out commands on her console and then leaned on the final button hard enough to lift her boots off the Velcro.

"Got him!" Stromsen exulted. "That's one laser that won't bother us again."

Yang and Feeney were grinning. Hazard asked the communications officer, "Let me hear what the *Graham* has been saying."

It was Buckbee's voice on the tape. "Hazard, you are not to attempt to change your orbital altitude. If you don't return to your original altitude immediately, we will fire on you."

"Well, they know by now that we're not paying attention to them," Hazard said to his three young officers. "If I know them, they're going to take a few minutes to think things over, especially now that we've shown them we're ready to hit back. Stromsen, get into your suit. Feeney, you're next, then Yang. Move!"

It took fifteen minutes before the three of them were back in the CIC inside the bulky space suits, flexing gloved fingers, glancing about from inside the helmets. They all kept their visors up, and Hazard said nothing about it. Difficult enough to work inside the damned suits, he thought. They can snap the visors down fast enough if it comes to that.

The compact CIC became even more crowded. Despite decades of research and development, the space suits still bulked nearly twice as large as an unsuited person.

Suddenly Hazard felt an overpowering urge to get away from the CIC, away from the tension he saw in their young faces, away from the sweaty odor of fear, away from the responsibility for their lives.

"I'm going for my suit," he said, "and then a fast inspection tour of the station. Think you three can handle things on your own for a few minutes?"

Three heads bobbed inside their helmets. Three voices chorused, "Yes, sir."

"Fire on any satellite that fires at us," he commanded. "Tape all incoming messages. If there's any change in their tune, call me on the intercom."

"Yes, sir."

"Feeney, how long until we reach our final altitude?"

"More than an hour, sir."

"No way to move her faster?"

"I could get outside and push, I suppose."

Hazard grinned at him. "That won't be necessary, Mr. Feeney." Not yet, he added silently.

Pushing through the hatch into the passageway, Hazard saw that there was one pressure suit hanging on its rack in the locker just outside the CIC hatch. He passed it and went to his personal locker and his own suit. It's good to leave them on their own for a while, he told himself. Build up their confidence. But he knew that he had to get away from them, even if only for a few minutes.

His personal space suit smelled of untainted plastic and fresh rubber, like a new car. As Hazard squirmed into it, its joints felt stiff—or maybe it's me, he thought. The helmet slipped from his gloved hands and went spinning away from him, floating off like a severed head. Hazard retrieved it and pulled it on. Like the youngsters, he kept the visor open.

His first stop was the bridge. Varshni was hovering in the companionway just outside the airtight hatch that sealed off the devastated area. Two other space-suited men were zippering an unrecognizably mangled body into a long black-plastic bag. Three other bags floated alongside them, already filled and sealed.

Even inside a pressure suit, the Indian seemed small, frail, like a skinny child. He was huddled next to the body bags, bent over almost into a fetal position. There were tears in his eyes. "These are all we could find. The two others must have been blown out of the station completely."

Hazard put a gloved hand on the shoulder of his suit.

"They were my friends," Varshni said.

"It must have been painless," Hazard heard himself say. It sounded stupid.

"I wish I could believe that."

"There's more damage to inspect, over by the power generator area. Is your team nearly finished here?"

"Another few minutes, I think. We must make certain that all the wiring and air lines have been properly sealed off."

"They can handle that themselves. Come on, you and I will check it out together."

"Yes, sir." Varshni spoke into his helmet microphone briefly, then straightened up and tried to smile. "I am ready, sir."

The two men glided up a passageway that led to the outermost level of the station, Hazard wondering what would happen if a laser attack hit the area while they were in it. Takes a second or two to slice the hull open, he thought. Enough time to flip your visor down and grab on to something before the air blowout sucks you out of the station. Still, he slid his visor down and ordered Varshni to do the same. He was only mildly surprised when the Indian replied that he already had.

Wish the station were shielded. Wish they had designed it to withstand attack. Then he grumbled inwardly, Wishes are for losers; winners use what they have. But the thought nagged at him. What genius put the power generator next to the unarmored hull? Damned politicians wouldn't allow shielding; they *wanted* the stations to be vulnerable. A sign of goodwill, as far as they're concerned. They thought nobody would attack an unshielded station because the attacker's station is also unshielded. We're all in this together, try to hurt me and I'll hurt you. A hangover from the old mutual-destruction kind of dogma. Absolute bullshit.

There ought to be some way to protect ourselves from lasers. They shouldn't put people up here like sacrificial lambs.

Hazard glanced at Varshni, whose face was hidden behind his helmet visor. He thought of his son. Sheila had ten years to poison his mind against me. Ten years. He wanted to hate her for that, but he found that he could not. He had been a poor husband and a worse father. Jon Jr. had every right to loathe his father. But dammit, this is more important than family arguments! Why can't the boy see what's at stake here? Just because he's sore at his father doesn't mean he has to take total leave of his senses.

They approached a hatch where the red warning light was blinking balefully. They checked the hatch behind them, made certain it was airtight, then used the wall-mounted keyboard to start the pumps that would evacuate that section of the passageway, turning it into an elongated air lock.

Finally they could open the farther hatch and glide into the wrecked storage magazine.

Hazard grabbed a handhold. "Better use tethers here," he said.

Varshni had already unwound the tether from his waist and clipped it to a hold.

It was a small magazine, little more than a closet. In the light from their helmet lamps, they saw cartons of pharmaceuticals securely anchored to the shelves with toothed plastic straps. A gash had been torn in the hull, and through it Hazard could see the darkness of space. The laser beam had penetrated into the cartons and shelving, slicing a neat burned-edge slash through everything it touched.

Varshni floated upward toward the rent. It was as smooth as a surgeon's incision, and curled back slightly where the air pressure had pushed the thin metal outward in its rush to escape to vacuum.

"No wiring here," Varshni's voice said in Hazard's helmet earphones. "No plumbing either. We were fortunate."

"They were aiming for the power generator."

The Indian pushed himself back down toward Hazard. His face was hidden behind the visor. "Ah, yes, that is an important target. We were *very* fortunate that they missed."

"They'll try again," Hazard said.

"Yes, of course."

"Commander Hazard!" Yang's voice sounded urgent. "I think you should hear the latest message from *Graham*, sir."

Nodding unconsciously inside his helmet, Hazard said, "Patch it through."

He heard a click, then Buckbee's voice. "Hazard, we've been very patient with you. We're finished playing games. You bring the *Hunter* back to its normal altitude and surrender the station to us or we'll slice you to pieces. You've got five minutes to answer."

The voice shut off so abruptly that Hazard could picture Buckbee slamming his fist against the Off key.

"How long ago did this come through?"

"Transmission terminated thirty seconds ago, sir," said Yang.

Hazard looked down at Varshni's slight form. He knew that Varshni had heard the ultimatum just as he had. He could not see the Indian's face, but the slump of his shoulders told him how Varshni felt.

Yang asked, "Sir, do you want me to set up a link with *Graham*?"

"No," said Hazard.

"I don't think they intend to call again, sir," Yang said. "They expect you to call them."

"Not yet," he said. He turned to the wavering form beside him. "Better straighten up, Mr. Varshni. There's going to be a lot of work for you and your damage-control team to do. We're in for a rough time."

Ordering Varshni back to his team at the ruins of the bridge, Hazard made his way toward the CIC. He spoke into his helmet mike as he pulled himself along the passageways, hand over hand, as fast as he could go:

"Mr. Feeney, you are to fire at any satellites that fire on us. And at any ABM satellites that begin maneuvering to gain altitude so they can look down on us. Understand?"

"Understood, sir!"

"Miss Stromsen, I believe the fire-control panel is part of your responsibility. You will take your orders from Mr. Feeney."

"Yes, sir."

"Miss Yang, I want that simulation of our position and altitude updated to show exactly which ABM satellites under hostile control are in a position to fire upon us."

"I already have that in the program, sir."

"Good. I want our four lifeboats detached from the station and placed in positions where their heat shields can intercept incoming laser beams."

For the first time, Yang's voice sounded uncertain. "I'm not sure I understand what you mean, sir."

Hazard was sweating and panting with the exertion of hauling himself along the passageway. This suit won't smell new anymore, he thought.

To Yang he explained, "We can use the lifeboats' heat shields as armor to absorb or deflect incoming laser beams. Not just shielding, but *active* armor. We can move the boats to protect the most likely areas for laser beams to come from."

"Like the goalie in a hockey game!" Feeney chirped. "Cutting down the angles."

"Exactly."

By the time he reached the CIC they were already working the problems. Hazard saw that Stromsen had the heaviest work load: all the station systems' status displays, fire control for the laser-armed ABM satellites, and control of the lifeboats now hovering dozens of meters away from the station.

"Miss Stromsen, please transfer the fire-control responsibility to Mr. Feeney."

The expression on her strong-jawed face, half hidden inside her helmet, was pure stubborn indignation.

Jabbing a gloved thumb toward the lightning-slash insignia on the shoulder of Feeney's suit, Hazard said,

"He *is* a weapons specialist, after all."

Stromsen's lips twitched slightly and she tapped at the keyboard to her left; the fire-control displays disappeared from the screens above it, only to spring up on screens in front of Feeney's position.

Hazard nodded as he lifted his own visor. "Okay, now. Feeney, you're the offense. Stromsen, you're the defense. Miss Yang, your job is to keep Miss Stromsen continuously advised as to where the best placement of the lifeboats will be."

Yang nodded, her dark eyes sparkling with the challenge. "Sir, you can't possibly expect us to predict all the possible paths a beam might take and get a lifeboat's heat shield in place soon enough . . ."

"I expect—as Lord Nelson once said—each of you to do your best. Now get Buckbee or Cardillo or whoever on the horn. I'm ready to talk to them."

It took a few moments for the communications laser to lock onto the distant *Graham*, but when Buckbee's face finally appeared on the screen, he was smiling—almost gloating.

"You've still got a minute and a half, Hazard. I'm glad you've come to your senses before we had to open fire on you."

"I'm only calling to warn you: any satellite that fires on us will be destroyed. Any satellite that maneuvers to put its lasers in a better position to hit us will also be destroyed."

Buckbee's jaw dropped open. His eyes widened.

"I've got fifteen ABM satellites under my control," Hazard continued, "and I'm going to use them."

"You can't threaten us!" Buckbee sputtered. "We'll wipe you out!"

"Maybe. Maybe not. I intend to fight until the very last breath."

"You're crazy, Hazard!"

"Am I? Your game is to take over the whole defense

system and threaten a nuclear-missile strike against any nation that doesn't go along with you. Well, if your satellites are exhausted or destroyed, you won't be much of a threat to anybody, will you? Try impressing the Chinese with a beat-up network. They've got enough missiles to wipe out Europe and North America, and they'll use them. If you don't have enough left to stop those missiles, then who's threatening whom?"

"You can't . . ."

"Listen!" Hazard snapped. "How many of your satellites will be left by the time you overcome us? How much of a hole will we rip in your plans? Geneva will be able to blow you out of the sky with ground-launched missiles by the time you're finished with us."

"They'd never do such a thing."

"Are you sure?"

Buckbee looked away from Hazard, toward someone off-camera. He moved off, and Cardillo slid into view. He was no longer smiling.

"Nice try, Johnny, but you're bluffing and we both know it. Give up now or we're going to have to wipe you out."

"You can try, Vince. But you won't win."

"If we go, your son goes with us," Cardillo said.

Hazard forced his voice to remain level. "There's nothing I can do about that. He's a grown man. He's made his choice."

Cardillo huffed out a long, impatient sigh. "All right, Johnny. It was nice knowing you."

Hazard grimaced. Another lie, he thought. The man must be categorically unable to speak the truth.

The comm screen blanked.

"Are the lifeboats in place?" he asked.

"As good as we can get them," Yang said, her voice doubtful.

"Not too far from the station," Hazard warned. "I don't want them to show up as separate blips on their radar."

"Yes, sir, we know."

He nodded at them. Good kids, he thought. Ready to fight it out on my say-so. How far will they go before they crack? How much damage can we take before they scream to surrender?

They waited. Not a sound in the womb-shaped chamber, except for the hum of the electrical equipment and the whisper of air circulation. Hazard glided to a position slightly behind the two women. Feeney can handle the counterattack, he said to himself. That's simple enough. It's the defense that's going to win or lose for us.

On the display screens he saw the positions of the station and the hostile ABM satellites. Eleven of them in range. Eleven lines straight as laser beams converged on the station. Small orange blips representing the four lifeboats hovered around the central pulsing yellow dot that represented the station. The orange blips blocked nine of the converging lines. Two others passed between the lifeboat positions and reached the station itself.

"Miss Stromsen," Hazard said softly.

She jerked as if a hot needle had been stuck into her flesh.

"Easy now," Hazard said. "All I want to tell you is that you should be prepared to move the lifeboats to intercept any beams that are getting through."

"Yes, sir, I know."

Speaking as soothingly as he could, Hazard went on, "I doubt that they'll fire all eleven lasers at us at once. And as our altitude decreases, there will be fewer and fewer of their satellites in range of us. We have a good chance of getting through this without too much damage."

Stromsen turned her whole space-suited body so that she could look at him from inside her helmet. "It's good of you to say so, sir. I know you're trying to cheer us up, and I'm certain we all appreciate it. But you are taking my attention away from the screens."

Yang giggled, whether out of tension or actual humor at Stromsen's retort, Hazard could not tell.

Feeney sang out, "I've got a satellite climbing on us!"

Before Hazard could speak, Feeney's hands were moving on his console keyboard. "Our beasties are now programmed for automatic, but I'm tapping in a backup manually, just in—ah! Got her! Scratch one enemy."

Smiles all around. But behind his grin, Hazard wondered, Can they gin up decoys? Something that gives the same radar signature as an ABM satellite but really isn't? I don't think so—but I don't know for sure.

"Laser beam . . . two of them," called Stromsen.

Hazard saw the display screen light up. Both beams were hitting the same lifeboat. Then a third beam from the opposite direction lanced out.

The station shuddered momentarily as Stromsen's fingers flew over her keyboard and one of the orange dots shifted slightly to block the third beam.

"Where'd it hit?" he asked the Norwegian as the beams winked off.

"Just aft of the emergency oxygen tanks, sir."

Christ, Hazard thought, if they hit the tanks, enough oxygen will blow out of here to start us spinning like a top.

"Vent the emergency oxygen."

"Vent it, sir?"

"Now!"

Stromsen pecked angrily at the keyboard to her left. "Venting. Sir."

"I don't want that gas spurting out and acting like a rocket thruster," Hazard explained to her back. "Besides, it's an old submariner's trick to let the attacker think he's caused real damage by jettisoning junk."

If any of them had reservations about getting rid of their emergency oxygen, they kept them quiet.

There was plenty of junk to jettison, over the next quarter of an hour. Laser beams struck the station repeatedly, although Stromsen was able to block most of the beams with the heat-shielded lifeboats. Still, despite the mobile shields, the station was being slashed apart, bit by bit. Chunks of the outer hull ripped away, clouds of air blowing out of the upper level to form a brief fog around the station before dissipating into the vacuum of space. Cartons of supplies, pieces of equipment, even spare space suits, went spiraling out, pushed by air pressure as the compartments in which they had been housed were ripped apart by the probing incessant beams of energy.

Feeney struck back at the ABM satellites, but for every one he hit, another maneuvered into range to replace it.

"I'm running low on fuel for the lasers," he reported.

"So must they," said Hazard, trying to sound calm.

"Aye, but they've got a few more than fifteen to play with."

"Stay with it, Mr. Feeney. You're doing fine." Hazard patted the shoulder of the Irishman's bulky suit. Glancing at Stromsen's status displays, he saw rows of red lights glowering like accusing eyes. *They're taking the station apart, piece by piece. It's only a matter of time before we're finished.*

Aloud, he announced, "I'm going to check with the damage-control party. Call me if anything unusual happens."

Yang quipped, "How do you define 'unusual,' sir?"

Stromsen and Feeney laughed. Hazard wished he could, too. He made a grin for the Chinese American, thinking, At least their morale hasn't cracked. Not yet.

The damage-control party was working on level three, reconnecting a secondary power line that ran along the overhead through the main passageway. A laser beam had burned through the deck of the second level and severed the line, cutting power to the station's main computer. A shaft of brilliant sunlight lanced down from the outer hull through two levels of the station and onto the deck of level three.

One space-suited figure was dangling upside down halfway through the hole in the overhead, splicing cable carefully with gloved hands, while a second hovered nearby with a small welding torch. Two more were working farther down the passageway, where a larger hole had been burned halfway down the bulkhead.

Through that jagged rip Hazard could see clear out to space and the rim of the Earth, glaring bright with swirls of white clouds.

He recognized Varshni by his small size even before he could see the Indian flag on his shoulder or read the name stenciled on the front of his suit.

"Mr. Varshni, I want you and your crew to leave level three. It's getting too dangerous here."

"But, sir," Varshni protested, "our duty is to repair damage."

"There'll be damage on level four soon enough."

"But the computer requires power."

"It can run on its internal batteries."

"But for how long?"

"Long enough," said Hazard grimly.

Varshni refused to be placated. "I am not risking lives unnecessarily, sir."

"I didn't say you were."

"I am operating on sound principles," the Indian insisted, "exactly as required in the book of regulations."

"I'm not faulting you, man. You and your crew have done a fine job."

The others had stopped their work. They were watching the exchange between their superior and the station commander.

"I have operated on the principle that lightning does not strike twice in the same place. In old-fashioned naval parlance this is referred to, I believe, as 'chasing salvos.'"

Hazard stared at the diminutive Indian. Even inside the visored space suit, Varshni appeared stiff with anger. Chasing salvos—that's what a little ship does when it's under attack by a bigger ship: run to where the last shells splashed, because it's pretty certain that the next salvo won't hit there. I've insulted his abilities, Hazard realized. And in front of his team. Damned fool!

"Mr. Varshni," Hazard explained slowly, "this battle will be decided, one way or the other, in the next twenty minutes or so. You and your team have done an excellent job of keeping damage to a minimum. Without you, we would have been forced to surrender."

Varshni seemed to relax a little. Hazard could sense his chin rising a notch inside his helmet.

"But the battle is entering a new phase," Hazard went on. "Level three is now vulnerable to direct laser damage. I can't afford to lose you and your team at this critical stage. Moreover, the computer and the rest of the most sensitive equipment are on level four and in the Combat Information Center. Those are the areas that need our protection and those are the areas where I want you to operate. Is that understood?"

A heartbeat's hesitation. Then Varshni said, "Yes, of course, sir. I understand. Thank you for explaining it to me."

"Okay. Now finish your work here and then get down to level four."

"Yes, sir."

Shaking his head inside his helmet, Hazard turned and pushed himself toward the ladderway that led down to level four and the CIC.

A blinding glare lit the passageway and he heard screams of agony. Blinking against the burning afterimage, Hazard turned to see Varshni's figure almost sliced in half. A dark burn line slashed diagonally across the torso of his space suit. Tiny globules of blood floated out from it. The metal overhead was blackened and curled now. A woman was screaming. She was up by the overhead, thrashing wildly with pain, her backpack ablaze. The other technician was nowhere to be seen.

Hazard rushed to the Indian while the other two members of the damage-control team raced to their partner and sprayed extinguisher foam on her backpack.

Over the woman's screams he heard Varshni's gargling whisper. "It's no use, sir . . . no use . . ."

"You did fine, son." Hazard held the little man in his arms. "You did fine."

He felt the life slip away. Lightning does strike in the same place, Hazard thought. You've chased your last salvo, son.

Both the man and the woman who had been working on the power cable had been wounded by the laser beam. The man's right arm had been sliced off at the elbow, the woman badly burned in the back when her life-support pack exploded. Hazard and the two remaining damage-control men carried them to the sick bay, where the station's one doctor was already working over three other casualties.

The sick bay was on the third level. Hazard realized how vulnerable that was. He made his way down to the CIC, at the heart of the station, knowing that it was protected not only by layers of metal but by human flesh as well. The station rocked again and Hazard heard the ominous groaning of tortured metal as he pushed weightlessly along the ladderway.

He felt bone-weary as he opened the hatch and floated into the CIC. One look at the haggard faces of his three young officers told him that they were on the edge of defeat as well. Stromsen's status display board was studded with glowering red lights.

"This station is starting to resemble a piece of Swiss cheese," Hazard quipped lamely as he lifted the visor of his helmet.

No one laughed. Or even smiled.

"Varshni bought it," he said, taking up his post between Stromsen and Feeney.

"We heard it," said Yang.

Hazard looked around the CIC. It felt stifling hot, dank with the smell of fear.

"Mr. Feeney," he said, "discontinue all offensive operations."

"Sir?" The Irishman's voice squeaked with surprise.

"Don't fire back at the sonsofbitches," Hazard snapped. "Is that clear enough?"

Feeney raised his hands up above his shoulders, like a croupier showing that he was not influencing the roulette wheel.

"Miss Stromsen, when the next laser beam is fired at us, shut down the main power generator. Miss Yang, issue instructions over the intercom that all personnel are to place themselves on level four —except for the sick bay. No one is to use the intercom. That is an order."

Stromsen asked, "The power generator . . . ?"

"We'll run on the backup fuel cells and batteries. They don't make so much heat."

There were more questions in Stromsen's eyes, but she turned back to her consoles silently.

Hazard explained, "We are going to run silent. Buckbee, Cardillo, and company have been pounding the hell out of us for about half an hour. They have inflicted considerable damage. However, they don't know that we've been able to shield ourselves with the lifeboats. They think they've hurt us much more than they actually have."

"You want them to think that they've finished us off, then?" asked Feeney.

"That's right. But, Mr. Feeney, let me ask you a hypothetical question . . ."

The chamber shook again and the screens dimmed, then came back to their normal brightness.

Stromsen punched a key on her console. "Main generator off, sir."

Hazard knew it was his imagination, but the screens seemed to become slightly dimmer.

"Miss Yang?" he asked.

"All personnel have been instructed to move down to level four and stay off the intercom."

Hazard nodded, satisfied. Turning back to Feeney, he resumed, "Suppose, Mr. Feeney, that you are in command of *Graham*. How would you know that you've knocked out *Hunter*?"

Feeney absently started to stroke his chin and bumped his fingertips against the rim of his helmet instead. "I suppose . . . if *Hunter* stopped shooting back, and I couldn't detect any radio emissions from her . . ."

"And infrared!" Yang added. "With the power generator out, our infrared signature goes way down."

"We appear to be dead in the water," said Stromsen.

"Right."

"But what does it gain us?" Yang asked.

"Time," answered Stromsen. "In another ten minutes or so we'll be within contact range of Geneva."

Hazard patted the top of her helmet. "Exactly. But more than that. We get them to stop shooting at us. We save the wounded up in the sick bay."

"And ourselves," said Feeney.

"Yes," Hazard admitted. "And ourselves."

For long moments they hung weightlessly, silent, waiting, hoping.

"Sir," said Yang, "a query from *Graham*, asking if we surrender."

"No reply," Hazard ordered. "Maintain complete silence."

The minutes stretched. Hazard glided to Yang's comm console and taped a message for Geneva, swiftly outlining what had happened.

"I want that tape compressed into a couple of milliseconds and burped by the tightest laser beam we have down to Geneva."

Yang nodded. "I suppose the energy surge for a low-power communications laser won't be enough for them to detect."

"Probably not, but it's a chance we'll have to take. Beam it at irregular intervals as long as Geneva is in view."

"Yes, sir."

"Sir!" Feeney called out. "Looks like *Graham*'s detached a lifeboat."

"Trajectory analysis?"

Feeney tapped at his navigation console. "Heading for us," he reported.

Hazard felt his lips pull back in a feral grin.

"They're coming over to make sure. Cardillo's an old submariner; he knows all about running silent. They're sending over an armed party to make sure we're finished."

"And to take control of our satellites," Yang suggested.

Hazard brightened. "Right! There're only two ways to control the ABM satellites—either from the station on patrol or from Geneva." He spread his arms happily. "That means they're not in control of Geneva! We've got a good chance to pull their cork!"

But there was no response from Geneva when they beamed their data-compressed message to IPF headquarters. *Hunter* glided past in its unusually low orbit, a tattered wreck desperately calling for help. No answer reached them.

And the lifeboat from *Graham* moved inexorably closer.

The gloom in the CIC was thick enough to stuff a mattress as Geneva disappeared over the horizon and the boat from *Graham* came toward them. Hazard watched the boat on one of Stromsen's screens: it was bright and shining in the sunlight, not blackened by scorching laser beams, unsullied by splashes of human blood.

We could zap it into dust, he thought. One word from me and Feeney could focus half a dozen lasers on it. The men aboard her must be volunteers, willing to risk their necks to make certain that we're finished. He felt a grim admiration for them. Then he wondered, Is Jon Jr. aboard with them?

"Mr. Feeney, what kind of weapons do you think they're carrying?"

Feeney's brows rose toward his scalp. "Weapons, sir? You mean, like sidearms?"

Hazard nodded.

"Personal weapons are not allowed aboard station,

sir. Regulations forbid it."

"I know. But what do you bet they've got pistols, at least. Maybe some submachine guns."

"Damned dangerous stuff for a space station," said Feeney.

Hazard smiled tightly at the Irishman. "Are you afraid they'll put a few more holes in our hull?"

Yang saw what he was driving at. "Sir, there are no weapons aboard *Hunter*—unless you want to count kitchen knives."

"They'll be coming aboard with guns, just to make sure," Hazard said. "I want to capture them alive and use them as hostages. That's our last remaining card. If we can't do that, we've got to surrender."

"They'll be in full suits," said Stromsen. "Each on his own individual life-support system."

"How can we capture them? Or even fight them?" Yang wondered aloud.

Hazard detected no hint of defeat in their voices. The despair of a half hour earlier was gone now. A new excitement had hold of them. He was holding a glimmer of hope for them, and they were reaching for it.

"There can't be more than six of them aboard that boat," Feeney mused.

I wonder if Cardillo has the guts to lead the boarding party in person, Hazard asked himself.

"We don't have any useful weapons," said Yang.

"But we have some tools," Stromsen pointed out. "Maybe . . ."

"What do the lifeboat engines use for propellant?" Hazard asked rhetorically.

"Methane and Oh-eff-two," Feeney replied, looking puzzled.

Hazard nodded. "Miss Stromsen, which of our supply magazines are still intact—if any?"

It took them several minutes to understand what he

was driving at, but when they finally saw the light, the three young officers went speedily to work. Together with the four unwounded members of the crew, they prepared a welcome for the boarders from *Graham*.

Finally, Hazard watched on Stromsen's display screens as the boat sniffed around the battered station. Strict silence was in force aboard *Hunter*. Even in the CIC, deep at the heart of the battle station, they spoke in tense whispers.

"I hope the bastards like what they see," Hazard muttered.

"They know that we used the lifeboats for shields," said Yang.

"Active armor," Hazard said. "Did you know the idea was invented by the man this station's named after?"

"They're looking for a docking port," Stromsen pointed out.

"Only one left," said Feeney.

They could hang their boat almost anywhere and walk in through the holes they've put in us, Hazard said to himself. But they won't. They'll go by the book and find an intact docking port. They've got to! Everything depends on that.

He felt his palms getting slippery with nervous perspiration as the lifeboat slowly, slowly moved around *Hunter* toward the Earth-facing side, where the only usable port was located. Hazard had seen to it that all the other ports had been disabled.

"They're buying it!" Stromsen's whisper held a note of triumph.

"Sir!" Yang hissed urgently. "A message just came in—laser beam, ultracompressed."

"From where?"

"Computer's decrypting," she replied, her snub-nosed face wrinkled with concentration. "Coming up on my center screen, sir."

Hazard slid over toward her. The words on the screen read:

From: IPF Regional HQ, Lagos.
To: Commander, battle station *Hunter*.
Message begins. Coup attempt in Geneva a failure, thanks in large part to your refusal to surrender your command. Situation still unclear, however. Imperative you retain control of *Hunter*, at all costs. Message ends.

He read it aloud, in a guttural whisper, so that Feeney and Stromsen understood what was at stake.

"We're not alone," Hazard told them. "They know what's happening, and help is on the way."

That was stretching the facts, he knew. And he knew *they* knew. But it was reassuring to think that someone, somewhere, was preparing to help them.

Hazard watched them grinning to one another. In his mind, though, he kept repeating the phrase "Imperative you retain control of *Hunter*, at all costs."

At all costs, Hazard said to himself, closing his eyes wearily, seeing Varshni dying in his arms and the others maimed. At all costs.

The bastards, Hazard seethed inwardly. The dirty, power-grabbing, murdering bastards. Once they set foot inside my station, I'll kill them like the poisonous snakes they are. I'll squash them flat. I'll cut them open just like they've slashed my kids . . .

He stopped abruptly and forced himself to take a deep breath. Yeah, sure. Go for personal revenge. That'll make the world a better place to live in, won't it?

"Sir, are you all right?"

Hazard opened his eyes and saw Stromsen staring at him. "Yes, I'm fine. Thank you."

"They've docked, sir," said the Norwegian.

"They're debarking and coming up passageway C, just as you planned."

Looking past her to the screens, Hazard saw that there were six of them, all in space suits, visors down. And pistols in their gloved hands.

"Nothing bigger than pistols?"

"No, sir. Not that we can see, at least."

Turning to Feeney. "Ready with the aerosols?"

"Yes, sir."

"All crew members evacuated from the area?"

"They're all back on level four, except for the sick bay."

Hazard never took his eyes from the screens. The six space-suited boarders were floating down the passageway that led to the lower levels of the station, which were still pressurized and held breathable air. They stopped at the air lock, saw that it was functional. The leader of their group started working the wall unit that controlled the lock.

"Can we hear them?" he asked Yang.

Wordlessly, she touched a stud on her keyboard.

". . . use the next section of the passageway as an air lock," someone was saying. "Standard procedure. Then we'll pump the air back into it once we're inside."

"But we stay in the suits until we check out the whole station. That's an order," said another voice.

Buckbee? Hazard's spirits soared. Buckbee will make a nice hostage, he thought. Not as good as Cardillo, but good enough.

Just as he had hoped, the six boarders went through the airtight hatch, closed it behind them, and started the pump that filled the next section of passageway with air once again.

"Something funny here, sir," said one of the space-suited figures.

"Yeah, the air's kind of misty."

"Never saw anything like this before. Christ, it's like Mexico City air."

"Stay in your suits!" It *was* Buckbee's voice, Hazard was certain of it. "Their life-support systems must have been damaged in our bombardment. They're probably all dead."

You wish, Hazard thought. To Feeney, he commanded, "Seal that hatch."

Feeney pecked at a button on his console.

"And the next one."

"Already done, sir."

Hazard waited, watching Stromsen's main screen as the six boarders shuffled weightlessly to the next hatch and found that it would not respond to the control unit on the bulkhead.

"Damn! We'll have to double back and find another route . . ."

"Miss Yang, I'm ready to hold converse with our guests," said Hazard.

She flashed a brilliant smile and touched the appropriate keys, then pointed a surprisingly well-manicured finger at him. "You're on the air!"

"Buckbee, this is Hazard."

All six of the boarders froze for an instant, then spun weightlessly in midair, trying to locate the source of the new voice.

"You are trapped in that section of corridor," Hazard said. "The mist that you see in the air is oxygen difluoride from our lifeboat propellant tanks. Very volatile stuff. Don't strike any matches."

"What the hell are you saying, Hazard?"

"You're locked in that passageway, Buckbee. If you try to fire those popguns you're carrying, you'll blow yourselves to pieces."

"And you too!"

"We're already dead, you prick. Taking you with us is the only joy I'm going to get out of this."

"You're bluffing!"

Hazard snapped, "Then show me how brave you are, Buckbee. Take a shot at the hatch."

The six boarders hovered in the misty passageway like figures in a surrealistic painting. Seconds ticked by, each one stretching excruciatingly. Hazard felt a pain in his jaws and realized he was clenching his teeth hard enough to chip them.

He took his eyes from the screen momentarily to glance at his three youngsters. They were just as tense as he was. They knew how long the odds of their gamble were. The passageway was filled with nothing more than aerosol mists from every spray can the crew could locate in the supply magazines.

"What do you want, Hazard?" Buckbee said at last, his voice sullen, like a spoiled little boy who had been denied a cookie.

Hazard let out his breath. Then, as cheerfully as he could manage, "I've got what I want. Six hostages. How much air do your suits carry? Twelve hours?"

"What do you mean?"

"You've got twelve hours to convince Cardillo and the rest of your pals to surrender."

"You're crazy, Hazard."

"I've had a tough day, Buckbee. I don't need your insults. Call me when you're ready to deal."

"You'll be killing your son!"

Hazard had half expected it, but still it hit him like a blow. "Jonnie, are you there?"

"Yes I am, Dad."

Hazard strained forward, peering hard at the display screen, trying to determine which one of the space-suited figures was his son.

"Well, this is a helluva fix, isn't it?" he said softly.

"Dad, you don't have to wait twelve hours."

"Shut your mouth!" Buckbee snapped.

"Fuck you," snarled Jon Jr. "I'm not going to get

myself killed for nothing."

"I'll shoot you!" Hazard saw Buckbee level his gun at Jon Jr.

"And kill yourself? You haven't got the guts," Jonnie sneered. Hazard almost smiled. How many times had his son used that tone on him.

Buckbee's hand wavered. He let the gun slip from his gloved fingers. It drifted slowly, weightlessly, away from him.

Hazard swallowed. Hard.

"Dad, in another hour or two the game will be over. Cardillo lied to you. The Russians never came in with us. Half a dozen ships full of troops are lifting off from IPF centers all over the globe."

"Is that the truth, son?"

"Yes, sir, it is. Our only hope was to grab control of your satellites. Once the coup attempt in Geneva flopped, Cardillo knew that if he could control three or four sets of ABM satellites, he could at least force a stalemate. But all he's got is *Graham* and *Wood*. Nobody else."

"You damned little traitor!" Buckbee screeched.

Jon Jr. laughed. "Yeah, you're right. But I'm going to be a *live* traitor. I'm not dying for the likes of you."

Hazard thought swiftly. Jon Jr. might defy his father, might argue with him, even revile him, but he had never known the lad to lie to him.

"Buckbee, the game's over," he said slowly. "You'd better get the word to Cardillo before there's more bloodshed."

It took another six hours before it was all sorted out. A shuttle filled with armed troops and an entire replacement crew finally arrived at the battered hulk of *Hunter*. The relieving commander, a stubby, compactly built black from New Jersey who had been a U.S. Air Force fighter pilot, made a grim tour of inspection with Hazard.

From inside his space suit he whistled in amazement at the battle damage. "Shee-it, you don't need a new crew, you need a new station!"

"It's still functional," Hazard said quietly, then added proudly, "and so is my crew, or what's left of them. They ran this station and kept control of the satellites."

"The stuff legends are made of, my man," said the new commander.

Hazard and his crew filed tiredly into the waiting shuttle, thirteen grimy, exhausted men and women in the pale-blue fatigues of the IPF. Three of them were wrapped in mesh cocoons and attended by medical personnel. Two others were bandaged but ambulatory.

He shook hands with each and every one of them as they stepped from the station's only functional air lock into the shuttle's passenger compartment. Hovering there weightlessly, his creased, craggy face unsmiling, to each of his crew members he said, "Thank you. We couldn't have succeeded without your effort."

The last three through the hatch were Feeney, Stromsen, and Yang. The Irishman looked embarrassed as Hazard shook his hand.

"I'm recommending you for promotion. You were damned cool under fire."

"Frozen stiff with fear, you mean."

To Stromsen, "You, too, Miss Stromsen. You've earned a promotion."

"Thank you, sir," was all she could say.

"And you, little lady," he said to Yang. "You were outstanding."

She started to say something, then flung her arms around Hazard's neck and squeezed tight. "I was so frightened!" she whispered in his ear. "You kept me from cracking up."

Hazard held her around the waist for a moment. As they disengaged he felt his face turning flame red. He turned away from the hatch, not wanting to see the expressions on the rest of his crew members.

Buckbee was coming through the air lock. Behind him were his five men. Including Jon Jr.

They passed Hazard in absolute silence, Buckbee's face as cold and angry as an antarctic storm.

Jon Jr. was the last in line. None of the would-be boarders was in handcuffs, but they all had the hangdog look of prisoners. All except Hazard's son.

He stopped before his father and met the older man's gaze. Jon Jr.'s gray eyes were level with his father's, unswerving, unafraid.

He made a bitter little smile. "I still don't agree with you," he said without preamble. "I don't think the IPF is workable—and it's certainly not in the best interests of the United States."

"But you threw your lot in with us when it counted," Hazard said.

"The hell I did!" Jon Jr. looked genuinely aggrieved. "I just didn't see any sense in dying for a lost cause."

"Really?"

"Cardillo and Buckbee and the rest of them were a bunch of idiots. If I had known how stupid they are I wouldn't . . ." He stopped himself, grinned ruefully, and shrugged his shoulders. "This isn't over, you know. You won the battle, but the war's not ended yet."

"I'll do what I can to get them to lighten your sentence," Hazard said.

"Don't stick your neck out for me! I'm still dead set against you on this."

Hazard smiled wanly at the youngster. "And you're still my son."

Jon Jr. blinked, looked away, then ducked through

the hatch and made for a seat in the shuttle.

Hazard formally turned the station over to its new
commander, saluted one last time, then went into the
shuttle's passenger compartment. He hung there
weightlessly a moment as the hatch behind him was
swung shut and sealed. Most of the seats were already
filled. There was an empty one beside Yang, but after
their little scene at the hatch Hazard was hesitant
about sitting next to her. He glided down the aisle and
picked a seat that had no one next to it. Not one of his
crew. Not Jon Jr.

There's a certain amount of loneliness involved in
command, he told himself. It's not wise to get too
familiar with people you have to order into battle.

He felt, rather than heard, a thump as the shuttle
disengaged from the station's air lock. He sensed the
winged hypersonic spaceplane turning and angling its
nose for reentry into the atmosphere.

Back to . . . Hazard realized that *home*, for him,
was no longer on Earth. For almost all of his adult life,
home had been where his command was. Now his
home was in space. The time he spent on Earth would
be merely waiting time, suspended animation until
his new command was ready.

"Sir, may I intrude?"

He looked up and saw Stromsen floating in the aisle
by his seat.

"What is it, Miss Stromsen?"

She pulled herself down into the seat next to him
but did not bother to latch the safety harness. From a
breast pocket in her sweat-stained fatigues she pulled
a tiny flat tin. It was marked with a red cross and some
printing, hidden by her thumb.

Stromsen opened the tin. "You lost your medication patch," she said. "I thought you might want a
fresh one."

She was smiling at him, shyly, almost like a daughter might.

Hazard reached up and felt behind his left ear. She was right, the patch was gone.

"I wonder how long ago . . ."

"It's been hours, at least," said Stromsen.

"Never noticed."

Her smile brightened. "Perhaps you don't need it anymore."

He smiled back at her. "Miss Stromsen, I think you're absolutely right. My stomach feels fine. I believe I have finally become adapted to weightlessness."

"It's rather a shame that we're on our way back to Earth. You'll have to adapt all over again the next time out."

Hazard nodded. "Somehow I don't think that's going to be much of a problem for me anymore."

He let his head sink back into the seat cushion and closed his eyes, enjoying for the first time the exhilarating floating sensation of weightlessness.

Space Weapons

Somehow I have gotten the reputation of being a hawk.

Apparently this stems from my advocacy of the Strategic Defense Initiative (a.k.a. "Star Wars"). There are some people—even people within the sophisticated science fiction community—who pin simpleminded labels on others, based on their own political prejudices.

It is sad to see reviews of my novels begin with statements such as, "Ben Bova, whose pro–Star Wars views are well known . . ." Sad because I know it's going to be an unfavorable review by a writer who lets his politics blind him to the beauties of my prose!

Perhaps this situation stems from the polarization of the Vietnam era. Or maybe it goes even deeper, back to the beginnings of science fiction fandom, in the fractious 1930s.

Whatever the roots, the result is that anyone who suggests that SDI might be a concept worth exploring, that laser-armed satellites might lead to a war-preventing International Peacekeeping Force, is branded as a warmongering hawk who wants to turn the pristine realms of outer space into a battlefield.

I don't consider myself a hawk. Or a dove. Maybe an owl. The owl is the mascot of my alma mater, Temple University. The owl is also sacred to Athena, the one goddess in all the world's religions who is worth worshiping. Originally a warrior-cult goddess, Athena grew into the patroness of wisdom and civilization, of arts and industries, of cities and democracy.

The arguments over SDI have been largely political debates. Although many prominent scientists (some of them friends and former colleagues of mine) have publicly claimed that SDI is technically impossible, no one really knows if "Star Wars" will be possible or not; that is why a multiyear research program is needed.

"Space Weapons" examines the heart of the controversy. Can weapons aboard satellites destroy ballistic missiles reliably enough to defend the world against nuclear-missile attack?

I try to give both sides of the technical debate, and show what the political consequences might be. I don't feel terribly hawkish—but I can't seem to escape the nagging memory that a dove is really a species of pigeon.

––––––––––––

When President Reagan gave his "Star Wars" speech, March 23, 1983, he proposed to "counter the awesome Soviet missile threat with measures that are defensive," measures that would "intercept and destroy strategic ballistic missiles before they reach our own soil or that of our allies."

Although the President gave no hint in his speech of what these defensive measures might be, aides later revealed to the news media that the basic concept hinges on placing weapons in orbital space.

Satellites in orbit a few hundred miles above the Earth's surface can be in a position to destroy hydrogen-bomb-carrying ballistic missiles within a few minutes after they are launched. While they are still rising above the Earth's atmosphere, and their boosting-rocket engines are still working, the missiles are very vulnerable. If they can be hit then, they can be destroyed relatively easily.

But a defensive shield in space could destabilize the balance of terror that has been the cornerstone of U.S. and Soviet relations for more than twenty years. The policy of mutual assured destruction (MAD) assumes that no defense against missile attack is possible: if one superpower launches a nuclear attack, the other can retaliate in kind. When Reagan proposed a defensive system that would "save lives rather than avenge them," the typical Russian response was, "Why do you want to attack us?" Soviet leaders see any attempt by the United States to defend itself against nuclear attack as a preparation for American nuclear attack on the Soviet Union.

Thus the arguments over "Star Wars" include questions of politics, policy, and technology. Is it necessary to put weapons in space? Should the Congress appropriate tens or hundreds of billions of dollars to build space-based defenses? Is it wise to shift American strategic policy away from MAD, a policy that —whatever its risks—has kept the superpowers from nuclear war for more than twenty years?

Before these questions can be gainfully addressed, the technology question must be considered. Will space-based weapons work? Will they be able to stop a nuclear missile attack?

Among the weapons being considered for the space-based ABM (antiballistic missile) role are high-power lasers, particle beam devices, small missiles, and electrically powered "rail guns" that fire small metal darts at very high velocities. Lasers and particle beam devices are often referred to as directed energy weapons (DEW) or, more simply, beam weapons.

Of these four types of weapons, lasers are the most commonly discussed and may well be the first type actually tested in space. The laser has distinct advantages as a space weapon. It fires a beam of light—pure energy. Nothing in the universe moves faster than light's velocity of 186,000 miles per *second*. By comparison, a missile flying at 15,000 to 20,000 miles per hour seems like a turtle. In the vacuum of space, the laser's beam moves in a perfectly straight line, undeflected by gravity, electric or magnetic fields, wind or weather. Not only is the laser "the fastest gun" in the universe; it can be the most accurate as well.

Small missiles are already being tested by the Air Force as an antisatellite (ASAT) weapon. Carried under the wing of a high-altitude F-15 jet fighter, the ASAT missile rockets into space, where it can seek out a satellite and destroy it by direct impact. Similar missiles could be used in the ABM role, carried aboard satellite "trucks" in orbit until they are needed to intercept enemy missiles. Their technology is well understood and highly developed. But missiles cannot give the speed and range that a powerful laser would. Laser beams could cross thousands of miles in a fraction of a second. This means that fewer defensive satellites would be needed, because each laser-armed satellite would have a "reach" that extends far beyond the limited range of small missiles.

Particle beam weapons are somewhat like lasers; they fire streams of subatomic particles such as protons and electrons instead of a beam of light. The particle beam can move at the speed of light. It must be an electrically neutral beam: negatively charged electrons or positively charged protons by themselves would be deflected by the Earth's magnetic field. While some analysts such as retired Air Force Major General George J. Keegan insist that the Soviet Union is pushing development of particle beam weapons, most Western scientists feel that such devices are not yet as fully developed as lasers.

Rail guns, which can accelerate dartlike fléchettes to velocities of better than 11,000 miles per hour in less than a second, are even less developed than particle beam devices.

Lasers have reached power levels where they can be used as weapons, although they may not yet be powerful enough to destroy missiles in space.

In 1983 the Air Force released news that a 400-kilowatt laser flown aboard its Airborne Laser Laboratory (a specially outfitted Boeing cargo jet) had successfully shot down five Sidewinder missiles fired at it by a jet fighter plane. The test took place high above the Navy Weapons Center testing grounds at China Lake, California. Sidewinders are the missiles that U.S. fighters use to destroy other planes: air-to-air missiles. Although the laser did not destroy the Sidewinders, it damaged their heat-seeking sensors so severely that the missiles could not find their target and crashed into the desert.

TRW Corporation has built a laser of 2.2 megawatts (2.2 million watts) output for the U.S. Navy. Although it is not intended to fly, this laser is approaching the power range of interest for orbital ABM weaponry. It is called MIRACL, a somewhat whimsical acronym for mid-infrared advanced chemical laser. Installed at the White Sands Missile Range in New Mexico, it is used by all three armed services to study the mechanisms by which laser energy damages target materials such as the metals and plastics of which aircraft and missiles are constructed.

Damage mechanisms are an important consideration in deciding which devices may be tested in space and eventually deployed. Missiles and rail-gun fléchettes use the "kinetic kill" approach: like supersophisticated shotgun pellets, they simply smash into the oncoming missile or bomb-carrying warhead. The target's own forward velocity of more than 15,000 miles per hour merely adds more kinetic energy to the shattering collision.

The basic kill mechanism of a laser beam is to heat the target's surface so quickly and intensely that the material is vaporized. A laser that can focus many kilowatts or megawatts of pure energy per square centimeter on its target will cause damage similar to the kind that Buck Rogers's "disintegrator" gun did in the comic strips of fifty years ago. The skin of a missile can be boiled away by the searing finger of a laser beam, which can punch a hole in the missile's skin in a second or less. If the missile's rocket engines are still burning, and its tanks still contain volatile rocket propellants, rupturing the tankage will blow the missile apart in a spectacular explosion.

However, the metal boiled up by the laser beam creates a cloud that tends to absorb incoming laser energy. To counter this, the beam might be pulsed many times per second, so that the cloud created by the first pulse of laser energy dissipates before the next pulse arrives. The pulses could be thousandths of a second in duration, or even shorter. Very high-energy pulses could also damage a missile or warhead by mechanical shock, literally shaking its innards apart. A very energetic pulse would blast a small crater in the target's surface and send a shock wave penetrating into its interior. A train of sufficiently energetic pulses could rattle a missile or hydrogen-bomb warhead to pieces.

A particle beam could also deliver a massive jolt of energy to its target. It would not be absorbed by clouds of gas, as a laser beam would be. Nor would it be reflected by a shiny surface or absorbed by an ablative coating. It could penetrate the metal skin of a missile or even the "hardened" heat shield of a reentry warhead within microseconds. The beam could shock-heat the inner workings of a nuclear bomb, destroying its electronic controls or damaging the triggering mechanism so badly that the bomb will not detonate.

There are many different kinds of lasers, but the type that appears to be closest to actual testing in space is the chemical laser, so called because its energy is derived from the chemical reaction of two or more "fuels," such as hydrogen and fluorine. Chemical lasers emit infrared energy, at wavelengths of light that are invisible to the human eye.

Edward Teller, "father of the H-bomb," is urging the development of a laser that produces X rays. It is powered by the explosion of a small nuclear bomb; thus the X-ray laser has been called a "third-generation nuclear device" (the first two generations being the fission-based atomic bomb and the hydrogen fusion bomb). Since the end product of Teller's third-generation bomb is a laser beam of X rays, the system is also called a "directed nuclear device."

The technical community is also excited by the more recent development of *excimer* lasers, which can emit energy at ultraviolet wavelengths.

But the basic question remains: Will lasers, or any of the proposed space weapons, actually be able to defend against a full-scale strategic missile attack? Many scientists and strategists believe that it will be impossible to destroy thousands of missiles and their multiple warheads with orbiting weaponry. Dr. Robert Bowman, former director of advanced space programs for the Air Force, says that "every dollar spent on defense can be neutralized by five cents of offense."

Perhaps the strongest voice speaking against the concept of space-based defense belongs to Kosta Tsipis, associate director of the MIT Physics Department's Program in Science and Technology for International Security.

"We are witnessing a tragedy . . . a cruel hoax," he told me, "a repetition of the pattern that saw the government spend two billion dollars on a nuclear-powered airplane in the 1950s."

Tsipis is convinced that neither lasers nor particle beams can be made to work well enough to serve as ABM weapons. Writing in *Scientific American*'s April 1979 and December 1981 issues (and later including much the same material in his book *Arsenal: Understanding Weapons in the Nuclear Age*), Tsipis concluded that "it is difficult to see how the development and deployment of such fragile, complex and expensive weapons would improve the military capability of a nation."

He says quite firmly that the "dream" of orbiting energy weapons capable of destroying ballistic missiles is simply "not physically possible. . . . There are no weapons applications for existing lasers," and even if much better lasers are developed, "the operational difficulties" will make orbital ABM systems impractical.

"The President has no sense of the physical reality" of such devices, Tsipis feels. He believes that Reagan is "trying to stampede the country" into pushing ahead with such a program because "it is good for the California industries, and good for negotiations" with the Soviets.

In his writings, Tsipis concludes that a laser ABM weapon cannot put enough energy on a missile to destroy it, especially within the few seconds after launch when the missile's rocket engines are still burning and it is most vulnerable. He believes that a laser-armed satellite would itself be so vulnerable to attack and so expensive that it would have no real military value. "We have concluded that lasers have little or no chance of succeeding as practical, cost-effective defensive weapons."

Tsipis shows that an orbiting laser must be pointed at its target with extraordinary accuracy: ". . . for a laser weapon to destroy its target, the position of the target must be known to within a distance equal to the shortest dimension of the target [the width of the ICBM booster rocket], and the laser must be pointed with the same precision."

He sets up a scenario in which fifty laser-armed ABM satellites face an attacking force of one thousand missiles, which they must destroy within eight minutes of launching. Under these conditions, only a single satellite would be in a position to engage the attacking force; the other forty-nine satellites would be orbiting over different areas of the globe, too far away to deal with the attacking missiles within the first eight minutes of their flight.

"Therefore," Tsipis writes, "the [lone] satellite could devote only about half a second to each missile." He estimates that a hundred-megawatt chemical laser would need a pointing mirror four meters wide (slightly more than thirteen feet) to put enough energy on a missile at one thousand kilometers' range to destroy it within a second. "Making such a mirror sufficiently rugged and of the necessary optical quality, however," he states, "is beyond the technical capabilities of the U.S. or any other nation."

Moreover, Tsipis calculates that the chemical laser would need nearly 1,500 pounds of fuel for each missile destroyed, which means that each satellite must be supplied with roughly 750 *tons* of laser fuel because one cannot tell in advance which satellite might face the entire attacking missile fleet. Since the space shuttle carries about 30 tons of payload, each satellite would require twenty-five shuttle flights just to "fill 'er up." The entire system of fifty satellites would require 1,250 shuttle missions merely to fuel the lasers. Even if shuttles were launched once a week to do nothing except carry fuel to the orbiting lasers, it would take more than twenty-four years to bring each of the fifty orbiting lasers to a condition of readiness.

Tsipis believes that even these conditions are "unrealistically optimistic," since a hundred-megawatt chemical laser does not exist "and there is no indication that such a device could be developed in the foreseeable future." Moreover, his calculations were based on a 100 percent efficiency for the laser, whereas in reality the best that might be expected is 30 to 40 percent efficiency. Thus the fuel requirements would balloon "by a factor of at least 10 and more likely 30."

Finally, Tsipis points out that laser-armed satellites would be vulnerable to countermeasures. They could be attacked while under construction in orbit, their sensors could be blinded by the attacker just before the ICBMs are launched, or their communications links to command centers could be jammed.

Bowman, Tsipis, and others have shown that the attacking missiles could be protected from laser beams by shiny, reflective coatings on their surfaces, or by blowing a stream of laser-absorbing fluid along the missiles' length. The reentry warheads are already coated with heat-absorbing ablative materials; the entire length of the missile could be "painted" with an ablative plastic. An even simpler countermeasure would be to increase the number of attacking missiles until the defensive system is overwhelmed.

Daniel Deudney, senior researcher at the Washington-based Worldwatch Institute, brought out another cautionary point in his 1983 testimony to the Senate Subcommittee on Arms Control:

"Large-scale space weapons would be an example of what I call a destruction entrusted automatic device [DEAD]. Space weapons could never be commanded and controlled by humans. A space laser, for example, would have about five minutes to detect, target and engage an ICBM in the boost phase. One Department of Defense analyst put it this way, 'We would have to delegate the decision-making to the weapon system itself and we have had no experience in that type of operational system.' To start a nuclear war in the MAD era would have required a major political misjudgment; with space weapons, a machine malfunction would be sufficient."

Tsipis and other scientists in the academic community complain about their lack of access to the President. "We don't have a voice in the Oval Office," he claims. "The White House has cut itself off almost completely from the academic community." He maintains that President Reagan relies on industrial scientists, especially those employed by the major aerospace corporations, for his scientific advice.

One of those "industrial scientists" is Edward T. Gerry, a youthful physicist who headed the effort at Avco Everett Research Laboratory, in Massachusetts, in the mid-1960s that produced the breakthrough to high-power lasers. A descendant of the Massachusetts politician from whom the word "gerrymander" arose, Gerry went into government service in the 1970s to become chief of all laser programs for the Defense Department's Advanced Research Projects Agency. Today he is president of W. J. Schafer Associates, a Washington-area research and development firm.

When I asked Gerry about the criticisms voiced by Tsipis and others, he said flatly, "Tsipis is wrong. The articles he's written are misleading. He sets up 'straw man' arguments that are based on false assumptions." He took Tsipis's example of a hundred-megawatt laser and analyzed the situation this way:

Such a laser is powerful enough to put at least ten to one hundred kilowatts per square centimeter of laser

energy on the skin of a missile, over a range of more
than one thousand miles. That much energy on the
missile will boil away enough of the metal within one
second to make the missile's structure crumple and
destroy the missile. While Tsipis makes the point that
"shiny aluminum" will reflect all but 4 percent of the
infrared energy from a chemical laser, Gerry maintains that 4 percent of the energy from a hundred-
megawatt laser is quite sufficient to destroy the
missile, even assuming that its metal skin is protected
by an ablative coating.

Every pound of material used to protect the missile,
Gerry points out, is a pound taken away from the
payload. For purposes of calculation, he assumed that
the protective ablative coating reduced the weight of
the missile's warhead by 20 percent. "The more
protection you build into the missile, the smaller its
payload [the warhead] becomes," he says. Protecting
the ballistic missile costs the attacker kilotons of
explosive power.

The biggest point of difference between Tsipis and
Gerry is over how many ABM satellites would actually be in position to engage an attacking force of one
thousand ICBMs. With fifty satellites in orbits about
six hundred miles high, Tsipis assumes that only one
will be in the right place at the right time, and
therefore one laser weapon must take on the entire
attacking force.

"But the missiles don't all come from the same
point," Gerry maintains. Soviet ICBM silo "farms"
are strung out over thousands of miles, mainly along
the Trans-Siberian Railroad. Gerry feels that at least
one quarter of the satellites—say, twelve of them
—will be in position to engage the attacking missiles.
This means that each laser weapon will have to engage
between eighty-three and eighty-four missiles within a

time period of roughly three hundred to four hundred seconds. That gives each laser somewhat more than one second to attack each missile, with another second to locate and target the next missile. "That's not pushing any physical limits whatever," Gerry claims.

One second is a very long time for modern electronic equipment. Human comprehension of time is based on the human pulse rate, less than one hundred beats per minute. Computers can perform operations in *nanoseconds*, billionths of a second, or less. There are as many nanoseconds in one second as there are seconds in thirty-two years.

Gerry flatly contradicts Tsipis's statement that a four-meter (thirteen-foot) mirror is "beyond the technical capabilities of the U.S. or any other nation." For a hundred-megawatt chemical laser, a four-meter-wide mirror would reflect eight hundred watts from each square centimeter of its surface. "Mirrors that handle a hundred times that flux have already been operated," Gerry says, although he admits that such mirrors have been considerably smaller than four meters. "But there's no reason why such mirrors can't be built."

Gerry agrees that it would take roughly a metric ton of laser fuels to shoot down a missile. But since he envisions a dozen satellites engaging the attacking missiles, it is not necessary to provide each and every satellite with enough fuel to destroy all one thousand ICBMs. One shuttle payload should be enough to down twenty-five missiles. Forty shuttle flights could carry the laser fuels to destroy a thousand missiles. But since only a quarter of the satellites in orbit will be in position to engage the attacker, each satellite must then carry four times as much laser fuel as the simple numbers would at first indicate. This means 160 shuttle flights should bring the fifty-satellite system to a state of readiness.

One hundred sixty shuttle flights is a formidable task. If all four existing space shuttles were devoted to nothing but such "fuel runs," and they were launched at a rate of one mission per week, it would still take slightly more than three years to "top off" all fifty satellites.

Lowell Wood, of the Lawrence Livermore National Laboratory in California, where the work on Teller's nuclear-powered X-ray laser is being carried out, is even harsher in his criticism of "Tsipis and his group at MIT." In an interview in *Defense Science and Electronics* magazine, Wood stated that Tsipis's December 1981 article in *Scientific American* "was premised on political and not technical grounds. It was riddled with fundamental technical faults. . . . These were not fundamental, unavoidable physics problems that Tsipis was pointing out. They were technological hurdles to be cleared. They have all been cleared. Tsipis was flogging a dead horse."

Although the scientists are at odds about the possibility of making laser weapons work well enough, and at powers high enough, to destroy ballistic missiles, the government is pushing ahead with its plans to do enough research and engineering to reach the point where decisions can be made about deploying a space-based system. Based on studies by panels of scientists and strategic analysts headed by Defense Under Secretaries Richard DeLauer and Fred Ikle, the research and engineering are estimated to cost between $18 billion and $27 billion.

Space-based defenses may one day be able to destroy ballistic missiles within minutes after they are launched. But what about nuclear bombs carried by airplanes or low-flying cruise missiles? What about nuclear devices smuggled into a city by terrorists aboard a ship or even in a smallish van?

There are three points to be made:

First, if space-based defenses do nothing more than prevent missile attack, they will have made an enormous contribution to peace and survival. They will have moved humankind away from the fearful specter of a thirty-minute push-button war that ends with the entire northern hemisphere devastated and the onset of Nuclear Winter.

Second, if missiles can be destroyed within minutes, much the same technology can be used to stop the slower airplanes and drones that might carry nuclear bombs. The defensive weaponry can be based on the ground, at sea, or aboard aircraft just as well as in satellites. While atmospheric effects may trouble laser and particle beam systems, the "kinetic kill" weapons will work just fine here on Earth. And the electronic detection, pointing, and tracking "brains" that run the ABM satellites will find supersonic aircraft easy targets. There are even a few bold scientists like Wood who hint that lasers will be able to destroy targets despite the absorption and beam-disrupting problems of the atmosphere.

Third, this kind of defensive weaponry will probably be of little use against suicidal terrorists armed with nuclear bombs. But that is a different order of problem. Terrorists may one day destroy a city, or several cities. But they will not be able to produce the kind of instantaneous holocaust that is threatened by the thousands of warheads resting atop their ballistic missiles today. Stopping terrorism calls for political action.

Space-based defenses can stop World War III. That should be a powerful incentive for moving ahead with the research needed to prove out the fundamental concepts.

We may be witnessing a new era in international politics, the first real change since the reign of nuclear terror began at Hiroshima. As Winston Churchill once said, "This is not the end. It is not even the beginning of the end. But it is, perhaps, the end of the beginning."

Nuclear Autumn ═══════════

The alternative to strategic defenses in space is *no* defense against nuclear attack, the policy called mutual assured destruction. MAD is essentially a mutual suicide pact between the superpowers: attack is deterred because neither side dares risk the other's devastating counterattack.

But there might be another way for a ruthless and calculating enemy to launch a nuclear attack and confidently expect no counterstrike at all.

The arguments over Nuclear Winter—the idea that a sufficient number of nuclear explosions in the atmosphere will plunge the whole world into an era of freezing darkness that will extinguish all life on Earth—is being hotly debated among scientists today.

Strangely, very little of this debate is being reported in the media. Even the science press is largely ignoring it. To the media, Nuclear Winter is a Truth. It was revealed through press conferences, a slickly illustrated book, and videotapes. No matter that the basic scientific underpinnings of the idea are under attack by many atmospheric physicists and other scientists. It is now embedded in cement in the mind-sets of the world's media—and many science fiction writers, too.

Critics of Nuclear Winter claim that its proponents used Joe McCarthy tactics to publicize what, to them, is a political idea rather than a scientific theory. They claim that Carl Sagan, Paul Ehrlich, et al made their publicity splash and "sold" the idea to the media, and only afterward quietly admitted that there are some doubts about the models and calculations they used.

On their side, Sagan, Ehrlich, and their colleagues insist that Nuclear Winter has been verified by extensive computer simulations, and is absolute proof that even a relatively small nuclear war threatens to end not only human life on Earth, but *all* life.

"Nuclear Autumn" takes it for granted that the Nuclear Winter theory is right. It shows one of the possible consequences. A very likely one, I fear.

"They're bluffing," said the President of the United States.

"Of course they're bluffing," agreed her science advisor. "They have to be."

The chairman of the Joint Chiefs of Staff, a grizzled old infantry general, looked grimly skeptical.

For a long, silent moment they faced each other in the cool, quiet confines of the Oval Office. The science advisor looked young and handsome enough to be a television personality, and indeed had been one for a while before he allied himself with the politician who sat behind the desk. The President looked younger than she actually was, thanks to modern cosmetics and a ruthless self-discipline. Only the general seemed to be old, a man of an earlier generation, gray-haired and wrinkled, with light brown eyes that seemed sad and weary.

"I don't believe they're bluffing," he said. "I think they mean exactly what they say—either we cave in to them or they launch their missiles."

The science advisor gave him his most patronizing smile. "General, they *have* to be bluffing. The numbers prove it."

"The only numbers that count," said the general, "are that we have cut our strategic ballistic missile force by half since this Administration came into office."

"And made the world that much safer," said the President. Her voice was firm, with a sharp edge to it.

The general shook his head. "Ma'am, the only reason I have not tendered my resignation is that I know full well the nincompoop you intend to appoint in my place."

The science advisor laughed. Even the President smiled at the old man.

"The Soviets are not bluffing," the general repeated. "They mean exactly what they say."

With a patient sigh, the science advisor explained, "General, they cannot—repeat, can*not*—launch a nuclear strike at us or anyone else. They know the numbers as well as we do. A large nuclear strike, in the three-thousand-megaton range, will so damage the environment that the world will be plunged into a Nuclear Winter. Crops and animal life will be wiped out by months of subfreezing temperatures. The sky will be dark with soot and grains of pulverized soil. The sun will be blotted out. All life on Earth will die."

The general waved an impatient hand. "I know your story. I've seen your presentations."

"Then how can the Russians attack us, when they know they'll be killing themselves even if we don't retaliate?"

"Maybe they haven't seen your television specials. Maybe they don't believe in Nuclear Winter."

"But they have to!" said the science advisor. "The numbers are the same for them as they are for us."

"Numbers," grumbled the general.

"Those numbers describe reality," the science advisor insisted. "And the men in the Kremlin are realists. They understand what Nuclear Winter means. Their own scientists have told them exactly what I've told you."

"Then why did they insist on this hot-line call?"

Spreading his hands in the gesture millions had come to know from his television series, the science advisor replied, "They're reasonable men. Now that they know nuclear weapons are unusable, they are undoubtedly trying to begin negotiations to resolve our differences without threatening nuclear war."

"You think so?" muttered the general.

The President leaned back in her swivel chair. "We'll find out what they want soon enough," she said. "Kolgoroff will be on the hot line in another minute or so."

The science advisor smiled at her. "I imagine he'll suggest a summit meeting to negotiate a new disarmament treaty."

The general said nothing.

The President touched a green square on the keypad built into the desk's surface. A door opened and three more people—a man and two women —entered the Oval Office: the Secretary of State, the Secretary of Defense, and the National Security Advisor.

Exactly when the digital clock on the President's desk read 12:00:00, the large display screen that took up much of the wall opposite her desk lit up to reveal the face of Yuri Kolgoroff, General Secretary of the Communist Party and President of the Soviet Union. He was much younger than his predecessors had been, barely in his midfifties, and rather handsome in a Slavic way. If his hair had been a few shades darker and his chin just a little rounder, he would have looked strikingly like the President's science advisor.

"Madam President," said Kolgoroff, in flawless American-accented English, "it is good of you to accept my invitation to discuss the differences between our two nations."

"I am always eager to resolve differences," said the President.

"I believe we can accomplish much." Kolgoroff smiled, revealing large white teeth.

"I have before me," said the President, glancing at the computer screen on her desk, "the agenda that our ministers worked out . . ."

"There is no need for that," said the Soviet leader. "Why encumber ourselves with such formalities?"

The President smiled. "Very well. What do you have in mind?"

"It is very simple. We want the United States to withdraw all its troops from Europe and to dismantle NATO. Also, your military and naval bases in Japan, Taiwan, and the Philippines must be disbanded. Finally, your injunctions against the Soviet Union concerning trade in high-technology items must be ended."

The President's face went white. It took her a moment to gather the wits to say, "And what do you propose to offer in exchange for these . . . concessions?"

"In exchange?" Kolgoroff laughed. "Why, we will allow you to live. We will refrain from bombing your cities."

"You're insane!" snapped the President.

Still grinning, Kolgoroff replied, "We will see who is sane and who is mad. One minute before this conversation began, I ordered a limited nuclear attack against every NATO base in Europe, and a counterforce attack against the ballistic missiles still remaining in your silos in the American Midwest."

The red panic light on the President's communications console began flashing frantically.

"But that's impossible!" burst the science advisor. He leaped from his chair and pointed at Kolgoroff's image in the big display screen. "An attack of that size will bring on Nuclear Winter! You'll be killing yourselves as well as us!"

Kolgoroff smiled pityingly at the scientist. "We have computers also, Professor. We know how to count. The attack we have launched is just below the threshold for Nuclear Winter. It will not blot out the sun everywhere on Earth. Believe me, we are not such fools as you think."

"But . . ."

"But," the Soviet leader went on, smile vanished and voice iron-hard, "should you be foolish enough to launch a counterstrike with your remaining missiles or bombers, that *will* break the camel's back, so to speak. The additional explosions of your counterstrike will bring on Nuclear Winter."

"You can't be serious!"

"I am deadly serious," Kolgoroff replied. Then a faint hint of his smile returned. "But do not be afraid. We have not targeted Washington. Or any of your cities, for that matter. You will live—under Soviet governance."

The President turned to the science advisor. "What should I do?"

The science advisor shook his head.

"What should I do?" she asked the others seated around her.

They said nothing. Not a word.

She turned to the general. "What should I do?"

He got to his feet and headed for the door. Over his shoulder he answered, "Learn Russian."

Freedom From Fear ═══════════

I stepped down from the editorship of *Analog* magazine in 1978, yet even to this day I am frequently introduced to science fiction audiences as "the man who filled John Campbell's shoes." (To those who are not familiar with the inner workings of science fiction, John Campbell was the editor of *Analog* from 1937—when it was known as *Astounding Stories*—until his sudden and totally unexpected death in 1971.)

One wag mused that since Campbell was an acknowledged giant of the field, I must therefore have extremely large feet. Which led me to ask myself, Since I also sat in Campbell's chair (literally), what does that mean about the size of my rump?

Be that as it may, while I was in the midst of writing *Star Peace: Assured Survival*, Stanley Schmidt (my successor at *Analog*) hinted to me that he was planning to take a short vacation from his duties as editor, and would appreciate it if someone would volunteer to write a guest editorial for the magazine.

After seven years of running *Analog*, I knew the pressures of coming up each month with an editorial that will excite the readers to send in angry letters and impel the writers to generate stories. So I volunteered and wrote the following guest editorial. Sure enough, it generated some waspish letters—and some supportive ones, too.

Did it generate any good stories? Well, there's one I

know of that I think of rather fondly. It is a novel called
Privateers. I wrote it.

Shakespeare's Hamlet, brooding on the attractions
of suicide over a continued life of anguish, concluded
that the fear of what lies beyond death is the great
deterrent to self-destruction:

> *And makes us rather bear those ills we have*
> *Than fly to others we know not of . . .*

So, too, much of today's academic community,
including many scholars who have spent most of their
professional lives in the field of nuclear strategy, have
decided they would rather "bear those ills" of our
twenty-year-old policy of mutual assured destruction
than "fly to others we know not of": namely, the
possibility of a space-based defense against nuclear
attack.

Most of these academics are so firmly wedded to
MAD that they view any attempt to protect ourselves
against nuclear devastation as not only politically
destabilizing, but morally reprehensible.

As I write this, just over a year has elapsed since
President Reagan's "Star Wars" speech of March 23,
1983. The concept of placing defensive weapons in
orbit, where they could blunt a nuclear missile attack,
is not new to the readers of *Analog.* But it caught most
of the rest of the world—including the academics
—by surprise.

In a small way, I was present at the birth of this new
idea. In 1965 I was manager of marketing for the Avco
Everett Research Laboratory, where the breakthrough

into truly high-power lasers was made. I helped to arrange the first top-secret briefing in the Pentagon, where Avco's scientists revealed to the Defense Department that lasers of incredible power could now be developed. I was privy to some of the earliest studies on the possible use of laser-armed satellites to destroy attacking ballistic missiles.

In the years since then, I have written about these possibilities in novels such as *Millennium* and *Kinsman*. I have just completed a nonfiction book, *Assured Survival*, that examines the technical, military, and political implications of space-based defenses and other high-technology approaches to preventing war.

In the course of these years, I have learned two things:

1. We have at our fingertips the means to prevent nuclear war.

2. Most of the entrenched academic scientists and strategic analysts will resist any move toward this new possibility.

Indeed, their resistance is already quite evident. The Union of Concerned Scientists has denounced the "Star Wars" concept of space-based missile defense as technologically infeasible and economically ruinous. Carl Sagan, Hans Bethe, and many former science advisors to presidents have similarly inveighed against placing weaponry in space.

Many strategic analysts have made it quite clear that they prefer MAD, in which the two superpowers disdain defending their cities and offer their own civilian populations as hostage to the goodwill of their adversary. Their tortured logic is that, by building defenses, we will so frighten the Soviets that they will launch the long-dreaded nuclear attack upon us. Defensive systems, they say, are not only impossible, immoral, and expensive, but destabilizing as well.

For forty years the world has witnessed an arms

race of steadily escalating, constantly more frightening weapons of attack. The atomic bomb and the V-2 rocket have evolved into the hydrogen bomb and the ICBM with its MIRVed warheads. The Cold War has been a natural consequence of this horrifying technology. With weapons that are too terrible to use, neither the United States nor Soviet Russia has dared to attack the other. But because each possesses such powerful weapons, neither one will back down and accommodate its adversary. The result, a stalemate of terror.

Now the technological drive is toward a new kind of weaponry, the weapons of defense: very high-power lasers and other energy weapons of pinpoint accuracy, directed by very smart computers, are beginning to give the defense its chance to catch up with the offense—after forty years.

But after two generations of equating weaponry with mass destruction, most of the academic community automatically reacts adversely to any talk of new weapons. The media depends on "knowledgeable" academics to inform the world of what is possible and impossible in the world of science. The media goes to these same academics to check on technological pronouncements coming out of the Department of Defense and other branches of government.

Most of these academics are poorly informed about the latest work in weaponry, in large part because such work is generally classified secret by the Pentagon. And their bias, fed by memories of Hiroshima and Vietnam, is against weapons development. Hence their resistance to weapons that can defend the world against nuclear missiles and more conventional machines of destruction.

The readers of *Analog* certainly are better informed than most Americans about the feasibility of high-tech weapons. Networks of satellites armed with lasers or other advanced defensive weapons will work, and they will be deployed in the 1990s. Even if the system costs a trillion dollars, no American government would be able to resist the pressure to defend this nation against missile attack—once the American public becomes convinced that such a system will work.

Will the deployment of defensive satellites trigger the nuclear holocaust we all want to avoid? Not likely. It will take many years, perhaps a decade, to establish an effective system. In that time, the Russians will either negotiate us out of it, build their own defensive system to keep abreast of us, or perhaps even join us in creating a global defensive system that will protect every nation on Earth against attack by any nation.

That last possibility seems as farfetched as flying to the Moon seemed in 1944. But it is equally inevitable. For just as the technologies of offensive weaponry led to the Cold War, the new technologies of defensive weaponry will eventually lead the politicians to create an international system where nuclear war—perhaps all kinds of war—will be sternly repressed by a true multinational peacekeeping force.

Perhaps we will have to come to the very brink of the nuclear abyss before we draw back and begin to place our reliance on defenses and new political arrangements that will make war impossible. Perhaps the mushrooms will have to bloom again, and it will take a nuclear engagement of some sort to make the nations realize that an international peacekeeping force is necessary.

But it will happen. And it will happen, most likely, in this way:

Both the United States and the Soviet Union will test defensive, antimissile weapons in orbit before the end of the 1980s. Despite the wailings of those who would rather live under the terror of nuclear annihilation, both superpowers will begin to deploy defensive systems in orbit during the 1990s. This will be a time of very high international tensions, as the two superpowers and their allies jockey for advantage, both in orbital space and at the conference table. A new arms race will have begun: a *defensive* arms race.

By the turn of the century, there may well be two separate networks of defensive satellites in orbit. Neither defensive system will be foolproof; the offense will always be able to get a few missiles through to their targets. But a few is not enough. The defensive systems in orbit will make it virtually impossible for either side to launch a nuclear attack upon the other. Slowly, but with the certainty of time, the nuclear-tipped missiles will become obsolete.

In time, the peoples of the world will become accustomed to having guardians orbiting overhead, preventing nuclear missile attack. The governments of the world will start to cooperate more as the terror of nuclear annihilation recedes. Eventually (and this may be a *long* time from now) the two orbital defensive systems will be merged into one, as even the two superpowers learn how to trust one another.

In 1941, as war raged in Europe and Asia and was soon to engulf the United States, President Franklin D. Roosevelt enunciated the Four Freedoms, which he wished to see promulgated everywhere in the world. Among them was *Freedom From Fear*. In today's world, where the nations spend more than $600 billion per year on armaments, the fear of war and annihilation is stronger than ever within us. But we can create a world without war, we can gain our freedom from fear, if we are wise enough to use the tools that technology is forging for us.

The ancient Greeks worshiped two war deities: Ares (the Roman Mars) was the aggressive, bloodthirsty god of violence who enjoyed nothing better than to see men fighting and killing each other; Athena, who sprang full-grown from the brow of Zeus bearing shield and spear, was originally a battle goddess. But as time evolved, Athena became the gray-eyed goddess of wisdom, of learning, of civilization and democracy. Her symbol was the owl, and ancient Athens became her special city. She remained a warrior goddess, but she represented to the Greeks the craft of defensive war, of strategy and planning, of careful preparations that can minimize bloodshed.

It is time that we, with this generation of awesome weapons in our hands, turn away from bloody Ares and his battle lust and turn toward wise Athena. It is time that we begin the long, difficult road toward a world of peace, a world that is freed from the crushing burden of armaments, a world where orbital guardians make it impossible for any nation to attack its neighbors, a world in which our children and our children's children will be free at last of the fear of war.

We have at our fingertips the tools to fulfill the ancient prophecy of Isaiah:

And they shall beat their swords into plowshares, and their spears into pruninghooks: nation shall not lift up sword against nation, neither shall they learn war any more.

Béisbol

There are other (better!) ways for nations to compete than by going to war. The Greeks figured that out more than two thousand years ago.

I got this crazy idea one day—if the United States began its rapprochement with Communist China by sending Ping-Pong players to Peking, maybe someday we would start to make up with Castro's Cuba by sending a baseball team to Havana. As I mulled it over in my mind, a certain Mr. Lucius J. Riccio, of New York City, suggested the same thing in a letter to *The New York Times* of March 3, 1985.

I realized that I could not waste time mulling. The idea would slip away from me if I didn't get the story onto paper.

The first draft of the tale was pretty dull. Thank heaven, I was smart enough to look up Alfred Bester, one of the great talents of our age—especially when it comes to sparking up a story idea. Alfie's mind works in leaps and bounds, and after an evening of swapping ideas and swilling booze, "Béisbol" just about wrote itself.

So thank you, Alfie. See you at the World Series. (Or maybe not. I'm a Red Sox fan, and I don't think I could stand another crushing blow like the 1986 Series.)

Nixon sat scowling in the dugout, his dark chin down on the letters of his baseball uniform, his eyes glaring. It wasn't us he was mad at; it was Castro.

Across the infield, the Cubans were passing out cigars in their dugout. Top of the ninth inning and they were ahead, 1–0. We had three more chances at their robot pitcher. So far, all the mechanical monster had done was strike out fourteen of us USA All-Stars and not allow a runner past first base.

Castro looked a lot older than I thought he'd be. His beard was all gray. But he was laughing and puffing on a big cigar as his team took the field and that damned robot rolled itself up to the mound.

Nixon jumped to his feet. He looked kind of funny in a baseball uniform, like, out of place.

"Men," he said to us, "this is more than a game. I'm sure you know that."

We all kind of muttered and mumbled and nodded our heads.

"If they win this series, they'll take over all of the Caribbean. All of Central America. The United States will be humiliated."

Yeah, maybe so, I thought. And you'll be a bum again, instead of a hero. But he didn't have to go up and try to bat against that Commie robot. From what we heard, they had built it in Czechoslovakia or someplace like that to throw hand grenades at tanks. Now it was throwing baseballs right past us, like a blur.

"We've got to win this game," Nixon said, his voice trembling. "We've *got* to!"

It had seemed like a good idea. Use baseball to reestablish friendly relations with Cuba, just like they had used Ping-Pong to make friends with Red China. So the commissioner personally picked an All-Star team and Washington picked Nixon to manage us. It would be a pushover, we all thought. I mean, the Cubans like baseball, but they couldn't come anywhere near matching us.

Well, pitching may be 80 percent of the game, but scouting is 200 percent more. We waltzed into Havana and found ourselves playing guys who were just about as good as we were. According to a CIA report, their guys were pumped up on steroids and accelerators and God knows what else. They'd never pass an Olympic Games saliva test, but nobody on our side had thought to include drug testing in the ground rules.

Oh, we won the first two games okay. But it wasn't easy.

And then the Commies used their first secret weapon on us. Women. It was like our hotel was all of a sudden invaded by them. Tall show-girl types, short little señoritas, redheads, blondes, dark flashing eyes and luscious lips that smiled and laughed. And boobs. Never saw so many bouncing, jiggling, low-cut bosoms in my life.

What could we do? Our third baseman hurt his back swinging by his knees from the chandelier in his room with a broad in one arm and a bottle of champagne in the other. Two of our best pitchers were so hung over that they couldn't see their catchers the next morning. And our center fielder, who usually batted cleanup, was found under his bed in a coma that lasted three days. But there was a big smile on his face the whole time.

By the time the Cubans had pulled ahead, three games to two, Nixon called a team meeting and put it to us but good.

"This has got to stop," he said, pacing back and forth across the locker room, hands locked behind his stooped back, jowls quivering with anger.

"These women are trained Communist agents," he warned us. "I've been getting intelligence reports from Washington. Castro has no intentions of establishing friendly relations with us . . ."

Somebody snickered at the words *friendly relations*, but quickly choked it off as Nixon whirled around, searching for the culprit like a schoolteacher dealing with a bunch of unruly kids.

"This isn't funny! If the Commies win this series, they'll go all through Latin America crowing about how weak the United States is. We'll lose the whole Caribbean, Central America, the Panama Canal —everything!"

We promised to behave ourselves. Hell, he was worried about Latin America, but most of us had more important problems. I could just imagine my next salary negotiation: "Why, you couldn't even beat a bunch of third-rate Cubans," the general manager would tell my agent.

More than that, I could see my father's face. He had spent many years teaching me how to play baseball. He had always told me that I could be a big leaguer. And he had always asked nothing more of me than that I gave my best out on the field. I wouldn't be able to face him, knowing that we had lost to Castro because we had screwed around.

We went out there that afternoon and tore them apart, 11–2. That tied the series. The seventh and final game would decide it all.

That's when they brought out their second secret weapon: Raoul the Robot, the mechanical monster, the Czechoslovak chucker, the machine that threw supersonic fastballs.

I thought Nixon would have apoplexy when the little robot rolled itself up to the pitcher's mound to start the game. It looked sort of like a water cooler, a squat metal cylinder with a glass dome on top. It had two "arms:" curved metal chutes that wound around and around several times and then fired the ball at you. Fast. Very fast.

Nixon went screaming out onto the field before our leadoff batter got to the plate. Castro ambled out, grinning and puffing his cigar. The huge crowd—the Havana stadium was absolutely jammed—gave him the kind of roar that American fans reserve for pitchers who throw no-hitters in the seventh game of the World Series. He turned, doffed his cap just like any big leaguer would, and then joined the argument raging at the mound.

Nixon did us proud. He jumped up and down. He threw his cap on the dirt and kicked it. He turned red in the face. He raged and shouted at the umpires —two of them from the States, two from Cuba.

The crowd loved it. They started shouting "*Ole!*" every time he kicked up some dirt.

The umpires went through the rule book. There's no rule that says all the players have to be human beings. So Raoul the Robot stayed on the mound.

He struck out the side in the first inning. Leading off the second inning, our cleanup hitter, well rested after his three-day coma, managed to pop a fly to center field. But the next two guys struck out.

And so it went. Raoul had three basic pitches: fast, faster, and fastest. No curve, no slider, no change-up. His fastballs were pretty straight, too. Not much of a hop or dip to them. They just blazed past you before you could get your bat around. And he could throw either right-handed or left-handed, depending on the batter.

He couldn't catch the ball at all. After each pitch the catcher would toss the ball to the shortstop, who would come over to the mound and stick the ball in a round opening at the top of the robot's glassed-in head. Then the machine would be ready to wind up and throw.

"Hit him in the head," Nixon advised us. "Break that glass top and knock him the hell out of there."

Easy to say. Through the first four innings we got exactly one man on base, a walk. Their catcher adjusted the little gizmo he had clipped to his chest protector, and the mechanical monster started throwing strikes again.

By the time the ninth inning came around, we had collected two hits, both of them bloop pop-ups that just happened to fall in between fielders. Raoul had struck out fourteen. Nixon was glaring pure hatred across the infield. Castro was laughing and passing out cigars in the Cubans' dugout.

Our own pitcher had done almost as well as the robot. But an error by our substitute third baseman, a sacrifice fly, and a squeeze bunt had given the Cubans a 1–0 lead. That one run looked as big as a million.

Our shortstop led off the ninth inning and managed to get his bat on the ball. A grounder. He was out by half a step. The next guy popped up—not bad after three strikeouts.

I breathed a sigh of relief. The next man up, Harry Bates, would end the game, and that would be that. I was next after him, and I sure didn't want to be the guy who made the last out. I went out to the on-deck circle, kneeled on one knee, and watched the final moment of the game.

"Get it over with, Harry," I said inside my head. "Don't put me on the spot." I was kind of ashamed of myself for feeling that way, but that's how I felt.

Raoul cranked his metal slingshot arm once, twice, and then fired the ball. It blurred past the batter. Strike one. The crowd roared. "*Ole!*" The catcher flipped the ball to the shortstop, who trotted over to the mound and popped the ball into the robot's slot like a guy putting money into a video game.

The curved metal arm cranked again. The ball came whizzing to the plate. Strike two. "*Ole!*" Louder this time. Castro leaned back on the dugout bench and clasped his hands behind his head. His grin was as wide as a superhighway.

But on the third pitch Harry managed to get his bat around and cracked a solid single, over their short-stop's head. The first real hit of the day for us.

The crowd went absolutely silent.

Castro looked up and down his bench, then made a big shrug. He wasn't worried.

I was. It was my turn at bat. All I had to show for three previous trips to the plate was a strikeout and two pop flies.

Automatically, I looked down to our third-base coach. He was staring into the dugout. Nixon scratched his nose, tugged at the bill of his cap, and ran a hand across the letters on the front of his shirt. The coach's eyes goggled. But he scratched his nose, tugged at his cap, and ran his hand across the letters.

Hit and run.

Damn! I'm supposed to poke the first pitch into right field while Harry breaks for second as soon as the pitcher starts his—its—delivery. Terrific strategy, when the chances are the damned ball will be in the catcher's mitt before I can get the bat off my shoulder. Nixon's trying to be a genius. Well, at least when they throw Harry out at second, the game'll be over and I won't have to make the final out.

The mechanical monster starts its windup, Harry breaks from first, and *wham*! the ball's past me. I wave my bat kind of feebly, just to make the catcher's job a little bit tougher.

But his throw is late. Raoul's windup took so much time that Harry made it to second easy.

I look down to the third-base coach again.

Same sign. Hit and run. Sweet Jesus! Now he wants Harry to head for third. I grit my teeth and pound the bat on the plate. Stealing second is a lot easier than stealing third.

Raoul swings his mechanical arm around, Harry breaks for third, and the ball comes whizzing at me. I swing at it but it's already in the catcher's mitt and he's throwing to third. Harry dives in headfirst and the umpire calls him safe. By a fingernail.

The crowd is muttering now, rumbling like a dark thundercloud. The tying run's on third.

And I've got two strikes on me.

Nixon slumps deeper on the bench in the dugout, his face lost in shadow. Both Harry and our third-base coach are staring in at him. He twitches and fidgets. The coach turns to me and rubs his jaw.

Hit away. I'm on my own.

No, my whole life didn't flash before my eyes, but it might as well have. Old Raoul out there on the mound hadn't thrown anything but strikes since the fourth inning. One more strike and I'm out and the game's over and we've lost. The only time I got any wood on the ball I produced a feeble pop fly. There was only one thing I could think of that had any chance.

You can throw, you goddamned Commie tin can, I said silently to the robot. But can you field?

Raoul cranked up his metal arm again, and I squared away and slid my hand halfway up the bat. Out of the corners of my eyes I could see the Cuban infielders suddenly reacting to the idea that I was going to bunt. The first and third basemen started rushing in toward me. But too late. The pitch was already on its way.

Harry saw it, too, and started galloping for home.

I just stuck my bat in front of the ball, holding it limply to deaden the impact. I had always been a good bunter, and this one had to be perfect.

It damned near was. I nudged the ball right back toward the mound. It trickled along the grass as I lit out for first, thinking, "Let's see you handle that, Raoul."

Sonofabitch if the mechanical monster didn't roll itself down off the mound and scoop up the ball as neatly as a vacuum cleaner picking up a fuzzball. I was less than halfway to first and I knew that I had goofed. I was dead meat.

Raoul the Robot sucked up the ball, spun itself around to face first base, and fired the baseball like a bullet to the guy covering the bag. It got there ten strides ahead of me, tore the glove off the fielder's hand, and kept on going deep into right field, past the foul line.

My heart bounced from my throat to my stomach and then back again. Raoul had only three pitches: fast, faster, and fastest. The poor sucker covering first base had never been shot at so hard. He never had a chance to hold on to the ball.

Harry scored, of course, and I must have broken the world record for going from first to third. I slid into the bag in a storm of dust and dirt, an eyelash ahead of the throw.

The game was tied. The winning run—me!—was on third base, ninety feet away from home.

And the stadium was dead quiet again. Castro came out to the mound and they didn't even applaud him. The catcher and the whole infield clustered around him and the robot. Castro, taller than all his players, turned and pointed at somebody in the dugout.

"He's bringin' in a relief pitcher!" our third-base coach said.

No such luck. A stumpy little guy who was built kind of like the robot himself, thick and solid, like a fireplug, came trudging out of the dugout with something like a tool kit in one hand. He was wearing a mechanic's coveralls, not a baseball uniform.

They tinkered with Raoul for about ten minutes, while the crowd got restless and Nixon shambled out of our dugout to tell the umpires that the Cubans should be penalized for delaying the game.

"This ain't football, Mr. President," said the chief umpire.

Nixon grumbled and mumbled and went back inside the dugout.

Finally, the repair job at the mound was finished. The infielders dispersed and the repairman trotted off the field. Castro stayed at the mound while Raoul made a few practice pitches.

Kee-rist! Now he didn't wind up at all. He just swung the arm around once and fired the ball to the catcher. Faster than ever.

And our batter, Pedro Valencia, had struck out three straight times. Never even managed to tick the ball foul. Not once. Nine pitches, nine strikes, three strikeouts.

I looked at the coach, a couple of feet away from me. No sign. No strategy. I was on my own.

Pedro stepped into the batter's box. Raoul stood up on the mound. His mechanical arm swung around and something that looked like an aspirin tablet whizzed into the catcher's mitt. "*Ole!*" Strike one.

I took a good-sized lead off third base. Home plate was only a dozen strides away. The shortstop took the catcher's toss and popped the ball into the robot's slot.

If I stole home, we would win. If I got thrown out, we would lose for sure. Raoul could keep pitching like that all day, all night, all week. Sooner or later we'd tire out and they'd beat us. We'd never get another runner to third base. It was up to me. Now.

I didn't wait for the damned robot to start his pitch. He had the ball, he was on the mound, nobody had called time out. I broke for the plate.

Everything seemed to happen in slow motion. I could see the surprised expression on Pedro's face. But he was a pro; he hung in there and swung at the pitch. Missed it. The catcher had the ball in his mitt and I was still three strides up the line. I started a slide away from him, toward the pitcher's side of the plate. He lunged at me, the ball in his bare hand.

I felt him tag my leg. And I heard the umpire yell, "Out . . . no, *safe!*"

I was sitting on the ground. The catcher was on top of me, grabbing for the ball as it rolled away from us both. He had dropped it.

Before I could recover from the shock, he whispered from behind his mask, "You ween. Now we have to play another series. In the States, no?"

I spit dust from my mouth. He got to his feet. "See you in Peetsborgh, no?"

He had dropped the damned ball on purpose. He wanted to come to the States and play for my team, the Pirates.

By now the whole USA team was grabbing me and hiking me up on their shoulders. Nixon was already riding along, his arms upraised in his old familiar victory gesture. The fans were giving us a grudging round of applause. We had won—even if it took a deliberate error by a would-be defector.

In the locker room, news correspondents from all the Latin American nations descended on us. Fortunately, my Spanish was up to the task. They crowded around me, and I told them what it was like to live in Miami and get the chance to play big-league baseball. I told them about my father, and how he had fled from Cuba with nothing but his wife and infant son—me—twenty-three years ago. I knew we had won on a fluke, but I still felt damned good about winning.

Finally the reporters and photographers were cleared out of the locker room, and Nixon stood on one of the benches, a telegram in his hand, tears in his eyes.

"Men," he said, "I have good news and bad news."

We clustered around him.

"The good news is that the President of the United States," his voice quavered a little, "has invited all of us to the White House. You're all going to receive medals from the President himself."

Smiles all around.

"And now the bad news," he went on. "The President has agreed to a series against a Japanese team —the Mitsubishi Marvels. They're all robots. Each and every one of them."

The Jefferson Orbit

In 1975 my beautiful wife, Barbara, and I traveled to Melbourne for the World Science Fiction Convention. While in Australia we met many, many wonderful people. The Aussies are fine and hospitable hosts. We didn't draw a sober breath for two weeks.

Back then, if you had more than a single beer with an Aussie, he would fix you with a beady stare and mutter, "By heaven, Yank, if the America's Cup races were sailed here, we'd win!" To which I would always reply, "Well, maybe. But first you've got to go to Newport and win the Cup." Which they have since done, and more credit to them.

But at one particular cocktail party, one of the top lawyers in Australia was crying in his beer (literally!) because he was having enormous difficulties getting a fair trial for a group of prison convicts he was representing. The convicts had staged a sit-down strike or some such, if memory serves me, and the prison guards had thoroughly and methodically beaten them with billy clubs. Our lawyer friend was trying to get the convicts' case heard in court. No go. The courts refused to hear it.

"And the newspapers won't even print the story," he complained bitterly.

I was shocked. "What do you mean they won't print the story?" I'm a former newspaper reporter, and my blood was up. (Heavily fortified with alcohol.)

"They can't. Government won't let them."

"That's impossible!" I cried. "We've got freedom of the press!"

"No, Yank," he said sadly. "*You've* got freedom of the press. We have a government censor."

That is when it hit me. Every nation in the world has a government censor. Except one.

"The Jefferson Orbit" looks at how our ideas of freedom of expression are faring in the world of communications satellites. To summarize, it's Jefferson 1, Censorship 102.

————————————

It's called the Clarke Orbit, that lovely band in space 22,300 miles above Earth's equator, where a satellite's revolution around the planet exactly matches the Earth's own rotation, so that the satellite hangs over the same spot on the equator all the time.

It's the ideal location for communications satellites, as Arthur C. Clarke figured out in 1945: hence the orbit is named for him.

But it is also the site for a quietly intense struggle between those who believe in Jeffersonian freedom and those who don't—which is why this "far frontier" of human technology might also be dubbed the Jefferson Orbit.

Futurists (i.e., science fiction writers who are dull) are fond of predicting that our rapidly advancing communications technology will soon create a "global village," where ancient differences and animosities among people and nations will be washed away by a new wave of electronic information and understanding.

Perhaps so. But most of the governments of the world are fighting their hardest to prevent this bright new vision from becoming reality. They do not want to become members of a "global village." They would rather keep the walls around their borders high and tight.

If eternal vigilance is the price of liberty, then we had better look to the skies, and especially to the Clarke Orbit. For the nations of the world are arguing over who may use that orbit, and how. In that battle the United States is a lonely and outnumbered champion of the Jeffersonian ideal of freedom of information. Practically every other nation in the world is lined up against us, in favor of censorship.

The direct broadcast satellite is what the battle is all about: a bitter lesson in how politics can sidetrack the futurists' dreams of better living through technology.

We tend to take communications satellites for granted, like weather satellites and interplanetary probes and space shuttles. Last week I picked up my telephone and chatted for half an hour with Arthur Clarke. He was at his home in Sri Lanka, I in my home in Connecticut. Except for a barely noticeable lag caused by the travel time of the microwave signals over a nearly 50,000-mile distance up to the commsat and back, the conversation was as normal as a call to the folks next door.

A few days later I conversed with a group of students and teachers at the University of Honolulu over a closed-circuit slow-scan television link. We sent pictures back and forth in much the same way that *Voyager* spacecraft have sent pictures from Jupiter and Saturn. Again, our communications link was relayed by a geostationary communications satellite.

Satellites are revolutionizing our communications systems, and the revolution has just barely begun. NASA and General Electric have developed a portable communications system that fits into two suitcases; it can send messages, relayed by satellite, to almost anyplace in the western hemisphere. Technology available today can produce wrist communicators that are telephones, television sets, and computers, all in one compact package. Professor Gerard O'Neill, father of the L5 space-colony concept, is marketing a hand-sized navigational aid that will pinpoint your location to within a couple of feet, anywhere on Earth, once the proper satellites have been hung in the geostationary orbit.

But the biggest change to affect the communications industry, and the change that will show its effects the soonest, is the direct broadcast satellite (DBS). This change began in 1974, when the United States orbited its ATS-6 satellite over the Indian Ocean; for more than a year this satellite beamed farming, hygiene, and safety information to more than four thousand villages in India. Thanks in large part to Clarke, the villages received from the Indian government inexpensive antenna "dishes" that could pick up the signal broadcast across the entire subcontinent by ATS-6. This was the first practical test of DBS.

The basic idea of DBS is elegantly simple: transmit television broadcasts directly from an orbiting satellite to individual homes. No need for television broadcasting or cable stations on the ground; a single satellite can beam its signal to almost half the world at once. Already today, the Japanese Broadcast Company, NHK of Tokyo, sells a two-foot-wide "dish" antenna to receive DBS signals for less than $350.

Today, you can see larger antenna dishes sitting on the parking lots behind motels, on the roofs of office buildings, even alongside private homes. These dishes are aimed at existing geostationary satellites, and they take in the television signals broadcast by those satellites—directly, without going through an intermediary broadcasting or cable station.

For less than the price of an automobile, you can buy one of those satellite dishes and tune in directly to the television signals broadcast your way. But you will not be tuning in to direct broadcast satellites. Instead, you will be eavesdropping on signals intended for the receiving antennas of commercial broadcasting stations or cable stations.

However, satellites that *do* broadcast directly to individual rooftop or parking lot dishes are now going into orbit. And the new technology of DBS has caused a furor in the international political arena.

For although the United States, with its Jeffersonian tradition of freedom of expression, is wholeheartedly in favor of DBS, most of the other nations of the world are much more cautious about opening the skies to direct satellite-to-home broadcasting.

The basic idea behind DBS is simple enough. Space technology has reached the point where satellites of considerable size and sophistication can be orbited rather routinely. *Telstar I*, launched in 1962, weighed 170 pounds and could handle twelve phone circuits or one television channel. *Intelsat V*, launched in 1980, weighs 2,200 pounds and carries twelve thousand voice circuits plus two television channels.

With the advent of the space shuttle, it is now possible to build much larger and more complex satellites in space, even linking modules together in low Earth orbit and then, after checking out the assembled satellite, sending it on to an assigned position in geostationary orbit.

The more powerful and sophisticated the satellite, the simpler and cheaper can be the ground antennas that receive the satellite's signals. Thus the DBS idea is to put most of the complexity and expense into the satellite, so that the cost of the ground antennas will be so low that millions of customers can afford to buy them.

Jerry Nelson, chairman of the board of Antenna Technology Corporation of Orlando, Florida, has watched the market for satellite antennas explode over the past few years. Antenna Technology sells mainly to the commercial market: business offices, hotels, and the like. Sales are climbing steeply, he says, and the market for home antennas will reach the multimillions when DBS comes on the domestic scene.

But it may still be too soon to rush out and buy a dish, because powerful forces within the international political community are working hard to prevent DBS from becoming a reality.

These forces are led by the so-called Group of 77, a bloc of Third World nations that now numbers more than 120 countries. The basic goal of the Group of 77 is to create a "new international economic order" based on the rationale that "fundamental justice requires that those who receive the raw materials and natural resources that fuel and feed industrialized economies *must be required* to pay a significant share of their economic wealth in exchange for access to those resources." (Italics added.)

One of the "resources" that the Third World claims is the geostationary orbit itself. In 1976 the equator-straddling nations of Brazil, Colombia, Congo, Ecuador, Indonesia, Kenya, Uganda, and Zaire signed the Declaration of Bogotá, in which they claimed possession of the Clarke Orbit. The industrialized nations, including the United States and the Soviet Union, have denounced this claim, and insist that the geostationary orbit is in free, international space as defined by the Outer Space Treaty of 1967.

But how many satellites can fit along that one choice orbit? And who decides which satellites will get the preferred slots up there?

According to Comsat Corporation's "Geosynchronous Satellite Log," there are 126 communications satellites functioning in the Clarke Orbit at present, plus another 29 meteorological, scientific, and experimental satellites also in the twenty-four-hour orbit. Of the communications satellites, 32 are Russian, 31 are American (19 of those are Defense Department satellites), and 2 belong to NATO. Six of those satellites are DBSs. Direct broadcast satellites have been orbited by the Soviet Union, a consortium of Western European nations, the People's Republic of China, Japan, West Germany, and France.

Added to these active satellites are an almost equal number of geostationary satellites that have ceased to function. Even so, at first glance it would seem that the geostationary orbit, which is slightly more than 140,000 miles in circumference, would scarcely be crowded.

Yet planners worry about crowding at certain preferred locations along the geostationary orbit. For example, more than forty commsats are either already in orbit or planned to be orbited between 60° and 150° west longitude, where they can "see"—and be seen by—most of North and South America.

While there is no danger of the satellites bumping each other in the vast emptiness of orbit, they still must be placed at least four degrees of arc apart from one another, so that their transmitting beams do not interfere with each other. This means that there are, at most, twenty-two available slots along the geostationary orbit between those two longitudes.

One way to resolve the crowding problem is to go to higher frequencies in the electromagnetic spectrum. Most commsats today operate at C-band frequencies, six and four gigahertz. One hertz equals one cycle per second. Household electrical current runs at sixty hertz. Six gigahertz is 6,000 million hertz.

Some satellites are already operating in the Ku-band, at fourteen and twelve gigahertz, where they can use ten-foot-wide antennas instead of the thirty-foot-wide dishes required for C-band. The Ka-band, at thirty and twenty gigahertz, can shrink antenna requirements to five-foot diameters, and offers more than three times the message-carrying capacity of C-band. Satellites operating at these frequencies can be spaced only one degree apart without fear of signal overlap.

Engineers are satisfied that Ka-band equipment can meet the expected growth in communications demand, including DBS's, through the 1990s.

But while the electronics technology may be ready to face the remaining years of this century, the politics of communications satellites—and especially DBS—lags behind.

Many national governments do not want their citizens to receive television broadcasts from other nations. Dr. Jerry Grey, author of *Beachheads in Space* (Macmillan, 1983) and a veteran of many international meetings and conferences on astronautics, says, "Television is too powerful a medium; they're afraid of it. Most of the governments of the world don't want TV broadcasts going directly from a satellite to their citizens."

Most of the world's governments are authoritarian, if not outright dictatorships. Freedom of speech, taken for granted by Americans, is a rarity elsewhere. But signals beamed from a satellite to the ground are very difficult to jam. To stop DBS, governments have turned to legalistic formulations.

Dr. Grey, in *Beachheads in Space*, traces the political turmoil succinctly:

International opposition [to DBS] arises from ... national sovereignty concerns. ... Unlike radio [which can be jammed], direct-to-citizen television was seen by many governments as too powerful a medium to be allowed to develop along the same relatively open lines as international radio. [Ordinary] television could be received only by relatively large, expensive ground stations, from which any retransmissions could be controlled. . . . But direct citizen access to geostationary satellites whose coverage could conceivably range over a third of the globe was worrisome to many governments.

Those governments, mostly Third World and Eastern Bloc nations, pushed through a ruling in the United Nations that the U.N.'s Committee on the Peaceful Uses of Outer Space should set up controls to regulate DBSs.

"The vote," Dr. Grey reports, "was 102 to 1, the United States alone defending vigorously its established policy of unrestricted free flow of information."

As a result, regulations were approved in which every nation, no matter how small, was awarded a geostationary orbital slot and five DBS channels. Thus the small nations have gained control of most of the future slots along the geostationary orbit. They are apparently willing to sell or lease those slots to nations that can actually place DBSs in orbit, providing that they have some measure of control over the programming being beamed to the ground.

This ruling applied, essentially, to the eastern hemisphere—the nations of Europe, Asia, and Africa—although the precedent can and probably will affect the availability of future orbital slots for North and South America.

As far as communications technology is concerned, this ruling makes certain that nations cannot place DBSs in orbit on a haphazard, first-come, first-served basis, which could result in a chaos of satellites beaming signals that overlap and interfere with each other, producing bedlam on the ground.

On the political side it ensures that virtually any nation on Earth can exert a controlling power over the transmissions beamed from DBSs to its citizens. These nations have the right to refuse to allow another nation or consortium to place a DBS in an orbital position assigned to them, unless and until they are satisfied that the satellite will not broadcast anything which that government does not want its citizens to receive.

For example, suppose France wants to place a DBS in an orbital slot above the Pacific, where it would beam transmissions to the islands of French Polynesia. The French would have to borrow, rent, or buy a slot from one of the nations that has been assigned an orbital position above the Pacific Ocean. That nation's government, presumably, could extract a promise from France not to broadcast any material to which the "host" government might object.

Another way that governments may restrict their citizens' access to foreign DBS signals is to control the frequencies that each satellite uses *and* the frequencies receivable by the TV sets owned by their citizens. Thus a government might prohibit the sale, within its borders, of TV sets that can receive broadcasts from neighboring nations.

The Group of 77's "New International Order" includes a "New World Information Order" in which, among other things, news correspondents would have to be licensed by the nations they are reporting about, and data from Earth-resources satellites could not be disseminated without the permission of the nation whose territory was surveyed. Jeffersonian freedom of information is antithetical to such attitudes, and the

Group of 77 will continue to use its voting power at the United Nations to place as many restrictions on DBSs as possible.

The struggle, then, is between those nations that insist on an unrestricted flow of information and those that insist that every nation has the right of prior approval of the information transmitted to its citizens. Of the former, only the United States has voted consistently in favor of Jefferson. Our allies have often deserted us, either abstaining from critical votes or voting with the other side.

Nandasiri Jasentuliyana, of Sri Lanka, the executive secretary of the U.N. Conference on Outer Space, points out that many of the nations of the world believe that their national sovereignty is just as important as Western ideas of freedom of speech. Even leaving aside the political aspect, he says that a nation's internal social and cultural values must also be carefully considered.

"Who am I to say, for example," he asks, "that one religion's ideas on family planning and birth control should or should not be broadcast to people of a different religion?"

To Americans raised on Jeffersonian ideas of free speech and tolerance for ideas different from our own, such regulation of DBSs smacks of censorship. Certainly a relatively closed society such as the Soviet Union would not want its citizens to see American situation comedies or game shows. Would Americans tolerate the six o'clock news as Tass would transmit it?

But Antenna Technology's chairman Nelson appears unworried by the Third World or even the Soviet-dominated Second World:

"Once people realize that they can put up a cheap antenna and get television programs from all over the world, no government on Earth will be able to hold them back."

Perhaps he is right. Certainly many engineers and industrialists see a brilliant future for commsats in general and DBSs in particular. After all, the biggest auction ever held by Sotheby Park Bernet was in 1981, when the famed auction house sold off seven-year leases for seven channels in an RCA satellite for a grand total of $90.1 million.

The ever-optimistic Clarke even foresees the advent of a global communications network that transcends national boundaries and, more important, national politics.

"During the coming decade," he believes, "more and more businessmen, well-heeled tourists, and virtually *all* newspersons will be carrying attaché case-sized units that will permit direct two-way communications with their homes or offices, via the most convenient satellite. These will provide voice, telex, and video facilities. . . . As these units become cheaper, they will make travelers *totally independent of national communications systems*." (Clarke's italics.)

Commsats, according to Clarke, can help to unify the world. "It means the end of closed societies." Nations that refuse to allow visitors to bring "such subversive machines across their borders" will face economic suicide, "because very soon they would get no tourists, and no businessmen offering foreign currency. They'd get only spies, who would have no trouble at all concealing the powerful new tools of their ancient trade."

Even if the politicians are dragging their feet, satellite communications is already a big business —and it is growing.

But like it or not, the fact is that DBS broadcasts are now, and will continue to be, under the control of national governments that have scant tolerance for freedom of information.

Despite the technology of DBS, we have a long way to go before that "global village" opens its gates. And the Jeffersonian struggle of knowledge over ignorance, of freedom over despotism, has found a new battleground in space.

Isolation Area ═══════════════

Like the Earth, space is not for the military alone, thank goodness!

If you have read *Prometheans*, a collection of fact and fiction published in 1986 by Tor Books, you have already met Sam Gunn. He's the feisty little astronaut who . . . Well, if you've read the story, you already know, and if you haven't, I shouldn't spoil it for you.

"Isolation Area" deals with a later period of Sam's life, when he takes that first scary step toward becoming the solar system's premier big-time space entrepreneur. In a subtler way it is also the story of the friendship between two men, and of the new freedoms that we will find as we begin to live and work—and love—in space.

Incidentally, the best way to see that the military role in space is minimal is to maximize the peaceful, civilian, commercial aspects of space development. In his own cash-and-carry way, Sam Gunn strikes a blow against militarism with every sale he makes.

───────────────

They faced each other suspiciously, floating weightlessly in emptiness.

The black man was tall, long-limbed, loose, gangling; on Earth he might have made a pro basketball player. His utilitarian coveralls were standard issue,

frayed at the cuffs and so worn that whatever color
they had been originally had long since faded into a
dull gray. They were clean and pressed to a razor
sharpness, though. The insignia patch on his left
shoulder said *Administration*. A strictly nonregula-
tion belt of royal blue, studded with rough lumps of
meteoric gold and clamped by a heavy gold buckle,
cinched his narrow waist and made him look even
taller and leaner.

He eyed the reporter warily. She was young, and the
slightly greenish cast to her pretty features told him
that she had never been in orbit before. Her pale
blond hair was shoulder length, he judged, but she
had followed the instructions given to groundlings
and tied it up in a zero-gee snood. Her coveralls were
spanking new white. She filled them nicely enough,
although she had more of a figure than he cared for.

Frederick Mohammed Malone was skeptical to the
point of being hostile toward this female interloper.
The reporter could see the resentment smoldering in
the black man's eyes. Malone's face was narrow,
almost gaunt, with a trim little Vandyke jutting out
from his chin. His forehead was high, receding; his
hair cropped close to the skull. She guessed Malone's
age at somewhere in the early forties, although she
knew that living in zero gravity could make a person
look much younger than his or her calendar age.

She tried to restart their stalled conversation. "I
understand that you and Sam Gunn were, uh,
friends."

"Why're you doing a story on Sam?" Malone asked,
his voice low and loaded with distrust.

The two of them were in Malone's "office": actually
an observation blister in the central hub of space
station *Alpha*. Oldest and still biggest of the Earth-
orbiting stations, *Alpha* was built on the old wheels-
within-wheels scheme. The outermost rim, where

most of the staff lived and worked, spun at a rate that gave it almost a full Earth gravity. Two thirds of the way toward the hub there was a wheel that spun at the Moon's one-sixth gee. The hub itself, of course, was for all practical purposes at zero gee, weightless.

Malone's aerie consisted of one wall, on which were located a semicircular sort of desk and communications center, a bank of viewing screens that were all blankly gray at the moment, and an airtight hatch that led to the spokes that radiated out to the various wheels. The rest of the chamber was a transparent plastic bubble, from which Malone could watch the station's loading dock—and the overwhelming majesty of the huge, curved, incredibly blue and white-flecked Earth as it slid past endlessly, massive, brilliant, ever-changing, ever-beautiful.

To the reporter, though, it seemed as if they were hanging in empty space itself, unprotected by anything at all, and falling, falling, falling toward the ponderous world of their birth. The background rumble of the bearings that bore the massive station's rotation while the hub remained static sounded to her like the insistent bass growl of a giant grinding wheel that was pressing the breath out of her.

She swallowed bile, felt it burn in her throat, and tried to concentrate on the job at hand.

She said to Malone, "I've been assigned to do a biography of Mr. Gunn for the Solar Network . . ."

Despite himself, Malone suddenly grinned. "First time I ever heard him called *Mr.* Gunn."

"Oh?" The reporter's microchip recorder, clipped to her belt, was already on, of course. "What did the people here call him?"

That lean, angular face took on an almost thoughtful look. "Oh . . . Sam, mostly. 'That tricky bastard,' a good many times." Malone actually laughed. "Plen-

ty times I heard him called a womanizing sonofabitch."

"What did you call him?"

The suspicion came back into Malone's eyes. "He
was my friend. I called him Sam."

Silence stretched between them, hanging as weightlessly as their bodies. The reporter turned her head
slightly and found herself staring at the vast bulk of
Earth. Her mind screamed as if she were falling down
an elevator shaft. Her stomach churned queasily. She
could not tear her eyes away from the world drifting
past, so far below them, so compellingly near. She
felt herself being drawn toward it, dropping through
the emptiness, spinning down the deep swirling
vortex . . .

Malone's long-fingered hand squeezed her shoulder
hard enough to hurt. She snapped her attention to his
dark, unsmiling face as he grasped her other shoulder
and held her firmly in his strong hands.

"You were drifting," he said, almost in a whisper.

"Was I . . . ?"

"It's all right," he said. "Gets everybody at first.
Don't be scared. You're perfectly safe."

His powerful hands steadied her. She fought down
the panic surging inside.

"If you got to upchuck, go ahead and do it. Nothing
to be ashamed of." His grin returned. "Only, use the
bags they gave you, please."

He looked almost handsome when he smiled, she
thought. After another moment, he released her. She
took a deep breath and dabbed at the beads of
perspiration on her forehead. The retch bags that the
technicians had attached to her belt were a symbol to
her now. I won't need them, she insisted to herself.
I'm not going to let this get me.

"Feel better?" he asked.

There was real concern in his eyes. "I think I'll be all right. Thanks."

"*De nada*," he said. "I appreciate your coming out here to the hub for the interview."

His attitude had changed, she saw. The sullenness had thawed. He had insisted on conducting the interview in the station's zero-gravity area. He had allowed no alternative. But she was grateful that the shell of distrust seemed to have cracked.

It took several moments before she could say, "I'm not here to do a hatchet job on Mr. Gunn."

Malone made a small shrug. "Doesn't make much difference, one way or t'other. He's dead; nothing you say can hurt him now."

"But we know so little about him. I suppose he's the most famous enigma in the solar system."

The black man made no response.

"The key question, I guess . . . the thing our viewers will be most curious about, is why Sam Gunn exiled himself up here. Why did he turn his back on Earth?"

Malone snorted with disdain. "He didn't! Those motherfuckers turned their backs on him."

"What do you mean?"

"It's a long story," Malone said.

"That's all right. I've got as much time as it takes." Even as she said it, the reporter wished that Malone would volunteer to return back to the outer wheel, where gravity was normal. But she dared not ask the man to leave his office. Once a subject starts talking, never interrupt! That was the cardinal rule of a successful interview. Besides, she was determined not to let weightlessness get the better of her.

"Would you believe," Malone was saying, "that it all started with a cold?"

"A cold?"

"Sam came down with a cold in the head. That's

how the whole thing began."

"Tell me about it."

Sam was a feisty little bastard—Malone reminisced —full of piss and vinegar. If there were ten different ways in the regulations to do a job, he'd find an eleventh, maybe a twelfth or a fourteenth, just because he couldn't abide being bound by the regs. A free spirit, I guess you'd call him.

He'd had his troubles with the brass in Houston *and* Washington. Why he ever became an astronaut in the first place is beyond me. Maybe he thought he'd be like a pioneer out on the frontier, on his own, way out in space. *How* he made it through training and into flight operations is something I'll never figure out. I just don't feature Sam sitting still long enough to get through kindergarten, let alone flight school and astronaut training.

Anyway, when I first met him, he was finished as an astronaut. He had put in seven years, which he said was a biblical amount of time, and he wanted out. And the agency was glad to get rid of him, believe me. But he had this cold in the head, and they couldn't let him go back Earthside until it cleared up.

"Six billion people down there with colds, the flu, bad sinuses, and postnasal drips, and the assholes in Houston won't let me go back until this goddamned sniffle clears up."

Those were the first words Sam ever said to me. He had been assigned to my special isolation ward, where I had reigned alone for nearly four years. *Alpha* was under construction then. We were in the old Mac-Dac Shack, a glorified tin can that passed for a space station back in those primitive days. It didn't spin, it just hung there; everything inside was weightless.

My isolation ward was a cramped compartment with four zero-gee bunks jammed into it, together with lockers to stow personal gear. Nobody but me had ever been in it until that morning. Sam shuffled over to the bed next to mine, towing his travel bag like a kid with a sinking balloon.

"Just don't sneeze in my direction, Sniffles," I growled at him.

That stopped Sam for about half a second. He gave me that lopsided grin of his—his face sort of looked like a scuffed-up soccer ball, kind of round, scruffy. Little wart of a nose in the middle of it. Longest hair I ever saw on a man who works in space; hair length was one of the multitudinous points of contention between Sam and the agency. His eyes sparkled. Kind of an odd color, not quite blue, not really green. Sort of in between.

"Malone, huh?" He read the name tag clipped over my bunk.

"Frederick Mohammed Malone."

"Jesus Christ, they put me next to an Arab!"

But he stuck out his hand. Sam was really a little guy; his hand was almost like a baby's. After a moment's hesitation I swallowed it in mine.

"Sam," he told me, knowing I could see his last name on the name tag pinned to his coveralls.

"I'm not even a Muslim," I said. "My father was, though. First one in Arkansas."

"Good for him." Sam disengaged his cleated shoes from the grillwork floor and floated up onto the cot. His travel bag hung alongside. He ignored it and sniffed at the air. "Goddamned hospitals all smell like somebody's dying. What're you in for? Hangnail or something?"

"Something," I said. "Acquired immune deficiency syndrome."

His eyes went round. "AIDS?"

"It's not contagious. Not unless we make love."

"I'm straight."

"I'm not."

"Terrific. Just what I need, a gay black Arab with AIDS." But he was grinning at me.

I had seen plenty of guys back away from me once they knew I had AIDS. Some of them had a hang-up about gays. Others were scared out of their wits that they would catch AIDS from me, or from the medical personnel or equipment. I had more than one reason to know how a leper felt, back in those days.

Sam's grin faded into a frown. "How the hell did the medics put me in here if you've got AIDS? Won't you catch my cold? Isn't that dangerous for you?"

"I'm a guinea pig . . ."

"You don't look Italian."

"Look," I said, "if you're gonna stay in here, keep off the ethnic jokes, okay?"

He shrugged.

"The medics think they've got my case arrested. New treatment that the genetic researchers have come up with."

"I get it. If you don't catch my cold, you're cured."

"They never use words like 'cured.' But that's the general idea."

"So I'm a guinea pig, too."

"No, you are a part of the apparatus for this experiment. A source of infection. A bag of viruses. A host of bacteria. Germ city."

Sam hooked his feet into his bunk's webbing and gave me a dark look. "And this is the guy who doesn't like ethnic jokes."

The Mac-Dac Shack was one of the first space stations the agency had put up. It wasn't fancy, but for years it had served as a sort of research laboratory, mainly for medical work. Naturally, with a lot of M.D.s in it, the Shack sort of turned into a floating hospital in orbit. With all the construction work going on in those days, there was a steady stream of injured workmen and technicians.

Then some bright bureaucrat got the idea of using the Shack as an isolation ward, where the medics could do research on things like AIDS, Legionnaires' disease, the New Delhi virus, and various paralytic afflictions that required either isolation or zero gravity or both. The construction-crew infirmary was moved over to the yet-unfinished *Alpha*, while the Shack was turned into a pure research facility with various isolation wards for guinea pigs like me.

Sam stayed in my ward for three, four days; I forget the exact time. He was like an energetic little bee, buzzing all over the place, hardly ever still for a minute. In zero gee, of course, he could literally climb the curved walls of the ward and hover up on the ceiling. He terrified the head nurse in short order by hanging near the ceiling or hiding behind one of the bunks and then launching himself at her like a missile when she showed up with the morning's assortment of needles.

Never once did Sam show the slightest qualm at having his blood sampled alongside mine. I've seen guys get violent from their fear that they'd get a needle contaminated by me, and catch what I had. But Sam never even blinked. Me, I never liked needles. Couldn't abide them. Couldn't look when the nurse stuck me; couldn't even look when she stuck somebody else.

"All the nurses are women," Sam noticed by the end of his first day.

"All six of them," I affirmed.

"The doctors are all males?"

"Eight men, four women."

"That leaves two extra women for us."

"For you. I'm on the other side."

"How come all women nurses?" he wondered.

"I think it's because of me. They don't want to

throw temptation in my path."

He started to frown at me but it turned into that lopsided grin. "They didn't think about *my* path."

He caused absolute havoc among the nurses. With the single-minded determination of a sperm cell seeking blindly for an ovum, Sam pursued them all: the fat little redhead, the cadaverous ash-blonde, the really good-looking one, the kid who still had acne—all of them, even the head nurse, who threatened to inject him with enough estrogen to grow boobs on him if he didn't leave her and her crew alone.

Nothing deflected Sam. He would be gone for long hours from the ward, and when he'd come back, he would be grinning from ear to ear. As politely as I could, I'd ask him if he had been successful.

"It matters not if you win or lose," he would say. "It's how you play the game . . . as long as you get laid."

When he finally left the isolation ward, it seemed as if we had been friends for years. And it was damned quiet in there without him. I was alone again. I missed him. I realized how many years it had been since I'd had a friend.

I sank into a real depression of self-pity and despair. I had caught Sam's cold, sure enough. I was hacking and sneezing all day and night. One good thing about zero gravity is that you can't have a postnasal drip. One bad thing is that all the fluids accumulate in your sinuses and give you a headache of monumental proportions. The head nurse seemed to take special pleasure in inflicting upon me the indignity of forcing tubes up my nose to drain the sinuses.

The medics were overjoyed. Their guinea pig was doing something interesting. Would I react to the cold like any normal person, and get over it after a few days? Or would the infection spread and worsen, turn into pneumonia or maybe kill me? I could see them writing their learned papers in their heads every time they examined me, four times a day.

I was really unfit company for anyone, including myself. I went on for months that way, just wallowing in my own misery. Other patients came and went: an African kid with a new strain of polio; an asthmatic who had developed a violent allergy to dust; a couple of burn victims from the *Alpha* construction crew. I stayed while they were treated and sent home. Then, without any warning, Sam showed up again.

"Hello, Omar, how's the tent-making business?" My middle name had become Omar as far as he was concerned.

I gaped at him. He was wearing the powder-blue coveralls and shoulder insignia of Global Technologies, Inc., which in those days was just starting to grow into the interplanetary conglomerate it has become.

"What the hell you doing back here?" My voice was a full octave higher than normal, I was so surprised. And glad.

"I work here."

"Say what?"

He ambled over to me in the zero-gee strides we all learn to make: maintain just enough contact with the grillwork on the floor to keep from floating off toward the ceiling. As Sam approached my bunk, the head nurse pushed through the ward's swinging doors with a trayful of the morning's indignities for me.

"Global Technologies just won the contract for running this tin can. The medical staff still belongs to the government, but everybody else will be replaced by Global employees. I'll be in charge of the whole place."

Behind him, the head nurse's eyes goggled, her mouth sagged open, and the tray slid from her hand. It just hung there, revolving slowly, as she turned a full one-eighty and flew out of the ward without a sound.

"You're in charge of this place?" I laughed. "No shit?"

"Only after meals," Sam said. "I've got a five-year contract."

We got to be *really* friends then. Not lovers. Sam was the most heterosexual man I have ever seen. One of the shrinks aboard the station said he had a Casanova complex: he had to take a shot at any and every female creature he saw. I don't know how good his batting average was, but he surely kept busy—and happy.

"The thrill is in the chase, Omar, not the capture," he said to me many times. Then he would always add, "As long as you get laid."

But Sam could be a true friend, caring, understanding, bringing out the best in a man. Or a woman, for that matter. I saw him help many of the station's female employees, nurses, technicians, scientists, completely aside from his amorous pursuits. He knew when to put his Casanova complex in the backseat. He was a helluva good administrator, and a leader. Everybody liked him. Even the head nurse grew to grant him a grudging respect, although she certainly didn't want anybody to know it, especially Sam.

Of course, knowing Sam, you might expect that he would have trouble with the chain of command. He had gotten himself out of the space agency, and it was hard to tell who was happier about it, him or the agency. You could hear sighs of relief from Houston and Washington all the way up where we were, the agency was so glad to be rid of the pestering little squirt who never followed regulations.

It didn't take long for Sam to find out that Global Technologies, Inc., had its own bureaucracy, its own set of regulations, and its own frustrations.

"You'd think a multibillion-dollar company would want to make all the profits it can," Sam grumbled to me about six months after he had returned to the Shack. "Half the facilities on *Alpha* are empty, right? They overbuilt, right? I show them how to turn *Alpha* into a tourist resort and they reject the goddamned idea. 'We're not in the tourism business,' they say. Goddamned assholes."

I found it hard to believe that Global Tech didn't understand what a bonanza they could reap from space tourism. But they just failed to see it. Sam spent weeks muttering about faceless bureaucrats who sat on their brains, and how much money a zero-gravity honeymoon hotel could make. It didn't do him a bit of good. At least, that's what I thought at the time.

The big crisis was mostly my fault. Looking back on it, if I could have figured out a different way to handle things, I would have. But you know how it is when your emotions are all churned up; you don't see any alternatives. Truthfully, I still don't see how I could have done anything else except what I did.

They told me I was cured.

Yeah, I know I said they never used words like that; but they changed their tune. After more than five years in the isolation ward of the station, the medics asked me to join them in the conference room. I expected another one of their dreary meetings; they made me attend them at least once a month, said it was important for me to "maintain a positive interaction with the research staff." So I dragged myself down to the conference room.

They were all grinning at me, around the table. Buckets of champagne stood at either end, with more bottles stashed where the slide projector usually hung.

I was cured. The genetic manipulations had finally worked. My body's immune system was back to normal. My case would be in the medical journals;

future generations would bless my memory (but not my name, they would protect my anonymity). I could go back home, back to Earth.

Only, I didn't want to go.

"You don't want to go?" Sam's pudgy little face was screwed up into an incredulous expression that mixed in equal amounts of surprise, disapproval, and curiosity.

"Back to Earth? No, I don't want to go," I said. "I want to stay here. Or maybe go live on *Alpha* or one of the new stations they're building."

"But why?" Sam asked.

We were in his office, a tiny little cubbyhole that had originally been a storage locker for fresh food. I mean, space in the Shack was *tight*. I thought I could still smell onions or something faintly pungent. Sam had walled the chamber with a blue-colored spongy plastic, so naturally it came to be known as the Blue Grotto. There were no chairs in the Grotto, we just hung in midair. You could nudge your back against the slightly rough wall surfacing and that would hold you in place well enough. There wasn't much room to drift around in. Two people were all the chamber could hold comfortably. Sam's computer terminal was built into the wall; there was no furniture in the Grotto, no room for any.

"I got nothing to go back there for," I answered, "and a lot of crap waiting for me that I would just as soon avoid."

"But it's *Earth*," he said. "The world . . ."

So I told him about it. The whole story, end to end.

I had been a soldier, back in that nasty little bitch of a war in Mexico. Nothing glamorous, not even patriotism. I had joined the army because it was the only way for a kid from my part of Little Rock to get a college education. They paid for my education, and right after they pinned a lieutenant's gold bars on my shoulders they stuck me inside a heavy tank. Well, you know how well the tanks did in those hills. Nothing to shoot at but cactus, and we were great big noisy targets for those smart little missiles they brought in from Czechoslovakia or wherever.

They knocked out my tank. I was the only one of the crew to survive, and I wound up in an army hospital where they tried to put my spine back together again. That's where I contracted AIDS, from one of the male nurses who wanted to prove to me that I hadn't lost my virility. He was a very sweet kid, very caring. But I never saw him again once they decided to ship me to the isolation ward up in orbit.

Now it was five years later. I was cured of AIDS, a sort of anonymous hero, but everything else was still the same. Earth would still be the same, except that every friend I ever knew was five years distance from me. My parents had killed themselves in an automobile wreck while I was in college. I had no sisters or brothers. I had no job prospects: soldiers coming back home five years after the war aren't greeted with parades and confetti, and all the computer stuff I had learned in college was obsolete by now. Not even the army used that kind of equipment anymore.

And Earth was dirty, crowded, noisy, dangerous —it was also *heavy*, a full one gee. I tried a couple of days in the one-gee wheel over at *Alpha* and knew that I could never live in Earth's full gravity again. Not voluntarily.

Sam listened to all this in complete silence, the longest I had ever known him to go without opening his mouth. He was totally serious, not even the hint of a smile. I could see that he understood.

"Down there I'd be just another nobody, an ex-soldier with no place to go. I can't handle the gravity, no matter what the physical therapists think they can do for me. I want to stay here, Sam. I want to make something of myself and I can do it here, not back there. The best I can be back there is another veteran on a disability pension. What kind of a job could I get? I can *be* somebody up here, I know I can."

He put his hand on my shoulder. "You're sure? You're absolutely certain this is what you want?"

I nodded. "I can't go back, Sam," I pleaded. "I just can't."

The faintest hint of a grin twitched at the corners of his mouth. "Okay, pal. How'd you like to go into the hotel business with me?"

You see, Sam had already been working for some time on his own ideas about space tourism. If Global Tech wouldn't go for a hotel facility over on *Alpha*, complete with zero-gee honeymoon suites, then Sam figured he could get somebody else interested in the idea. The people who like to bad-mouth Sam say that he hired me to cover his ass so he could spend his time working on his tourist hotel idea while he was still collecting a salary from Global. That isn't the way it happened at all; it was really the other way around.

Sam hired me as a consultant and paid me out of his own pocket. To this day I don't know where he got the money. I suspect it was from some of the financial people he was always talking to, but you never knew, with Sam. He had an inexhaustible fund of rabbits up his sleeves. Whenever I asked him about it, he just grinned at me and told me not to ask questions. I was never an employee of Global Technologies. And Sam worked full-time for them, eight hours a day, six days a week, and then some. They got his salary's worth out of him. More. But that didn't mean he couldn't spend nights, Sundays, and the odd holiday here and there wooing financiers and lawyers who might come up with the risk capital he needed for his hotel. Sure, sometimes he did his own thing during Global's regular office hours. But he worked plenty of overtime hours for Global, too. They got their money's worth out of Sam.

Of course, once I was no longer a patient whose bills were paid by the government, Global sent word up from corporate headquarters that I was to be shipped back Earthside as soon as possible. Sam interpreted that to mean when he was good and ready. Weeks stretched into months. Sam fought a valiant delaying action, matching every query of theirs with a detailed memorandum and references to obscure government health and safety regulations. It would take Global's lawyers a month to figure out what the hell Sam was talking about, and then frame an answer.

In the meantime, he moved me from the old isolation ward into a private room—a coffin-sized cubbyhole—and insisted that I start paying for my rent and food. Since Sam was paying me a monthly consultant's stipend, he was collecting my rent and food money out of the money he was giving me as his consultant. It was all done with the Shack's computer system, no cash ever changed hands. I had the feeling that there were some mighty weird subroutines running around inside that computer, all of them programmed by Sam.

While all this was going on, the Shack was visited by a rather notorious U.S. Senator, one of the most powerful men in the government. He was a wizened, shriveled old man who had been in the Senate almost half a century. I thought little of it; we were getting a constant trickle of VIPs in those days. The bigwigs usually went to *Alpha*, so much so that we began calling it the Big Wheel's Big Wheel. Most of them avoided the Shack; I guess they were scared of getting contaminated from our isolation ward patients. But a few of the VIPs made their way to the Shack now and then. Sam took personal charge of the Senator and his entourage, and showed him more attention and courtesy than I had ever seen him lavish upon a visitor before. Or since, for that matter. Sam, kowtowing to an authority figure? It astounded me at the time, but I laughed it off and forgot all about it soon enough.

Then, some six months after the Senator's visit, when it looked as if Sam had run out of time and excuses to keep me in the Shack and I would have to pack my meager bag and head down the gravity well to spend the rest of my miserable days in some overcrowded ghetto city, Sam came prancing weightlessly into my microminiaturized living quarters, waving a flimsy sheet of paper.

"What's that?" I knew it was a straight line, but he wasn't going to tell me unless I asked.

"A new law." He was smirking, canary feathers all over his chin.

"First time I ever seen you happy about some new regulation."

"Not a regulation," he corrected me. "A *law*. A federal law, duly passed by the U.S. Congress and just signed today by the President."

I wanted to play it cool, but he had me too curious. "What's it say? Why's it so important?"

"It says," he made a flourish that sent him drifting slowly toward the ceiling as he read, "'No person residing aboard a space facility owned by the United States or by a corporation or other legal entity licensed by the United States may be compelled to leave said facility without due process of law.'"

My reply was something profound, like, "Huh?"

His scrungy little face beaming, Sam said, "It means that Global can't force you back Earthside! As long as you can pay the rent, Omar, they can't evict you."

"You joking?" I couldn't believe it.

"No joke. I helped write this masterpiece, kiddo,"

he told me. "Remember when old Senator Winnebago was up here last year?"

The Senator was from Wisconsin, but his name was not Winnebago. He had been a powerful enemy of the space program—until his doctors told him that degenerative arthritis was going to make him a pain-racked cripple unless he could live in a low-gee environment. All of a sudden he became a big space freak. His visit to the Shack had proved what his doctors had told him: in zero gee the pains that hobbled him disappeared and he felt twenty years younger. That's when Sam convinced him to sponsor the "pay your own way" law, which provided that neither the government nor a private company operating a space facility could force a resident out as long as he or she was able to pay the going rate for accommodations.

"Hell, they've got laws that protect tenants from eviction in New York and every other city," Sam said. "Why not here?"

I was damned glad of it. Overjoyed, in fact. It meant that I could stay, that I wouldn't be forced to go back Earthside and drag myself around at my full weight. What I didn't realize at the time, of course, was that Sam would eventually have to use that law for himself. Obviously, *he* had seen ahead far enough to know that he would need such protection, sooner or later. Did he get the law written for his own selfish purposes? Sure he did. But it served *my* purpose, too, and Sam knew that when he was bending the Senator's tin ear. That was good enough for me. Still is.

For the better part of another year I served as Sam's legman—a job I found interesting and amusingly ironic. I shuttled back and forth from the Shack to *Alpha*, generally to meet big-shot business persons visiting the Big Wheel. When Sam was officially on duty for Global, which was most of the time, he'd send me over to *Alpha* to meet the visitors, settle them down, and talk to them about the money that a tourist facility would make. I would just try to keep them happy until Sam could shake loose and come over to meet them himself. Then he would weave a golden web of words, describing how fantastic an orbital tourist facility would be, bobbing weightlessly around the room in his enthusiasm, pulling numbers out of the air to show how indecently huge would be the profit that investors would make.

"And the biggest investors will get their own suites, all for themselves," Sam promised, "complete with every luxury—and every service that the staff can provide." He would wink hard enough to dislocate an eyelid at that point, to make certain the prospective investor knew what he meant.

I met some pretty interesting people that way: Texas millionaires, Wall Street financiers, Hollywood sharks, a couple of bullnecked types I thought might be Mafia but turned out to be in the book and magazine distribution business, even a few very nice young ladies who were looking for "good causes" in which to invest. Sam did not spare them his "every service that the staff can provide" line, together with the wink. They giggled and blushed.

"It's gonna happen!" Sam kept saying. Each time we met a prospective backer his enthusiasm rose to a new pitch. No matter how many times the prospect eventually turned sour, no matter how often we were disappointed, Sam never lost his faith in the idea or in the inevitability of its fruition.

"It's gonna happen, Omar. We're going to create the first tourist hotel in space. And you're going to have a share of it, pal. Mark my words."

When we finally got a tentative approval from a consortium of Greek and Italian shipping people, Sam nearly rocked the old Shack out of orbit. He whooped and hollered and zoomed around the place like a crazy billiard ball. He threw a monumental party for everybody in the Shack, doctors, nurses, patients, technicians, administrative staff, security guards, visitors, and even the one consultant who lived there: me. Where he got the caviar and fresh Brie and other stuff, I still don't know. But it was a party none of us will ever forget. The Shack damned near rocked out of orbit. It started Saturday at five P.M., the close of the official workweek. It ended, officially, Monday at eight A.M. There are those who believe, though, that it's still going on over there at the Shack.

Several couples sort of disappeared during the party. The Shack isn't so big that people can get lost in it, but they just seemed to vanish. Most of them showed up, looking tired and sheepish, by Monday morning. Three of those couples eventually got married. One pair of them was stopped by a security guard when they tried to go out an air lock while stark naked.

Sam himself engaged in a bit of EVA with one of the nurses, a tiny little elf of fragile beauty and uncommon bravery. She snuggled into a pressure suit with Sam, and the two of them made several orbits around the Shack, outside, propelled by nothing more than their own frenetic pulsations and Newton's Third Law of Motion.

Two days after the party, however, the Beryllium Blonde showed up.

Her real name was Jennifer Marlow, and she was as splendidly beautiful as a woman can be. A figure right out of a high school boy's wettest dreams. A perfect face, with eyes of china blue and thickly glorious hair like a crown of shining gold. She staggered every male who saw her, she stunned even me, and she sent Sam into a complete tailspin.

To top things off, she was Global Technology's ace

troubleshooter. Her official title was Administrative Assistant (Special Projects) to the President. The word we got from Earthside was that she had a mind like a steel trap, and a vagina much the same.

The official reason for her visit was to discuss Sam's letter of resignation with him.

"You stay right beside me," Sam insisted as we drifted down the Shack's central corridor, toward the old conference room. "I won't be able to control myself if I'm in there alone with her."

His face was as white as the Moon's. He looked like a man in shock.

"Will you be able to control yourself *with* me in there?" I wondered.

"If I can't, rap me on the head. Knock me out. Give me a Vulcan nerve pinch. Anything! Just don't let me go zonkers over her."

I smiled.

"I'm not kidding, Omar!" Sam insisted. "Why do you think they sent her up here, instead of some flunky? They know I'm susceptible. God knows how many scalps she's got nailed to her teepee."

I grabbed his shoulder and dug my cleats into the corridor's floor grid. We skidded to a stop.

"Look," I said, "maybe you want to avoid meeting with her altogether. I can represent you. I'm not . . . uh, susceptible."

His eyes went so wide I could see white all around the pupils. "Are you nuts? Miss a chance to be in the same room with her? I want to be protected, Omar, but not that much!"

What could I do with him? He was torn in half. He knew the Beryllium Blonde was here to talk him out of resigning, but he couldn't resist the opportunity of letting her try her wiles on him any more than Odysseus could resist listening to the Sirens.

Like a couple of schoolboys dragging ourselves

down to the principal's office, we made our way slowly along the corridor and pushed through the door to the conference room. She was already seated at the head of the table, wearing a Chinese-red jumpsuit that fit her like skin. I gulped down a lump in my throat at the sight of her. She smiled a dazzling smile and Sam gave a little moan and rose right off the floor.

He would have launched himself at her like a missile if I hadn't grabbed his belt and yanked him down into the nearest chair. Wishing there were safety harnesses on the seats, I sat down next to Sam, keeping the full length of the polished imitation-wood table between us and the Blonde.

"I think you know why I'm here," she said. Her voice was music.

Sam nodded dumbly, his jaw hanging open. I thought I saw a bit of saliva bubbling at the corner of his mouth.

"Why do you want to leave us, Sam? Don't you *like* us anymore?"

It took three tries before Sam could make his voice work. "It's . . . not that. I . . . I . . . I want to go into business for myself."

"But your employment contract has almost two full years more to run."

"I can't wait two years," he said in a tiny voice. "This opportunity won't keep . . ."

"Sam, you're a very valued employee of Global Technologies, Incorporated. We want you to stay with us. *I* want you to stay with us."

"I . . . can't."

"But you signed a contract with us, Sam. You gave us your word."

I stuck in my dime's worth. "The contract doesn't prohibit Sam from quitting. He can leave whenever he wants to."

"But he'll lose all his pension benefits and health-care provisions."

"He knows that."

She turned those heartbreakingly blue eyes on Sam again. "It will be a big disappointment to us if you leave, Sam. It will be a *personal* disappointment to me."

To his credit, Sam found the strength within himself to hold his ground. "I'm awfully sorry . . . but I've worked very hard to create this opportunity and I can't let it slip past me now."

She nodded once, as if she understood. Then she asked, "This opportunity you're speaking about: does it have anything to do with the prospect of opening a tourist hotel on space station *Alpha*?"

"That's right. Not just a hotel, a complete tourist facility. Sports complex, entertainment center, zero-gravity honeymoon suites . . ." He stopped abruptly and his face turned red. Sam *blushed*! He actually blushed.

Miss Beryllium smiled her dazzling smile at him. "But Sam, that idea is the proprietary property of Global Technologies. Global owns the idea, not you."

For a moment the little conference room was absolutely silent. I could hear nothing except the faint background hum of the air-circulation fans. Sam seemed to have stopped breathing.

Then he squawked, "*What?*"

With a sad little shake of her gorgeous head, the Blonde replied, "Sam, you developed that idea while an employee of Global Technologies. We own it."

"But you turned it down!"

"That makes no difference, Sam. Read your employment contract. It's ours."

"But I made all the contacts. I raised the funding. I worked everything out—on my own time, goddammit! *On my own time!*"

She shook her head again. "No, Sam. You did it while you were a Global employee. It's not your possession. It belongs to us."

Sam leaped from his chair and bounded to the ceiling. This time he was ready to make war, not love. "You can't do this to me!"

The Blonde looked completely unruffled by his display. She sat there patiently, a slightly disappointed little frown on her face, while I calmed Sam down and got him back into his chair.

"Sam, dear, I know how you must feel," she said. "I don't want us to be enemies. We'd be happy to have you take part in the tourist hotel program—as a Global employee. There could even be a raise in it for you."

"It's mine, dammit!" Sam screeched. "You can't steal it from me! It's mine!"

She shrugged. "Well, I expect our lawyers will have to settle it with your lawyers. In the meantime, I suppose there's nothing for us to do but accept your resignation. With reluctance. With my personal and very sad reluctance."

That much I saw and heard with my own eyes and ears. I had to drag Sam out of the conference room and take him back to his own quarters. She had him whipsawed, telling him that he couldn't claim possession of his own idea, and at the same time practically begging him to stay on with Global and run the tourist project for them.

What happened next depends on whom you ask. There are as many different versions of the story as there are people who tell it. As near as I can piece it all together, though, it went this way:

The Beryllium Blonde had figured that Sam's financial partners would go along with Global Technologies once they realized that Global had muscled Sam out of the tourist business. But she probably wasn't as sure of everything as she tried to make Sam think. After all, these backers had made their deal with the little guy; maybe they wouldn't want to do business with a big multinational corporation. Worse still, she didn't know exactly what kind of deal Sam had cut with his backers; if Sam had a legally binding contract with them that named him as their partner, they might scrap the whole project when they learned that Global had cut Sam out.

So she showed up at Sam's door that night. He told me that she was still wearing the same jumpsuit, with nothing underneath it except her own luscious body. She brought a bottle of incredibly rare and expensive wine with her. "To show there's no hard feelings."

The Blonde's game was to keep Sam with Global and get him to go through with the tourist hotel idea. Apparently, once Global's management got word that Sam had actually closed a deal for building a tourist facility on *Alpha*, they figured they might as well go into the tourist business for themselves. *Alpha* was still underutilized; a tourist facility suddenly made sense to those jerkoffs.

So instead of shuttling back to Phoenix, as we had thought she would, the Blonde knocked on Sam's door that night. The next morning I saw him floating along the Shack's central corridor. He looked kind of dazed.

"She's staying here for a few more days," Sam mumbled. It was like he was talking to himself instead of to me.

But there was a happy little grin on his face.

Everybody in the Shack started to make bets on how long Sam could hold out. The best odds had him capitulating in three nights. Jokes about Delilah and haircuts became uproariously funny to everybody —except me. My future was tied up with Sam's; if the tourist hotel project collapsed, it wouldn't be long before I was shipped back Earthside, I knew.

After three days there were dark circles under Sam's eyes. He looked weary. The grin was gone.

After a week had gone by, I found Sam snoring in the Blue Grotto. As gently as I could I woke him.

"You getting any food into you?" I asked.

He blinked, gummy-eyed. "Chicken soup. I been taking chicken soup. Had some yesterday . . . I think it was yesterday . . ."

By the tenth day, more money had changed hands among the bettors than on Wall Street. Sam looked like a case of battle fatigue. His cheeks were hollow, his eyes haunted.

"She's a devil, Omar," he whispered hoarsely. "A devil."

"Then get rid of her, man!" I urged.

He smiled wanly. "And quit show business?"

Two weeks to the day after she arrived, the Blonde packed up and left. Her eyes were blazing anger. I saw her off at the docking port. She looked just as perfectly radiant as she had the day she first arrived at the Shack. But what she was radiating now was rage. *Hell hath no fury . . .* I thought. But I was happy to see her go.

Sam slept for two days straight. When he managed to get up and around again, he was only a shell of his old self. He had lost ten pounds. His eyes were sunken into his skull. His hands shook. His chin was stubbled. He looked as if he had been through hell and back. But his crooked little grin had returned.

"What happened?" I asked him.

"She gave up."

"You mean she's going to let you go?"

He gave a deep, soulful, utterly weary sigh. "I guess she figured she couldn't change my mind and she couldn't kill me—at least not with the method she was using." His grin stretched a little wider.

"We all thought she had you wrapped around her . . . eh, her little finger," I said.

"So did she."

"You outsmarted her!"

"I outlasted her," Sam said, his voice low and suddenly sorrowful. "You know, at one point there, she almost had me convinced that she had fallen in love with me."

"In love with you?"

He shook his head slowly, like a man who had crawled across miles of burning sand toward an oasis that turned out to be a mirage.

"You had me worried, man."

"Why?" His eyes were really bleary.

"Well . . . she's a powerful hunk of woman. Like you said, they sent her up because you're susceptible."

"Yeah. But once she tried to steal my idea from me, I stopped being susceptible anymore. I kept telling myself, 'She's not a gorgeous hot-blooded sexpot of a woman, she's a company stooge, a bureaucrat with boobs, an android they sent here to nail you.'"

"And it worked," I said.

"By a millimeter. Less. She damned near beat me. She damned near did. She should have never mentioned marriage. That woke me up."

What had happened, while Sam was fighting the Battle of the Bunk, was that when Sam's partners realized that Global was interested in the tourist facility, they become absolutely convinced that they had a gold mine and backed Sam to the hilt. *Their* lawyers challenged Global's lawyers, and once the paper-shufflers in Phoenix saw that, they realized that Miss Beryllium's mission at the Shack was doomed to fail. The Blonde left in a huff when Phoenix ordered her to return. Apparently, either she was enjoying her work or she thought that she had Sam weakening.

"Now lemme get another week's worth of sleep, will you?" Sam asked me. "And, oh, yeah, find me about a ton of vitamin E."

So Sam became the manager and part-owner of the human race's first extraterrestrial tourist facility. I was his partner and, the way he worked things out, a major shareholder in the project. Global got some rent money out of it. Actually, so many people enjoyed their vacations aboard the Big Wheel so much that a market eventually opened up for low-gravity retirement homes. Sam beat Global on that, too. But that's another story.

Malone was hanging weightlessly near the curving transparent dome of his chamber, staring out at the distant Moon and the cold, unblinking stars.

The reporter had almost forgotten her fear of weightlessness. The black man's story seemed finished; she blinked and adjusted her attention to here and now. Drifting slightly closer to him, she turned the recorder off with an audible click, then thought better of it and clicked it on again.

"So that's how this facility came into being," she said.

Malone nodded, turning in midair to face her. "Yep. Sam got it built, got it started, and then lost interest in it. He had other things on his mind. He went into the advertising business, you know . . ."

"Oh, yes, everybody knows about that," she replied. "But what happened to the woman, the Beryllium Blonde? And why didn't Sam ever return to Earth again?"

"Two parts of the same answer," Malone said. "Miss Beryllium thought she was playing Sam for a fish, using his Casanova complex to literally screw him out of the hotel deal. Once she realized that *he* was playing *her*, fighting a delaying action until his partners got their lawyers into action, she got damned mad. Powerfully mad. By the time it finally became clear back at Phoenix that Sam was going to beat them, she took her revenge on Sam."

"What do you mean?"

"Sam wasn't the only one who could riffle through old safety regulations and use them for his own benefit. She found a few early NASA regs, then got some bureaucrats in Washington—from the Office of Safety and Health, I think—to rewrite them so that anybody who'd been living in zero gee for a year or more had to undergo six months' worth of retraining and exercise before he could return to Earth."

"Six months? That's ridiculous!"

"Is it?" Malone smiled without humor. "That regulation is still on the books, lady. Nobody pays any attention to it anymore, but it's still there."

"She did that to spite Sam?"

"And she made sure Global put all its weight behind enforcing it. Made people think twice before signing an employment contract for working up here. Stuck Sam, but good. He wasn't going to spend any six months retraining! He just never bothered going back to Earth again."

"Did he want to go back?"

"Sure he did. He wasn't like me. He *liked* it back there. There were billions of women on Earth! He wanted to return, but he just couldn't take six months out of his life for it."

"That must have hurt him."

"Yeah, I guess. Hard to tell with Sam. He didn't like to bleed where people could watch."

"And you never went back to Earth," the reporter said.

"No," Malone said. "Thanks to Sam, I stayed up here. He made me manager of the hotel, and once Sam bought the rest of this Big Wheel from Global, I became the manager of the entire *Alpha* station."

"And you've never had the slightest yearning to see Earth again?"

Malone gazed at her solemnly for long moments before answering. "Sure I get the itch. But when I do, I go down to the one-gee section of the Wheel here. I sit in a wheelchair and try to get around with these crippled legs of mine. The itch goes away then."

"But they have prosthetic legs that you can't tell from the real thing," she said. "Lots of paraplegics . . ."

"Maybe *you* can't tell them from the real thing, but I guarantee you that any paraplegic who uses those things can tell." Malone shook his head. "No, once you've spent some time up here in zero gee, you realize that you don't need legs to get around. You can live a good and useful life here, instead of being a cripple back down there."

"I see," the reporter said.

"Yeah. Sure you do."

An uncomfortable silence stretched between them. She turned off the recorder on her belt, for good this time. Finally Malone softened. "Hey, I'm sorry. I shouldn't be nasty with you. It's just that . . . thinking about Sam again. He was a great guy, you know. And now he's dead and everybody thinks he was just a trouble-making bastard."

"I don't, not anymore," she said. "A womanizing sonofabitch, like you said. A male chauvinist of the first order. But after listening to you tell it, even at that he doesn't sound so terrible."

The black man smiled at her. "Look at the time! No wonder I'm hungry! Can I take you down to the dining room for some supper?"

"The dining room in the full-gravity area?"

"Yes, of course."

"Won't you be uncomfortable there? Isn't there a

dining area in the low-gravity section?"

"Sure, but won't you be uncomfortable there?"

She laughed. "I think I can handle it."

"Really?"

"Certainly. And maybe you can tell me how Sam got himself into the advertising business."

"All right. I'll do that."

As she turned, she caught sight of the immense beauty of Earth sliding past the observation dome; the Indian Ocean a breathtaking swirl of deep blues and greens, the subcontinent of India decked with purest white clouds.

"But . . ." she looked at Malone, then asked in a whisper, "don't you miss being home, being on Earth? Don't you feel isolated here, away from . . ."

His booming laughter shocked her. "Isolated? Up here?" Malone pitched himself forward into a weightless somersault, then pirouetted in midair. He pointed toward the ponderous bulk of the planet and said, "*They're* the one's who're isolated. Up here, I'm free!"

He offered her his arm and they floated together toward the gleaming metal hatch, their feet a good eight inches above the chamber's floor.

Space Station ════════════════

In the grief and turmoil following the January 1986 explosion of the space shuttle *Challenger*, most of the world lost sight of NASA's program to build a permanent manned orbiting station.

A few weeks after that tragic accident, the Soviet Union launched *Mir*, the eighth space station it has placed in orbit since 1971. *Mir* is apparently a permanent station. Two cosmonauts are working in it as I write these words. I doubt that we will ever see a day again when there are not at least a few human beings living and working in space.

NASA's space station is still the most important project in the American *civilian* space program. It is the key to all the future explorations and development of the solar system, a base in orbit from which we can go on to the Moon, to Mars—eventually, to the stars.

Soon after I wrote this piece I was invited to give a lecture in Pittsburgh. My hosts provided a lovely suite in a downtown hotel that overlooks the spot where the Allegheny and Monongahela rivers join to form the Ohio. From my hotel window I looked down at the little park there and saw the foundations of the original Fort Pitt.

It struck me that *this* was the frontier less than three centuries ago. Fort Pitt was a bare little outpost in the wilderness then. It has grown into a giant modern city, headquarters of mammoth corporations such as USX (formerly U.S. Steel), Rockwell International, Alcoa Aluminum, and many others.

Less than three hundred miles overhead, a bare little outpost will be built in space. And for the same reasons of industry and exploration that turned Fort Pitt into modern Pittsburgh, that space station will grow into a city of commerce and industry and science.

And it won't take two centuries to make it happen. Not if we act with vigor and intelligence.

"When you think of this thing being a little over four times as long as a shuttle, it is a *big* piece of equipment."

Neil Hutchinson paused for a moment, then added, "And that's just the initial station that we're trying to put up there."

Hutchinson was manager of the Space Station Program Office at NASA's Johnson Space Center, outside Houston. He was in charge of building the largest structure ever placed into space.

To Philip Culbertson, Hutchinson's boss at NASA headquarters in Washington, the size of the space station was not as important as its permanency.

"We want this thing to fly for twenty-five or thirty years," said Culbertson, pointing to an artist's rendering of NASA's planned space station. "It *must* be an evolutionary design."

He tapped the picture on his conference table. "The space station may not be very graceful-looking," he said, but since it will be assembled in orbit from pieces carried aloft by the space shuttle, there will be no need to make it streamlined. No winds will rock the space station, no weather will threaten it. It will not have to reenter the atmosphere and return to Earth. It is intended to be in space permanently. If it is eventually abandoned, it will be disassembled and sent back to Earth aboard space shuttles, reversing the technique by which it will be built.

Sitting beside Culbertson was his deputy, John Hodge. Assembling the station in space "just changes your whole attitude toward the design," he said. The space station can evolve and develop even after it begins operating in orbit.

A slow smile broke across Culbertson's face. "It's kind of nifty that we can attach pieces on the outside with no penalty."

The first modules of the space station are scheduled to be launched aboard the shuttle in the early 1990s, according to current NASA plans. The station should be complete and "ready for business" in the mid-1990s. Its initial mass will be more than fifty tons, with room for growth. At least six shuttle missions will be required to bring the station's primary components into orbit.

Total program cost was originally budgeted at $8 billion, but by 1987 the cost was more realistically pegged at $12.5 billion.

One year after President Reagan's go-ahead in 1984, NASA awarded some $200 million worth of Phase B advanced development contracts to eight competing teams of aerospace companies for detailed studies of the station's major systems and components.

"We want *a* space station designed, not *the* space station," says Hodge. There are still plenty of unknowns and variables to be settled before a definite design of *the* space station can be pinned down.

The idea of placing a permanent station in orbit around the Earth goes back to the beginnings of the space program. But the political pressures of the 1960s pushed NASA to send astronauts to the Moon without first erecting an orbiting way station. After the Apollo program was killed and funding for space shriveled, NASA devoted its major energies to developing the space shuttle.

But the shuttle was intended, from the first, to go back and forth to a permanent station in orbit. By January 1984, with the shuttle fleet working well, President Reagan announced in his State of the Union speech:

"Today I am directing NASA to develop a permanently manned space station and to do it within a decade. A space station will permit quantum leaps in our research in science, communications and in metals and life-saving medicines that can be manufactured only in space."

The station is intended to serve as a base for many different kinds of scientific research under long-term conditions of weightlessness; as a permanent observatory of the heavens and the Earth; as a "transportation node" where very complex spacecraft can be assembled, checked out, and launched on deep-space missions; as a facility for servicing and repairing satellites; and as a manufacturing facility where new materials and medicines can be made under zero-gravity conditions.

Opposition to the space station has been raised by some scientists who believe that manned space operations are more costly than they are worth. They insist that unmanned spacecraft can accomplish most of the tasks a space station would do, and at a fraction of the space station's cost. They fear that major manned programs such as Apollo, the space shuttle, and now the space station, siphon funding away from their own scientific efforts.

In May 1984 James Van Allen, discoverer of the radiation belts circling Earth, told the annual meeting of the American Geophysical Union, "The development of a space station is . . . premature, and will severely reduce the opportunities for advances in space science during the next decade."

In November 1984 the Office of Technology Assessment, the high-tech advisory arm of the Congress, issued a massive report that found "no compelling, objective, external case" for a space station. In essence, the report portrayed NASA as pushing the station project merely to keep up its budget and payroll.

NASA Administrator James Beggs blasted the OTA study when it was first released. "Not a professional piece of work." He claimed that the study was "laced with rhetoric." But a few weeks later, in testimony to Congress, Beggs said that the study actually makes a "very compelling case" for NASA's space station program.

Despite such arguments and criticisms, NASA is moving ahead, although many in the aerospace community worry that the space station program may be particularly vulnerable to congressional cost-cutters seeking to trim massive federal budget deficits.

Even the station's most important backer, President Reagan, proposed a $50-million decrease in the station's funds for fiscal year 1986, from $280 million to $230 million. Although space enthusiasts want to have the station in operation by 1992, the 500th anniversary of Columbus's discovery of the New World, the Administration's schedule now calls for the station to be operational "in the mid-1990s," meaning 1994 at the earliest.

At this early stage of the program, hardly any of the details of the station's design have been firmed up. NASA has been doing its own in-house studies for several years, and many aerospace companies have also been conducting studies on their own. Every major aerospace corporation is involved in this competition, from RCA to TRW, from Rockwell to Martin Marietta, from Ford Aerospace to General Electric, and more.

This much seems clear: the station will be "shuttle compatible"; that is, each component of the station will have to fit inside the shuttle's cargo bay. The station will be assembled in an orbit between 250 and 280 miles high. Its orbit will be inclined 28.5° from the equator, the latitude of the Kennedy Space Center, from which the components of the station will be launched.

This orbital inclination takes advantage of the Earth's spin to give the shuttle an extra bit of velocity, like a broad jumper getting a running start. That not only gives more boost per pound of rocket propellant, it also means that it will take less energy to send satellites from that orbit onward to the geosynchronous orbit, 22,300 miles above the equator.

The task of actually running the space station program and making it work was started in an unprepossessing cinder-block office building a few miles outside the Johnson Space Center, near Houston. The placard taped onto the rented building's glass door said "Space Station Program Office." But the engineers inside the place called it "the Skunk Works."

(A note on aerospace etymology: the Skunk Works was, and still is, an elite group of Lockheed engineers in California. This small, tightly knit, highly secret cadre designed such extraordinary aircraft as the U-2 reconnaissance plane and Mach 3 SR-71. The term was originally borrowed from Al Capp's comic strip, *Li'l Abner*.)

Strangely enough, NASA had space problems. The Johnson Space Center, the sprawling complex at Clear Lake, Texas, where all the manned space programs have been directed, did not have enough room to handle the ongoing shuttle program and the space station as well. So the fledgling space station offices were temporarily housed in the Skunk Works.

Neil Hutchinson, manager of the Space Station Program, is a "second generation" NASA man. At the age of forty-four, he cut a figure of youthful vigor, despite the fact that he had been with the agency since getting his bachelor's degree in math and physics from Willamette University, in Oregon. Tall, intense, his hair and full beard just starting to turn salt-and-pepper, Hutchinson had been a flight director for the final three Apollo missions, all three Skylab missions, the Apollo-Soyuz program, and the first two shuttle flights.

The Space Station Program is being handled differently from earlier NASA projects, Hutchinson pointed out. There will be no prime contractor. No industrial corporation will receive a contract from NASA to design and build the entire station.

"We're really trying to avoid the 'prime contractor syndrome,'" said Hutchinson. "We don't want to get into a position where, for the next twenty-five or thirty years, NASA's beholden to a single contractor."

Hutchinson's office will be responsible for integrating all the studies and designs and coming up with the final selection of systems and contractors. "We have broken the station program into chunks," he said, "and given primary technical responsibility for those chunks to different NASA field centers."

The various NASA centers started out by proposing different designs for the station, but by early 1984 Hutchinson's group had narrowed the possibilities down to three, all of them developed at Johnson.

The *Planar* concept called for an A-frame type of structure 300 feet long, with four large sets of solar panels mounted at each end of the framework and the pressurized habitation modules and laboratories located in the middle of the structure.

The *Delta* design was an inverted pyramid, its point facing the Earth, with its array of solar panels at the top and the living quarters at the bottom.

The *Power Tower*, however, was the design that Hutchinson favored. It is based on a central spine, a 400-foot-long aluminum "strongback" that holds all the station's pieces together. Compared to the Delta and the Planar concepts, says Hutchinson, the Power Tower offers advantages of lower drag and easier stabilization.

Even 250 miles high, the space station will encounter some drag from the wispy outermost fringes of the Earth's atmosphere. To counter this, the station will carry cold-gas thrusters capable of nudging it to higher altitude when necessary. The thrusters will squirt out a gas such as nitrogen, which can generate the thrust needed for attitude adjustment. Since the Power Tower design gives the least drag, it will save on the amount of propellant gas the thrusters must carry.

Because the Power Tower is rather like a long, lean pole, it can take advantage of the Earth's gravity to stabilize its attitude in orbit. This is called gravity-gradient stabilization: the more massive end of the Tower, where the habitation modules are clustered, will be attracted by the Earth's mass and will point solidly toward the center of the planet. This means that the Tower will be less inclined to wobble in space than the Planar or Delta configurations, which are "fatter" and less adapted to gravity-gradient stabilization.

Moreover, the Power Tower allows designers to place Earth-observing sensors at the "downward"-pointing end of the station, and astronomical instruments at the end pointing skyward.

Remote manipulator arms, similar to the Canadarm that has been so useful aboard the shuttles, will run on trolleys along the length of the Power

Tower's spine and out along the 200-foot-long cross-spar that will hold the station's solar panels.

The pressurized habitation modules will be at the "bottom" of the station. These will include two working laboratories, one module for crew quarters, one for logistics (a combination pantry and hardware storehouse), and a mission module from which the station is operated.

The station will need a minimum of seventy-five kilowatts of electrical power, which means that it will generate more electrical power in its first month of operation than all the manned spacecraft NASA has flown, from the first Mercury to the latest shuttle mission.

In all likelihood this power will be generated by solarvoltaic panels which convert sunlight directly into electricity. Solar panels have been thoroughly tested for years, and they work quite reliably. On shuttle mission 41-D in September 1984, a 102-foot array of solar cells was unfolded from the shuttle payload bay. The test showed that such large arrays can be deployed and remain stable in orbit.

Hutchinson, however, recognizes that sooner or later the power requirements for the space station will grow even larger, and there is a limit to how big a "farm" of solar panels the station can manage, and how much drag it can afford. He is interested, therefore, in "solar dynamic" electric power generators. These are generators that use mirrors to focus the sun's heat, which boils a working fluid that spins a turbine to generate electricity—rather like the steam turbogenerators used by commercial power plants on Earth, except that orbiting "solar dynamic" generators would be smaller, more efficient, and would most likely use a working fluid like liquefied sodium, rather than water.

NASA's Lewis Research Center, at Cleveland, is

directing the development of electrical power systems for the station.

The station will house six to eight people, who will probably stay in orbit for ninety-day periods. The jobs they will do will include:

● Scientific, medical, and industrial experiments that will take advantage of zero-gravity conditions for indefinitely long periods.

● Observations for astronomical and geophysical research.

● Servicing and repairing malfunctioning satellites so that they can be returned to useful life in orbit.

● Running manufacturing facilities for zero-gravity processing of medicines, plastics, crystals, metal alloys, and other materials.

● Assembling, checking out, and launching complex spacecraft carried to the station in modules by the space shuttle.

The Marshall Space Flight Center, at Huntsville, is responsible for the habitation modules in which the crews will work and live, and the station's environmental control systems. Huntsville was the lead NASA center for the Spacelab program. Like the Spacelabs (which were designed and built by the European Space Agency), the habitation modules will be "aluminum cans" sized to be carried aloft by the shuttle.

Johnson Space Center is taking charge of the station's superstructure, the radiator panels that will get rid of excess heat, the data management system, and the overall integration of all the station's components. Mock-ups of station modules are already being built at Johnson, and engineers are beginning to try out various configurations for crew quarters and station operations.

The station will not be alone in orbit. It will be accompanied by "free flyers," smaller unmanned platforms that will be released from the station for specific experiments or observations. One "free flyer" that is already a definite part of the program will be inserted into polar orbit, where it can observe every part of the Earth twice each day with sensors that can seek out natural resources and monitor pollution.

There will also be orbital maneuvering vehicles (OMVs) aboard the station. Developed from the manned maneuvering units already flown aboard the shuttle, the OMVs will allow astronauts to fly out and reach satellites or free-flying platforms and bring them to docking facilities at the station, where they can be repaired and serviced. The OMVs will be capable of being operated remotely, guided from the station's command center.

The station will be highly automated, according to Al Wetterstroem, lead engineer of the Space Station Crew Control Mock-Up. The mock-ups his team has built at Johnson Space Center are already more sophisticated than the famed bridge of *Star Trek*'s U.S.S. *Enterprise*. With a crew of only six or eight aboard, perhaps none of them trained as astronauts, the station needs highly automated systems to run its life-support equipment, logistics, and other facilities.

Typical of the problems the space station will face is the need for an excellent computer program in the area of logistics, to keep track of all the equipment, clothing, food, and other supplies brought aboard. Each item may be marked with a computer code symbol, like canned goods in a supermarket, to help the computer system keep track of them.

"We'll have plenty of computer power aboard," Wetterstroem said confidently. "There's no good reason not to carry sixteen megabytes." That is 250 times more computer power than the space shuttle carried on its first flights and twice the power of the Cray 1 supercomputer. Wetterstroem believes the

station's computer needs will grow to thirty-two megabytes easily.

Computer screens line the walls of the control
center mock-up. Touch a screen with your finger and a
complete schematic of the life-support system appears. Point to a symbol depicting a valve and it will
be closed. Or opened. Functions that now require an
astronaut to flick a dozen switches in precisely the
proper sequence will be automated so that the touch
of one fingertip will do the job.

Or maybe not even a fingertip will be needed.
"We're pushing hard on voice-actuated systems and
artificial intelligence," Wetterstroem said.

There will be moments when a station engineer
literally has his hands full. Imagine standing at a work
station in the control center, watching through the
window as you handle the controls of the remote
manipulator arm. Perhaps you are trying to place a
recaptured satellite gently in a servicing cradle, where
your crewmates will go out and repair it. Or maybe
you are placing a new sensing system at the far end of
the Tower, where it has an unobstructed view of the
celestial sphere.

There may come a moment when you need a third
hand. "Move the power pack ten centimeters to the
left," you say. And the voice-actuated control system
built into the station's command center hears and
obeys, like an electronic genie.

After a hard day's work, crew members will want
some comfort and privacy. Chris Perner, chief of the
Man-Systems Division at JSC, is responsible for the
crew's safety and living conditions.

"We've got to think about fifteen hundred meals at
a time," said Perner, an affable avuncular Texan,
discussing the problems of feeding six crew members
for ninety days.

On earlier space missions, including the shuttle and

even *Skylab*, precooked meals were carried aboard the spacecraft. "But now we're thinking about home cooking, dishwashers and clothes washers and a lot else."

"Personal hygiene is important," Perner said, pointing out that the station will need a better shower facility than the one on *Skylab*, which he regarded as "not satisfactory."

And the occasional problems with the toilets on the space shuttles will have to be solved. Thinking about having six or eight people living in the station for ninety days at a time, he said, "We certainly need *that* system to work extremely well."

Water will be recycled in the station. Frank Samonski, chief of environmental control and life-support systems, said, "I believe we can go with a system where the water is completely recycled, with no replenishments necessary."

Six to eight pounds of potable water per man-day are needed aboard the station, plus another thirty pounds per man-day for personal hygiene and washing clothes and dishes. Samonski foresees a two-quality system: potable water for drinking and cooking, and "gray" water for the rest. Among the unknowns: "We don't know how much water will be used for showering."

Samonski's team is building a testbed system at JSC for ninety-day trials of various water-recycling equipment.

Then there is the question of health. Perner wants to make sure that each crew aboard the station includes a medical doctor. Even so, there are problems to be faced. How do you administer an intravenous solution or a blood transfusion in zero gravity, where fluids do not flow the way they do on Earth?

Far from being dismayed by these problems, Perner is enjoying the challenges they present. "The space station is gonna be fun," he chuckled.

Privacy is important for crew morale and work efficiency. Each crew member will have private quarters in the habitation module. Mock-ups have been built at Johnson Space Center to test out different possible configurations for individual crew quarters.

In the mock-ups a crew member's private quarters looks only slightly larger than a telephone booth. A college dorm room seems enormous by comparison. Even a submarine begins to look spacious. But in zero gravity, Perner pointed out, where you can use all six surfaces of an enclosure and even float in the middle of it, space seems to expand. A telephone booth can seem almost roomy. Almost.

Each private compartment in the JSC mock-ups has a zero-gravity bedroll attached to one wall. The bedroll includes a head strap. Astronauts have learned that it is more comfortable to be zippered in while sleeping, rather than floating freely. And once the body relaxes in sleep, the pressure of blood pumping through the carotid arteries in the neck tends to make the head nod back and forth, often awakening the sleeper. Hence the head strap.

Early studies of the space station considered the idea of "hot beds": that is, sharing one living compartment between two crew members, one sleeping while the other is on shift. Perner was firmly opposed to that. "It's an absolute must that each crew member have his or her own private quarters," he insisted.

Although it will be possible to operate the station on a three-shift, twenty-four-hour-a-day basis, Perner saw NASA's thinking moving to one or, at most, two shifts per day, with the entire crew (except for the computers) sleeping at the same time. That is the way the flight-support teams on the ground work, and it makes sense to have the station crews follow the same routine.

Then there is the trash problem. "People are the dirtiest animals on Earth," Perner said, without a trace of malice. He and his human factors engineers are trying to determine how many shredders and trash compactors the station will need.

There are literally hundreds, perhaps thousands, of other problems that must be faced by a space station intended to remain on orbit for a quarter century or more. Exactly what construction techniques will be used to assemble the 400-foot-long aluminum "strongback" of the Power Tower? Will it be folded into the shuttle's cargo bay and then unfolded and locked rigid in orbit? Or will it be carried up in sections and bolted together by astronauts in EVA? Tests at Langley Research Center showed that the sections could be connected as quickly as one strut every thirty-eight seconds. But that was a test done on the ground, not in zero-gravity space. And there are some six hundred struts to the total station structure.

How will the habitation modules be attached to the strongback? How much will the constant fine, sifting infall of cosmic dust erode the structures? Must they be covered with protective coatings?

"There's a good chance that sometime during the station's lifetime it's going to get hit" by a piece of man-made space debris, according to Donald J. Kessler, an engineer at JSC. It may be necessary to place a "free flyer" satellite up with the station to monitor the amount of man-made clutter accumulating in orbit. Computers would then assess the likelihood of any individual piece striking the station, and astronauts would ride out to the threatening pieces and remove them from orbit.

But while NASA and the aerospace industry draw their plans for a space station that will remain active in orbit for at least twenty-five years, opposition on

Earth continues to criticize the decision to build a *manned* station at all.

The OTA report, in particular, was seized upon by opponents to the station and by the media. *The New York Times* editorialized, "Indeed, the Office of Technology Assessment experts say that everything NASA proposes can be done with an automated space station, if we're willing to wait the five years it would take to develop the necessary equipment."

Most space engineers disagree strongly. All the experience of space exploration and development to date shows that human beings are necessary for the success of complex space missions. The more complicated the equipment placed in space, the more needed are humans to operate and, often, repair the equipment or adapt it to be used in ways it was not originally intended.

Arthur C. Clarke, replying to the *Times* editorial, wrote that OTA's concept of building an automated space station "showed uncanny timing . . . in the very month when astronauts brilliantly improvised the salvage of two stray communications satellites."

While a small but vocal group of space scientists argue that the station will take funds away from their own programs, history shows that space science budgets tend to follow the size of the total NASA budget; big manned programs such as Apollo and the shuttle have usually been accompanied by increased budgets for space science. And a survey conducted in late 1984 by *Research and Development* magazine showed that 69 percent of the scientists polled said they would like to fly on the space shuttle and an overwhelming 79 percent said they would like to conduct their research in the space station.

NASA is keenly interested in getting the West European and Japanese space agencies to cooperate in building and using the space station. Early in 1985 the thirteen-nation European Space Agency announced it would join NASA's space station program with a program of its own, Columbus. While ESA has not yet decided if Columbus will be manned or unmanned, a free flyer or attached to the NASA station, the West European decision strengthens NASA's hand in dealing with critics of the space station program.

ESA estimates that Columbus will cost some $2 billion.

At least one American private company wants to hook up to the space station. Space Industries, Inc., of Houston, has proposed building an orbital industrial facility—essentially an operating industrial laboratory and manufacturing facility—that eventually can be attached to the space station and buy electrical power and housekeeping services from NASA.

Maxime A. Faget, president of Space Industries, is an old NASA hand, one of the principal designers of spacecraft from Mercury right up to the space shuttle. Space Industries hopes to put their industrial facility into orbit by 1988, riding the shuttle, and then perhaps attach it to the station as a sort of "private enterprise wing" once the station is operational.

The true importance of the space station, however, is that it marks the beginning of a *permanent* American presence in space. After a quarter century of exploring the solar system and finding the energy, raw materials, and environmental conditions that can generate enormous new industries and lead to historic new discoveries, the human race will at last have a permanent base from which new industries, new explorations, and new scientific research can be launched.

Two men who rarely see eye to eye on space objectives—astronomer Carl Sagan and former presidential science advisor George A. Keyworth II

—agree that a manned space station is an important step toward further, grander objectives.

Keyworth sees the space station as a stepping-stone for the eventual return of Americans to the Moon.

Sagan, often a critic of manned space missions, admitted in January 1985 that a space station would be useful as a place to assemble spacecraft for a manned mission to Mars.

Mark Twain once told a grumbling sailing ship captain who was complaining about the newfangled steam-powered ships, "When it's steamboat time, you steam." Despite the complaints and doubts about the space station, it is unquestionably the next logical step in the exploration and utilization of space. It is now definitely "space station time."

Primary

We have not yet begun to feel the true impact of computers in government and politics.

I can't really say more about this story without giving away some of its surprises. So, since, as Polonius once said, brevity is the soul of wit, I will be brief. (And, by implication, witty.)

Think about who—and *what*—you are voting for the next time you enter your polling booth.

So they bring us into the Oval Office and he sits himself down behind the big desk. It even has Harry Truman's old "The Buck Stops Here" sign on it.

He grins at that. He's good-looking, of course. Young, almost boyish, with that big flop of hair over his forehead that's become almost mandatory for any man who wants to be president of the United States. His smile is dazzling. Knocks women dead at forty paces. But his eyes are hard as diamond. He's no fool. He hasn't gotten into this office on that smile alone.

I want him to succeed. God knows we need a president who can succeed, who can pull this country together again and make us feel good about ourselves. But more than that, I want my program to succeed. Let him be the star of the press conferences. Let the women chase him. It's my program that's really at stake here, those intricate, invisible electronic swirls and bubbles that I'm carrying in my valise. That's what's truly important.

We're going to have a busy day.

There are four other people in the office with us, his closest aides and advisors: three men and one woman who have worked for him, bled for him, sweated for him since the days when he was a grassy-green, brand-new junior senator from Vermont. The men are his Secretaries of Defense, Commerce, and the Treasury. The lone woman is his Vice President, of course. There hasn't been a male veep since the eighties, a cause for complaint among some feminists who see themselves being stereotyped as perpetual Number Twos.

And me. I'm in the Oval Office, too, with my valise full of computer programs. But they hardly notice me. I'm just one of the lackeys, part of the background, like the portraits of former presidents on the walls or the model of the Mars Exploration Base that he insisted they set up on the table behind his desk, between the blue-and-gold-curtained windows.

My job is to load my program disks into the White House mainframe computer, buried somewhere deep beneath the West Wing. He thinks of it as *his* program, *his* plans and techniques for running the country. But it's mine, my clever blend of hardware and software that will be the heart and brains and guts of this Oval Office.

I sit off in the corner, so surrounded by display screens and keyboards that they can barely see the top of my balding head. That's okay. I like it here, barricaded behind the machines, sitting off alone like a church organist up in his secret niche. I can see them, all of them, on my display screens. If I want, I can call up X-ray pictures of them, CAT scans, even. I can ask the mainframe for the blueprints of our newest missile guidance system, or for this morning's roll call attendance at any army base in the world. No need for that, though. Not now. Not today. Too much work to do.

I give him a few minutes to get the feel of the big leather chair behind that desk, and let the other four settle down in their seats. Treasury takes the old Kennedy rocker; I knew he would.

Then I reach out, like God on the Sistine ceiling, and lay my extended finger on the first pressure pad of the master keyboard.

The morning Situation Report springs up on my central screen. And on the screen atop Our Man's desk. Not too tough a morning, I see. He's always been lucky.

Food riots in Poland are in their third day.

The civil war in the Philippines has reignited; Manila is in flames, with at least three different factions fighting to take command of the city.

Terrorists assassinated the President of Mexico during the night.

The stock market will open the day at the lowest point the Dow Jones has seen in fourteen years.

Unemployment is approaching the 20 percent mark, although this is no reflection on Our Man's economic policy (my program, really) because we haven't had time to put it into effect.

The dollar is still sinking in the European markets. Trading in Tokyo remains suspended.

Intelligence reports that the new Russian base on the Moon is strictly a military base, contrary to the treaties that both we and they signed back in the sixties.

All in all, the kind of morning that any American president might have faced at any time during the past several administrations.

"This Mexican assassination is a jolt," says the Secretary of Commerce. He's a chubby, round-cheeked former computer whiz, a multi-multimillionaire when he was in his twenties, a philanthropist in his thirties, and for this decade a selfless public servant. If you can believe that. He hired me, originally, and got me this position as Our Man's programmer. Still thinks he's up to date on computers. Actually, he's twenty years behind but nobody's got the guts to tell him. His beard is still thick and dark, but when I punch in a close-up on my screens, I can see a few gray hairs. In another couple of years he's going to look like a neurotic Santa Claus.

Our Man nods, pouting a little, as if the assassination of a president anywhere is a low blow and a personal affront to him.

"The situation in the Philippines is more dangerous," says the Defense Secretary. "If the Reds win there, they'll have Japan outflanked and Australia threatened."

I like his Defense Secretary. He is a careful old grayhair who smokes a pipe, dresses conservatively, and has absolute faith in whatever his computer displays tell him. He has the reputation for being one of the sharpest thinkers in Washington. Actually, it's his programmers who are sharp. All he does is read what they print out for him, between puffs on his pipe.

"Maybe we should get the National Security Advisor in on this," suggests Commerce, scratching at his beard.

"By all means," says Our Man.

We can't have the Security Advisor in the room, of course, but I call him up on the communications screen and presto! there he is, looking as baggy and sad-eyed as a hound.

"What do you make of the situation in the Philippines, Doc?" Our Man, with his warmth and wit, and power, is the only man on Earth who can get away with calling this distinguished, dour, pompously pontifical scholar *Doc*.

"Mr. President"—his voice sounds like the creaking of a heavy, ancient castle door—"it is just as I have outlined for you on many occasions in the past. The situation in the Philippines can no longer be ignored. The strategic value of this traditional ally of ours is vital to our interests throughout Asia and the Pacific."

As he gives his perfectly predictable little spiel, I call up the subroutine that presents the pertinent information about the Philippines: the screens throw up data on our military and naval bases there, the ocean trade routes that they affect, the number of American business firms that have factories in the Philippines and how losing those factories would affect the GNP, employment, the value of the dollar —that kind of stuff.

I put all this information on the secondary screens that line the wall to one side of the President's desk. His eyes ping-pong between them and the desktop display of the Security Advisor.

"Thanks, Doc," he says at last. "I appreciate your candor. Please stand by, in case I need more input from you."

He turns back to the little group by his desk. I freeze Doc's image and fling it electronically to my farthest upper-right screen, a holding spot for him.

"Much as I hate to say it," Defense mutters around his pipe, "we're going to have to make our presence felt in the Philippines."

"You mean militarily," says the Vice President, her nose wrinkling with distaste. She has been an excellent vote-getter all through her political career: a Mexican-American from San Antonio who looks sexy enough to start rumors about her and Our Man.

"Of course militarily," Defense replies with ill-concealed impatience. "Look at the data on the screens. We can't let the Philippines slip away from us."

"Why does it always have to be troops and guns?" the Veep grumbles.

"I was thinking more of ships and planes."

"A task force," says the man behind the big desk. "A carrier group. That can be pretty impressive."

While they discuss the merits of a carrier group versus one of the old resurrected battleships, and whether or not they should throw in a battalion of Marines just in case, I do a little anticipating and flick my fingers in a way that brings up the projected costs for such a mission and how it will affect DOD's budget.

And, just as surely as gold is more precious than silver, the Secretary of the Treasury bestirs himself.

"Hey, wait a minute. This is going to cost real heavy money."

He has a very practical attitude toward money: his, mine, or yours. He wants all of it for himself. The only black in Our Man's Cabinet, Treasury is a hardheaded pragmatist who took the paltry few million his father left him (from a restaurant chain) and parlayed them into billions on the stock market. For years he belonged to the Other Party, but when the last president failed to name him to his Cabinet, he switched allegiance and devoted his life, his fortune, and what was left of his honor to Our Man.

Now he calls for details on the cost projections and, thanks to the wizardry of binary electronics, I place before their eyes (on the wall screens) vividly colored graphs that show not only how much the carrier group's mission will cost, but my program's projections of what the Philippine rebels' likely responses will be. These include—but are not limited to—a wave of assassinations throughout the 7,100 islands and islets of the archipelago, a *coup d' état* by their army, terrorist suicide attacks on our aircraft carrier, and armed intervention by the People's Republic of China.

Our Man is fascinated by these possibilities. The more awful they are, the more intrigued he is.

"Let's play these out and see where they lead," he says. He doesn't realize that he's speaking to me. He's just making a wish, like the prince in a fairy tale, and I, his digital godfather, must make the wish come true.

For two hours we play out the various scenarios, using my programs and the White House mainframe's stored memory banks to show where each move leads, what each countermove elicits. It is like following a grand master chess tournament on your home computer. Some of the scenarios lead to a nuclear engagement. One of them leads to a full-scale nuclear war between the United States and the Soviet Union: Armageddon, followed by Nuclear Winter.

Our Man, naturally, picks out the scenario that comes up best for our side.

"Okay, then," he says, looking exhilarated. He's always enjoyed playing computer games. "We will forgo the naval task force and merely increase our garrisons at Subic Bay and Mindanao. Our best counter to the threat, apparently, is to withhold economic aid from the Philippine government until they open honest negotiations with their opposition."

"If you can believe the computer projections," grumbles Commerce. He doesn't trust any programs he can't understand, and he's so far out of date that he can't understand my program. So he doesn't trust me.

The Vice President seems happy enough with me. "We can form a Cease-Fire Commission, made up of members from the neighboring nations."

"It'll never work," mutters Commerce from behind his beard.

"The computer says it will," Defense points out. He doesn't look terribly happy about it, though.

"What I want to know," says Treasury, "is what this course of action is going to do to our employment problems."

And it goes on like that for the rest of the day. Every problem they face is linked with all the other problems. Every Marine sent overseas has an effect on employment. Every unemployed teenager in the land has an effect on the crime rate. Every unwed mother has an effect on the price of milk.

No human being, no Cabinet full of human beings, can grasp all these interlinks without the aid of a *very* sophisticated computer program. Let them sit there and debate, let Our Man make his speeches to the public. The real work is done by the machine, by my program, by the software that can encompass all the data in the world and display it in all its interconnected complexity. They think they're making decisions, charting the course for the nation to follow, leading the people. In reality, the decisions they make are the decisions that the computer allows them to make, based on the information presented to them. It's my program that's charting the course for the nation; those human beings sitting around the President's desk are puppets, nothing more.

And don't think that I consider myself to be the puppet master, pulling their strings. Far from it. I'm just the guy who wrote the computer program. It's the program that runs the show. The program, as alive as any creature of flesh and blood, an electronic person that feeds on data, a digital soul that aspires to know everything, everywhere. Even during this one day it has grown and matured, I can see it happening before my teary eyes. Like a proud father I watch my program learning from the White House's giant mainframe, becoming more sure of itself, reaching out questioning tendrils all across the world, and learning, learning, learning.

"Four o'clock," announces the studio director. "Time to wrap it up."

The overhead lights turn off as abruptly as the end of the world. Our Man flinches, looks up, his face showing vast disappointment, irritation, even anger. The others exhale sighingly, wipe their brows, get up from their chairs, and stretch their weary bones. It's been a long day.

The TV camera crews shuffle out of the studio as the director, earphone still clamped to his head, comes over to Our Man and sticks out his hand.

"You did an excellent job, sir. You've got my vote in November."

Our Man gives him the old dazzling smile. "Thanks. I'll need every vote I can get, I'm sure. And don't forget the primary!"

"April seventh." The studio director smiles back. "Don't worry, I'll vote for you."

He must tell that to all the candidates.

I remain at my post, hidden behind the computer consoles, and check the National Rating Service's computer to see how well Our Man *really* did. The screen shows a rating of 0.54. Not bad. In fact, the best rating for any candidate who's been tested so far. It will look really impressive in the media; should get a lot of votes for Our Man.

He still has to go through the primaries, of course, but that's done mainly by electronics. No more backbreaking campaigns through every state for month after month. The candidates appeal to the voters individually, through their TV screens and home computers, a personal message to each bloc of voters, tailored to each bloc's innermost desires, thanks to the polished techniques of psychological polling and videotaping.

But this test run in the simulated Oval Office is of crucial importance. Each candidate has got to show that he can handle the pressures of an average day in the White House, that he can make decisions that will be good, effective, and politically palatable. Excerpts from today's simulation test will be on the evening news; tomorrow's papers will carry the story on page one. And naturally, the entire day's test will be available on PBS and even videotape for any voter who wants to see the whole day.

Of course, what this day's simulation *really* tested was my program. I feel a little like Cyrano de Bergerac, ghostwriting letters to the woman he loves for another man to woo her.

Making sure that no one is watching, I tap out the code for the White House mainframe's most secret subroutine. Only a handful of programmers know about this part of the White House's machine. None of our candidates know of it.

In the arcane language that only we dedicated programmers know, I ask the mainframe how well my program did. The answer glows brilliantly on the central screen: 0.96. Ninety-six! The highest score any program has ever received.

I hug myself and double over to keep from laughing out loud. If my legs worked, I would jump up and dance around the studio. Ninety-six! The best ever!

No matter which candidate gets elected, no matter who votes for whom, the White House mainframe is going to pick *my* program. My program will be the one the next president uses for the coming four years. Mine!

With my heart thumping wildly in my chest, I shut

down the consoles. All the screens go dark. I spin my chair around and go wheeling through the emptied, darkened studio, heading for the slice of light offered by the half-open door. Already my mind is churning with ideas for improving the program.

After all, in another four years the primaries start all over again.

MHD

Now for a labor of love.

In 1959 I was commissioned by Avco Everett Research Laboratory to write a "background memo" about the world's first successful MHD power generator, in preparation for an important press conference. A "background memo" is an aid to media reporters, filling them in on the history, technical details, etc., of the story they are covering. My "backgrounder" appeared, virtually word for word, in *Time* magazine the week after the press conference.

That bit of writing started an association with Avco Everett that lasted through 1971. I joined the staff of the lab and eventually founded and directed their marketing office. Actually, being director of marketing for such a high-powered research laboratory was rather like being the resident science fiction writer. The major difference was that when I succeeded in getting funding for such "science fiction" ideas as high-power lasers, artificial hearts, superconducting magnets, and so forth, the "science fiction" swiftly became hard engineering reality.

The one real heartbreak we suffered was in the MHD generator project. As this article tells, MHD showed—and still shows—brilliant possibilities. But the technical successes of MHD have been buried beneath political and bureaucratic folderol.

We do not have MHD-generated electrical power in the

United States, and as a result you are paying approximately twice what you should for electricity. You are also paying for the environmental degradation of air and water pollution and acid rain.

If nothing else, the MHD story is a cautionary tale of how politicians often stand in the way of progress.

But there is one further aspect to the tale: MHD generators can be both compact enough and powerful enough to provide the electricity needed for orbiting energy weapons such as lasers. It may turn out, ironically, that MHD is "saved" in the United States by the Air Force and the Strategic Defense Initiative.

That possibility also throws a different light on the Soviet efforts in MHD.

Thirty-eight sturdy steel I-beams, painted bright blue, clamp the copper plates of the powerful electromagnet together. A jungle of pipes and wires snakes into one end, where the rocketlike combustion chamber stands.

Taller than the technicians working through its final checkout, massive enough to generate more than thirty megawatts of electrical power, the Mark V is the biggest MHD power generator ever built. It looks so impressive, in fact, that a visiting Russian scientist surreptitiously took out a pocket knife and scratched it against one of the I-beams, wanting to make certain it was real and not a wooden mock-up built by the capitalists to hoodwink foreign visitors.

In the control room, separated from the monstrous generator itself by more solid steel and a heavy shatterproof window, the engineers go through a countdown much like that for a rocket launch.

The second hand of the clock on the wall sweeps

inexorably. Once an explosion in a smaller generator started a fire so intense that the heat radiating through the window melted the instruments in the control room. No one was injured, but the roof was blown away by the blast.

"Three . . . two . . . one . . . *ignition!*"

A deafening roar erupts from the heart of the generator. You can feel it rattling your bones, flattening your eardrums.

But everyone is smiling. The gauges along the control board climb steadily, showing that millions of watts of electricity are being produced by the Mark V: ten megawatts, twenty . . . more than thirty.

The noise ends so abruptly that you feel like you've been pushed off a cliff. Your ears ring. The pointers on the gauges drop back to zero.

The test has been a success. Slightly more than thirty-two megawatts. The Mark V MHD generator has operated just as the scientists predicted it would. Theory has been matched by experiment. MHD is almost ready to leave the laboratory and enter the practical world of electrical power generation.

That scene took place more than twenty years ago, in Everett, Massachusetts, a few miles north of Boston.

There, at the Avco Everett Research Laboratory, a spirited team of scientists and engineers were developing a new kind of electrical power generator, based on a technology with the jawbreaking name of *magnetohydrodynamics*. MHD, for short.

I worked at Avco Everett from 1959 to 1971. I was there when the MHD program started, and I saw it founder and almost sink.

A quarter century ago, the head of the Avco Everett lab was so confident of MHD that he bet an executive from the electric utilities industry that MHD would be producing electricity for utility customers by 1970.

He lost that bet. As things stand now, MHD won't start producing commercial electrical power until the mid-1990s—if then.

MHD could have averted the acid rain problem that now plagues wide areas of the eastern United States and Canada. It would have allowed electric power plants to burn coal cleanly, using America's most abundant fuel without producing the pollution fallout that is now stripping forests bare and killing aquatic life in lakes and streams.

Studies have shown that MHD power generators can burn the dirtiest coal without polluting the air, and burn it so efficiently that they produce 50 percent more kilowatts per pound of fuel than ordinary generators. More kilowatts per dollar would mean lower electricity bills for the consumer.

But MHD is no closer to realization today than it was twenty years ago. The story of MHD is a story of technological daring and political timidity, a story of failed hopes and lost opportunities.

"It's a tragic story," says Arthur Kantrowitz. "It's a story of frustration that's been very painful to me."

Kantrowitz is universally acknowledged as the father of MHD power generation. Now a professor at Dartmouth College's Thayer School of Engineering, Kantrowitz was the founder of Avco Everett and the driving force behind the MHD program in the 1960s. He is a dynamic, barrel-chested man who created one of the nation's leading industrial research laboratories out of his own restless desire to do scientific research "that has an impact on the way people live."

MHD began in the bright promise of space-age research. In 1955 Kantrowitz left a professorship at Cornell University to found Avco Everett, bringing a handful of his brightest graduate students with him. The laboratory, originally housed in an abandoned warehouse, was created to solve the problems of reentry for ballistic missile "nose cones." The Air Force desperately needed to know how to design reentry vehicles that would not burn to cinders when returning from space.

Using shock tubes, Kantrowitz's Avco Everett team simulated the conditions a reentry vehicle would have to face and within six months provided the data needed for engineers to design survivable reentry vehicles. Eventually another division of Avco Corporation built all the reentry heat shields for the Apollo lunar spacecraft.

Using their newly won knowledge of the behavior of very hot gases, Kantrowitz and his young staff tackled the problem of MHD power generation.

Power generators convert heat to electricity. In today's electric utility power plants, this energy conversion is accomplished by turbogenerators. Heat is created either by burning a fossil fuel (oil, coal, or natural gas) or by the fissioning of atoms in a nuclear reactor. The heat boils water. The steam turns the blades of a turbine. The turbine is connected to a bundle of copper wires called an armature, which sits inside a powerful magnet. When the steam turns the turbine, and the turbine spins the armature within the magnetic field, an electric current is generated.

Michael Faraday discovered the principles of electrical power generation in the 1830s, in Britain. Thomas Edison made it all practical some fifty years later, and electrified the world. Edison's steam-turbine generators were about 40 percent efficient. The steam turbogenerators used today are no better.

Instead of turbines and armatures, MHD employs the roaring ultra-hot exhaust gas of a powerful rocket engine, so rich in energy that it contains megawatts of potential electrical power in every cubic meter of its stream. By running such a gas through a pipe, with a powerful magnet around it and durable electrodes inside it, a steady current of electricity can be tapped from the hot gas. That is an MHD generator. A *Saturn V* rocket bellowing up from Cape Canaveral on its way to the Moon could have produced enough electricity, through MHD, to light the entire eastern seaboard for as long as its engines were burning.

No moving parts. No turbines. The supersonically flowing hot gas is itself the "armature." Efficiencies of 60 percent or more are attainable. More kilowatts per pound of fuel. More electricity per dollar.

High temperature is the key to efficiency. Turbogenerators are limited to temperatures well below 1,000°F because the turbine blades cannot take more heat without breaking. In the rocketlike combustion chamber of an MHD generator, the fuel is burned either in pure oxygen or preheated air to raise the gas temperature to 5,000°F. A pinch of potassium "seeding" is added to the hot gas, because potassium ionizes easily at such temperatures and makes the gas an electrical conductor. Although thousands of times less conductive than copper, the ionized gas (physicists call it a plasma) conducts electricity well enough to become an effective armature.

The high temperature in an MHD generator creates problems that ordinary generators do not face. The combustion chamber, the MHD channel, and especially the electrodes inside the channel, must be able to stand the rigors of a supersonic flow of 5,000°F plasma that is choked with soot and corrosive combustion products while megawatts of electricity are blazing within it.

But those very conditions force the MHD system to be environmentally clean. Scrubbers in the smokestack downstream are economically necessary to recover the costly potassium seed so that it can be reused. They also take out the soot from the exhaust gas before it is released to the air. Thus the cost of soot removal is built into the original cost of the MHD power plant and is not an expensive add-on.

Sulfur and nitrogen compounds that might cause smog and acid rain are removed from the hot gas by completely conventional equipment before they leave the MHD system. There is so much of these pollutants in the hot plasma stream that it becomes economically attractive to remove them and convert them into fertilizers, to be sold in the agricultural market. Again, the antipollution equipment is built into the MHD system for sound economic reasons. Nothing goes up the smokestack except warm carbon dioxide and a few impurities, well within the current clean-air standards set by the Environmental Protection Agency.

The first working MHD generator was built in 1959 at Avco Everett. It produced ten kilowatts (ten thousand watts) for a few seconds. The laboratory's parent, Avco Corporation, in conjunction with a group of electric utility companies, funded a fast-paced research and development effort under Kantrowitz's direction.

The program followed a two-pronged approach. Large MHD generators tested the ability to produce multimegawatts of power. Smaller generators tested the durability of the materials and components of an MHD generator over long time periods. By 1966 Avco's Mark V had generated more than thirty-two megawatts, and smaller machines had been operated for hundreds of hours continuously.

Kantrowitz and his team were ready, they believed, to build a demonstration power plant: an MHD generation station that would deliver some fifty megawatts of electricity and serve as a model for full-scale commercial power stations.

The demonstration plant was never built. Although Kantrowitz was confident that his team was ready to build it, hardly anyone else was.

The pilot plant would have cost $30 million in the mid-1960s. Avco and the electric utilities consortium were prepared to put up only $13 million. Kantrowitz and Philip Sporn, who headed the utilities group backing MHD, went to Washington and proposed to Stewart Udall, then Secretary of the Interior, a program funded fifty-fifty by the government and the Avco-utilities group.

But two "terrible blows," as Kantrowitz puts it, hit MHD and almost destroyed the program utterly.

First, Sporn reached mandatory retirement age and was forced out of his powerful position at American Electric Power Company. He had been a major figure in the utility industry, a leader with the drive and vision to equal Kantrowitz's own. The two men were well matched and made an effective team. Kantrowitz's bet about having MHD "on-line" by 1970—a symbolic bet of one dollar—had been with Sporn. Once Sporn lost his power base and was no longer able to keep prodding his colleagues, the electric utilities began to lose interest in MHD.

At about the same time, President Lyndon Johnson announced that cheap nuclear energy was at hand. "This wasn't true," Kantrowitz asserts, but with the White House pushing nuclear power, no one in Washington was willing to back an alternative such as coal-burning MHD.

John T. Conway, a vice-president of New York's Con Edison power company, was on the staff of the U.S. Congress Joint Committee on Atomic Energy in the mid-1960s.

He does not see the MHD decision as being pronuclear at the expense of coal. "In fact, we were trying to make coal and nuclear developments a joint effort," he says. "We knew that nuclear energy by itself couldn't handle all the nation's needs. We knew we needed nuclear *and* coal."

MHD lost out, according to Conway, for several reasons—none of them having anything to do with the technical performance of MHD generators.

First, the coal industry itself was "terribly fragmented" by battles between labor and management. As a result, there was no unified position from the coal industry backing MHD as a user of the nation's most abundant fuel.

Second, according to Conway, "When you get to the big bucks that hardware requires, you reach a natural checkpoint." The plans for an MHD demonstration plant were competing with requests for expensive new "atom-smashing" particle accelerators for high-energy physics experiments. The accelerators got the funding.

Most important, though, was Sporn's sudden departure. "Sporn was a hardheaded engineer," Conway recalls, "like a Rickover." Once the program lost his "drive and authority," the decision-makers in Washington lost confidence in MHD.

Princeton University's Jonathan C. Coopersmith, in his 1978 analysis of the MHD programs in the United States and Soviet Russia, concluded:

> Exactly why the [MHD] project was not approved by the government is not clear. The enthusiasm for nuclear power . . . undoubtedly had a great deal to do with the lack of similar enthusiasm for coal in government circles. Funding constraints imposed by Johnson's Great Society programs and the Vietnam War also had a negative impact. . . .

As the sixties staggered to their end under the burden of Vietnam and civil unrest, there was a general decline in government support of research and development. Hardly anyone in Washington, or anywhere else in the nation, would back a new energy technology. The Yom Kippur War, the Arab oil embargo, and the energy crisis were less than five years away. Protests and demonstrations against nuclear power plants were already beginning; the Three Mile Island fiasco was ten years in the future.

Because he was a corporate vice-president and member of the Avco board of directors, Kantrowitz could keep his MHD program inching along on corporate funds. But the kind of money needed to build the pilot plant could be found only in Washington. No private investors were willing to take the risk, and corporations that were already heavily involved in building conventional power generators saw no incentive in helping to develop competition for their existing products.

Researchers at Westinghouse and General Electric maintained comparatively low-level efforts in MHD, and several universities such as Stanford and Tennessee carried on MHD studies.

Kantrowitz and fellow Avco Corporation board member George Allen found a sympathetic ear in Clark Clifford, a longtime Washington "insider" who had served briefly as Johnson's Secretary of Defense after Robert McNamara left the Cabinet.

"We told him MHD would be good for the country," Kantrowitz remembers, "but no private company could justify risking the money to develop it."

Clifford began "knocking on doors" in Washington. The only one that opened was that of Senator Mike Mansfield, Democrat from Montana and majority leader of the Senate. Montana is a state that is rich in coal but poor in water resources. MHD is an energy system that could burn Montana's coal without using up its scarce water.

"I don't know how Mansfield reached the decision

that he would grab on to it," says Kantrowitz. "But he made the decision that he wanted MHD for Montana."

Suddenly the obscure Office of Coal Research, buried deep within the Department of the Interior, began funding MHD. The budget rose quickly from a few hundred thousand dollars to some $70 million per year by the mid-1970s.

But the money was not being spent on Kantrowitz's dream of a pilot plant. Every private and university laboratory engaged in MHD research lined up for a piece of the pie, and the funding was dutifully parceled out to government labs and private companies —including Avco Everett—and to universities such as Stanford, Tennessee, and the University of Montana, where a Mansfield-inspired MHD Institute and testing facility were built.

In the words of one disgruntled researcher, "They were spending more on MHD than ever, and getting less results." The program had no real goal, no focus.

"By that time the estimates of the cost of a pilot plant were $200 to $300 million," Kantrowitz says. "Nobody had the courage to undertake that risk."

Undaunted, Kantrowitz urged Mansfield to push for an MHD program that would produce megawatts instead of research reports.

The senator told Kantrowitz to write out a plan of action and Kantrowitz did, on a single sheet of paper. "I said we should build a pilot plant, and that's it," Kantrowitz recalls. The plan was enacted by the Congress, tacked onto another bill as a rider, and in 1976 Mansfield personally presented it to President Gerald Ford for his signature.

But even that failed to produce an MHD pilot plant. There were no teeth in the law. "I was stupid enough to think that if the Congress passed the MHD action plan, it would result in action," says

Kantrowitz ruefully. "It did absolutely nothing." The Department of Energy has been "studying" the plan for nearly ten years.

By 1978 it was Kantrowitz's turn to face mandatory retirement. He left Avco Everett and accepted a professorship at Dartmouth. "It's very painful to retire when you've still got things to do," he says.

When the Reagan Administration swept into Washington early in 1981, one of its avowed aims was to dismantle the Department of Energy and all of its programs.

But the new head of Avco Everett, R. W. ("Dutch") Detra, and Vincent J. Coates, director of Special Projects, began a campaign with MHD enthusiasts in Montana and elsewhere. Working with congressmen and senators who opposed dissolving the Department of Energy, they were able to keep MHD funded at about $30 million per year through the first Reagan Administration.

"The Massachusetts congressional delegation has been very helpful," Coates says. "Particularly Nicholas Mavroules, Silvio Conte, and Edward P. Boland." Congressmen from Montana and Tennessee, where MHD research efforts are under way, have also staunchly supported the program. So has powerful Senator John Stennis of Mississippi, who believes energy technology is vital to national defense.

Like ancient Gaul, the Department of Energy's MHD program is divided into three major parts. Avco Everett is concentrating on the MHD channel, the pipe at the heart of the generator that extracts electrical energy from the ultra-hot stream of gas flowing through it. TRW Corporation's Energy Technology Division in Redondo Beach, California, is developing special coal burners. And Babcock & Wilcox is building boilers that can take the still-hot gas coming out of an MHD generator and make steam that will run a conventional generator "downstream" of the MHD system.

Robert Kessler is Avco Everett's vice-president for energy technology, head of the MHD effort. He sees a pilot plant being built by 1995.

"The Department of Energy plan calls for retrofitting an existing power plant with an MHD system in the early to mid-1990s," says Kessler.

But privately, many scientists who have worked on MHD nearly all their lives admit that even that date—twenty-five years later than Kantrowitz's original estimation—may not be met. William D. Jackson, the "J" of HMJ Corporation, a small Washington-based energy research and development company, says, "A pilot plant in the early 1990s is just flat optimistic." He believes that DOE's current program of $30 million per year is far too small; $100 million per year is needed, Jackson claims.

Kessler says, "What we're trying to achieve is reliable operation of MHD equipment at sizes that are practical for commercial power generation. At this stage of the game, efficiency is not so important as predictability, economics, and reliability." He lays heavy emphasis on reliability.

Jackson agrees. "They've got to build something that a utility company would allow into one of its power plants!"

The DOE plan calls for an MHD generator to be installed in an existing power plant as a "topping unit." That is, the MHD system will start the process of converting heat to electricity. As the hot gas leaves the MHD generator, after having surrendered as much as fifty megawatts of electrical energy, it will be fed into the special boilers that will raise steam for the plant's conventional turbogenerators, which will then make even more electricity from the same original coal-fired heat input.

DOE has already indicated that it expects the MHD program's industrial participants to share the costs of the pilot plant. The government will not foot the bill on tax money alone. Joseph McElwain, chairman and chief executive officer of Montana Power Company, has offered one of his utility's power plants as the site for the demonstration retrofit. But the other industrial partners are looking askance at the idea of cost-sharing.

"It could take twenty years before the money invested in a demonstration plant shows any profit," says Avco Everett chief Detra. "Can a corporation afford to tie up millions of dollars for such a long time?"

Kantrowitz now serves as one of fifteen advisors to the MHD Industrial Forum, an organization created by the companies involved in MHD development. To him, all this should have happened twenty years ago.

"If we had built a pilot plant in the sixties," he insists, "it wouldn't have worked—at first. Then we'd figure out why it didn't work, we'd fix it, and it would have worked." A pilot plant in the 1990s will go through the same evolution. "It won't work. You'll have to fix it. What you might hope for is that you have a larger background of knowledge from which to fix it."

Kessler almost agrees. "If they'd built the pilot plant back in the sixties, we'd be ahead of where we are today."

But Jackson disagrees. If a pilot plant had been built in the 1960s and failed, "it would have killed MHD," he says. "Just absolutely killed it."

Some of the scientists and engineers involved in the program today are deeply pessimistic. "The only kinds of experiments we do are the kinds that entail no risks," says one of them. "That's no way to make progress."

"The MHD program has become a minor pork barrel," says another. "Its real aim is to satisfy the political forces that exist in Massachusetts, Montana, and Tennessee."

"We're no closer to a pilot plant now than we were eighteen years ago," Kantrowitz asserts flatly.

Perhaps the gloomiest statement came from an engineer who has worked almost his entire professional life on MHD. "I used to hope to see MHD become practical and useful in my lifetime. Now I don't think it will. I think I've been wasting my time."

"From the technical point of view there's no reason why MHD can't become commercially viable," says Richard Rosa, the man who built the first working MHD generator, at Avco Everett in 1959. Now a professor of mechanical engineering at the University of Montana, at Bozeman, Rosa is still carrying out MHD research and consulting with the nearby MHD Institute at Butte.

The annual Washington budget battle, however, "really tears up the program," according to Rosa. "Half the year everybody's on hold." He believes that the utility industry's bad experiences with technological innovations such as nuclear power is discouraging the industry from investing the money required to make a commercial success of MHD.

So the program is totally dependent on federal funding, with "a crisis every year."

The fear of massive budget deficits now pervading Washington led David Stockman's Office of Management and Budget to "zero out" MHD in the fiscal year 1986 federal budget. This was not the first time MHD has been dropped from the White House's budget plans. Similar efforts to stop all government funding of MHD have been successfully fought before. But there is more pressure now than ever to get the government out of the MHD business.

The House of Representatives Science and Technology Subcommittee on Energy Development and Applications approved a $28-million authorization for MHD. Coates believes the pro-MHD forces in Congress may eke out a budget somewhere between $25 and $30 million. But there is pressure from the White House to drop the program, once and for all.

"At best, we'll be able to keep the program alive from year to year," Coates says. "But as long as we have this polite antagonism between government and private industry, the U.S. runs the risk of losing its lead in technology to countries where government and industry work together."

Japan, China, and the Soviet Union are pursuing their own MHD programs, based on the work originally done in the United States, Coates points out. "We may have to buy MHD generators from them," he says.

In September 1983 Kantrowitz was invited to Moscow to receive the Faraday Medal, presented by UNESCO to him and Soviet scientist A. E. Sheindlin for their contributions to MHD.

Ironically, he never went to accept the medal. As he was preparing to leave for Moscow, the Soviets shot down Korean Air Lines flight 007. Kantrowitz canceled his trip. UNESCO sent the medal to his home in New Hampshire.

"It's the last thing of significance that I've had to do with MHD," he says sadly. "A medal instead of a pilot plant."

But a pilot plant *was* built in the 1960s. Near Moscow. Based largely on the work done in Massachusetts, the Russians have pushed ahead with the kind of MHD program that Kantrowitz was looking for. The Russian U-25 MHD plant worked well enough so that the Soviet government is starting construction of a 250-megawatt MHD plant at Ryazan, a city some 130 miles southeast of Moscow. Called the U-500, this power plant is expected to be delivering electricity before the end of the decade.

It may be that the only way the United States will get MHD power plants in the 1990s will be to buy them from the Soviet Union—if the Russians will be willing to sell our own technology back to us.

Born Again ════════════════

Assuming the UFO believers are right, and we *are* being infiltrated by a generally benign race of intelligent extra-terrestrials, why have they come to Earth and what do they want of us?

In an earlier story, "A Small Kindness" (see *Promethe-ans*, published by Tor Books in 1986), we saw the first meeting between Jeremy Keating and the alien Black Saint of the Third World, Kabete Rungawa.

Now we see the result of that meeting, and how it changes Keating's life. Changes it? In a literal sense, it *ends* his life.

Which leads to the title of the story.

────────────────

The restaurant's sign, out on the roadside, said *Gracious Country Dining*. There was no indication that just across the Leesburg Pike the gray unmarked headquarters of the Central Intelligence Agency lay screened behind the beautifully wooded Virginia hills.

Jeremy Keating sat by force of old habit with his back to the wall. The restaurant was almost empty, and even if it had been bursting with customers, they would all have been agency people—almost. It was the *almost* that would have worried him in the old days.

Keating looked tense, expectant, a trimly built six-footer in his late thirties, hair still dark, stomach still flat, wearing the same kind of conservative bluish-gray three-piece suit that served almost as a uniform for agency men when they were safely home.

Only someone who had known him over the past five years would realize that the pain and the sullen, smoldering anger that had once lit his eyes were gone now. In their place was something else, equally intense but lacking the hate that had once fueled the flames within him. Keating himself did not fully understand what was happening to him. Part of what he felt now was excitement, a fluttering, almost giddy anticipation. But there was fear inside him, too, churning in his guts.

It had been easy to get into the agency; it would not be so easy getting out.

He was halfway finished with his fruit-juice cocktail when Jason Lyle entered the quiet dining room and threaded his way through the empty tables toward Keating. Although he had never been a field agent, Lyle moved cautiously, walking on the balls of his feet, almost on tiptoe. Watching him, Keating thought that there must be just as many booby traps in the corridors of bureaucratic power as there are in the field. You don't get to be section chief by bulling blindly into trouble.

Keating rose as Lyle came to his table and extended his hand. They exchanged meaningless greetings, smiling at each other and commenting on the unbelievably warm weather, predicted an early spring and lots of sunshine, a good sailing season. When their waitress came, Lyle ordered a vodka martini; Keating asked for another glass of grapefruit juice.

The last time Keating had seen Jason Lyle, the section chief had ordered him to commit a murder. *Terminate with extreme prejudice* was the term used. Keating had received such orders, and obeyed them willingly, half a dozen times over the previous four years. Until this last one, a few weeks ago.

Now Lyle sat across the small restaurant table, in this ersatz rustic dining room with its phony log walls and gingham tablecloths, and gave Keating the same measured smile he had used all those other times. But Lyle's eyes were wary, probing, trying to see what had changed in Keating.

Lyle was handsome in a country-club, old-money way: thick silver hair impeccably coiffed, his chiseled features tanned and taut from years of tennis and sailing. He was vain enough to wear contact lenses instead of bifocals, and tough enough to order death for his own agents, once he thought they were dangerous to the organization—or to himself.

Keating listened to the banalities and let his gaze slide from Lyle to the nearby windows where the bright Virginia sunshine was pouring in. He knew that Lyle had carefully reviewed all the medical reports, all the debriefing sessions and psychiatric examinations that he had undergone in the past three weeks. They had wrung his brain dry with their armory of drugs and electronics. But there was one fact Keating had kept from them, simply because they had never in their deepest probes thought to ask the question. One simple fact that had turned Keating's life upside down: the man that he had been ordered to assassinate was not a human being. He had not been born on Earth.

Keating nodded at the right places in Lyle's monologue and volunteered nothing. The waitress took their lunch order, went away, and came back eventually with their food.

Finally, as he picked up his fork and stared down at what the menu had promised as sliced Virginia ham, Lyle asked as casually as a snake gliding across a meadow:

"So tell me, Jeremy, just what happened out there in Athens?"

Keating knew that the answers he gave over this luncheon would determine whether he lived or died.

"I got a vision of a different world, Jason," he answered honestly. "I'm through with killing. I want out."

Lyle's eyes flashed, whether at Keating's use of his first name or his intended resignation or his mention of a vision, it was impossible to tell.

"It's not that simple, you know," he said.

"I know." And Keating did. Lyle had to satisfy himself that this highly trained agent had not been turned around by the Soviets. Or, worse still, by the fledgling World Government.

"Why?" Lyle asked mildly. "Why do you want to quit?"

Keating closed his eyes for a moment, trying to decide on the words he must use. Each syllable must be chosen with scrupulous care. His life hung in the balance.

But in that momentary darkness, alone with only his own inner vision, Keating saw the man he had been, the life he had led. The years as an ordinary Foreign Service officer, a very minor cog in the giant bureaucratic machinery of the Department of State, moving from one embassy to another every two years. He saw Joanna, young and loving and alive, laughing with him on the bank of the Seine, dancing with him on the roof garden of the hotel that steaming-hot Fourth of July in Delhi, smiling at him through her exhaustion as she lay in the hospital bed with their newborn son at her breast.

And he saw her being torn apart by the raging mob attacking the embassy at Tunis. While Qaddafi's soldiers stood aside and watched, grinning. Saw his infant son screaming his life away as typhus swept the besieged embassy. Saw himself giving his own life, his body and mind and soul—gladly—to avenge their deaths. The training, where his anger and hatred had been honed to a cutting edge. The missions to track and kill the kind of men whom he blamed for the murder of his wife and child. Missions that always began in Lyle's office, in the calm, climate-controlled sanctuary of the section chief, and his measured reptilian smile.

Keating opened his eyes. "You let them take me, that first mission, didn't you?"

The admission was clear on Lyle's surprised face. "What are you talking about?"

"My first mission for you, the job in Jakarta. You allowed them to find me, didn't you? You tipped them off. Those interrogation sessions, that slimy little colonel of theirs with his razor—he was the final edge on my training, wasn't he?"

"That's crazy," Lyle snapped. "We shot our way in there and saved your butt, didn't we?"

Keating nodded. "At the proper moment."

"That was years ago."

But I still carry the scars, Keating replied silently. They still burn.

Lyle fluttered a hand in the air, as if waving away the past. Leaning forward across the table slightly, he said in a lowered voice, "I need to know, Jeremy. What happened to you in Athens? Why do you suddenly want to quit?"

Keating did not close his eyes again. He had seen enough of the past, and the shame of it seethed inside him. "Let's just say that I experienced a religious conversion."

"A *what*?"

"I've been reborn." Keating smiled, realizing the aptness of it. "I have renounced my old life."

For the first time in the years Keating had known the man, Lyle made no attempt to mask his feelings. "Born again? Fat chance! I've heard a lot of strange stories in my time, but this one . . ."

"Is the truth."

"Just tell me what happened to you in Athens," Lyle insisted. "I've got to know. It's important to both of us."

"So that you can decide whether to terminate me?"

"We don't do that," Lyle snapped.

"No, of course not. But I just might happen to have a car accident, or take an overdose of something."

Lyle glowered at him. "You hold a lot of very sensitive information inside your skull, Jeremy. We have to protect you."

"And yourself. It wouldn't look good on your record to have a trained assassin going over to the other side."

The section chief actually smiled with relief, and Keating could see that Lyle was grateful that the subject had finally been brought out into the open.

"Have you, Jeremy?" he asked in a whisper.

"Gone over? Which side would I go to? The Soviets? But we're working under the table with them these days, aren't we? Neither the Russians nor the Americans want the World Government running things. We're both trying to bring the World Government down before it gets a firm control over us."

"The World Government," Lyle said slowly, testingly.

Keating shook his head. "If I admit to that, I'm a dead man, and we both know it. I'm not that foolish, Jason."

Lyle said nothing, but looked unconvinced.

"There's the Third World," Keating went on. "They love the World Government, with its one-nation, one-vote system. They're using the World Government to bleed the rich nations white; you told me that yourself. But then, the rich nations are almost all white to begin with, aren't they?"

"This is no time for jokes!"

"A sense of humor helps, Jason. Believe me. But you can't picture me working for a bunch of blacks and browns and yellows, can you? That's so completely against your inner convictions that you can't imagine a fellow WASP going over to the Third World."

"Perhaps I can imagine it, at that," Lyle said, with dawning apprehension lighting his eyes. "Your assignment was to terminate Rungawa . . ."

"Ah, yes," Keating said. "Kabete Rungawa. The Black Saint of the Third World. The spiritual leader of the poor nations."

Lyle almost spat. "That old bastard is as spiritual as . . ."

"As Gandhi," Keating said, sudden steel in his voice. "And as powerful politically. That's why you want him terminated."

Lyle stared at Keating for long, silent moments before saying, "Rungawa. *He* turned you around! Jesus Christ, you fell for that black bastard's mealy-mouthed propaganda line."

"Yes, I did," said Keating. "Not in the way you're thinking, though. Rungawa is quite a person. He made me see that murdering him would be a horrible mistake. He opened my eyes."

"You admit it?"

"Why not? It's already in the debriefing reports, isn't it?"

The glitter in Lyle's cold blue eyes told Keating that it was.

"But here's something that isn't in the reports,

Jason. Something so utterly fantastic that you won't believe it."

The section chief leaned forward in anticipation. Hearing secrets was his trade.

"Kabete Rungawa is an extraterrestrial."

"What?"

"He looks human, but he's actually from another world."

Lyle's mouth hung open for a second, then clicked shut. "Are you joking, Jeremy, or what?" he asked angrily.

"That's what he told me," Keating said.

"And you believed him?"

Keating felt a smile cross his lips as he recalled that cold, rainy night in front of the Parthenon. His mission had been to terminate Rungawa, and he had finally tracked the Black Saint to the Acropolis.

"He was very convincing," Keating said softly. "Very convincing."

Lyle looked down at his untouched lunch, then back into Keating's eyes. "Jeremy, either you're lying in your teeth or you've gone around the bend."

"It's the truth, Jason."

"You want me to believe that you *think* it's the truth."

"Would I tell such a crazy story if it weren't the truth?"

The section chief seemed to suddenly realize that he held a knife and fork in his hands. He attacked the Virginia ham vigorously as he said, "Yes, I think you might. A completely wild story might make us believe that you've flipped out, might convince us that you ought to be retired."

"To a mental institution?"

"This isn't Russia," Lyle snapped. But then, looking up from his platter at Keating again, he added, "A good long rest might be what you need, though. You wouldn't be the first field agent to suffer from burn-out."

"A permanent rest?" Keating asked.

Lyle turned his attention back to his food. "Just relax and eat your lunch. We'll take care of you, Jeremy. The agency takes care of its own."

Keating took the afternoon off and drove far out into the wooded Virginia hills, without any conscious destination, merely drove through the late March sunshine in his agency-furnished inconspicuous gray Ford. He did not have to be told that it was bugged; that anything said inside the car would be faithfully recorded back at headquarters. And there were tracking transmitters built into the car, naturally. Even if he drove it to Patagonia, satellite sensors would spot him as plainly as they count missile silos in Siberia.

And he knew, just as surely, that he expected a contact, a message, a set of instructions or some sort of help from the entity he had refrained from killing that rainy night atop the Acropolis.

How can I be so certain that he'll help me? Keating asked himself as he drove. There's no doubt in my mind that he is what he said he is: an extraterrestrial, a creature from another world, sent here to keep us from blowing ourselves to kingdom come with our nuclear toys. But will he help *me*? Am I important enough to his plans to be rescued? Does he know what Lyle is going to do to me? Does he give a damn?

No answers came out of the sky as Keating drove blindly toward Charlottesville. It was not until he turned onto Interstate 64 and saw the signs for Monticello that he realized where he was heading.

He joined a group of five Japanese tourists and followed the guides through Thomas Jefferson's home, half listening to the guides' patter, half looking at the furnishings and gadgets of the brightest man ever to live in the White House. In the back of his mind Keating realized that he had slept in hotel rooms far more luxurious than Jefferson's bedroom. Was *he* one of them? he wondered. Were they tinkering with our world's politics that far back?

Keating kept pace with the other tourists, but his attention was actually focused on a message that never came. He felt certain that they—whoever they were—would contact him. But by the time his group had been ushered back to the main entrance of the house, at the end of the tour, there had been no contact. He was out in the cold, completely alone.

He drove back in darkness to the apartment in Arlington that the agency had provided for him. It was a pleasant-enough set of rooms, with a view of the Washington Monument and the Capitol dome. Keating could sense the bugs that infested the walls, the phone, most likely the entire building. A fancy jailhouse, he knew.

His apartment was on the top floor of the six-story building. Death row? Very likely. Lyle could not risk letting him go loose. And there were no close relatives or friends to raise a fuss about him.

He knew that he had to make a break for it, and it had to be tonight. If Rungawa and his people would not help him, then he would have to do it alone. Have dinner, then take the car and drive out to the nearest shopping mall. Use the crowds to lose whatever tails they've put on me. Then get to Rungawa, one way or another. He owes me a favor.

Keating took a frozen dinner from the refrigerator, microwaved it into a semblance of food, and sat in front of the living room TV set to eat what might be his last meal. But after a few bites of the lukewarm Salisbury steak, he felt himself nodding off. For a moment he felt panic surge through him like an electric current, but long years of practice damped it down. A short nap won't hurt, he told himself. Forty winks. He drowsed off in the comfortable reclining chair, while the TV screen played out a drama about corporate power and sexual passion in the cosmetics business.

"Mr. Keating."

He awoke with a start, looked around the living room. No one.

"Here, Mr. Keating. Here."

The TV screen showed the kindly looking face of an elderly black man: Kabete Rungawa.

"You!"

Rungawa smiled and lowered his eyes briefly, almost as if embarrassed.

"Forgive this unorthodox way of communicating with you. Your erstwhile colleagues have listening devices on the telephone . . ."

"And in the walls," Keating said.

Rungawa replied, "They will not hear this conversation. As far as their devices are concerned, you are still asleep and the eleven o'clock news is on the air."

Hunching forward in his chair, Keating asked, "How do I know that I'm *not* asleep, and that this isn't just a dream?"

"That is a question of faith, Mr. Keating," said the black man gravely. "Can you trust your own senses? Only your own inner faith can give you the answer."

"They're going to kill me," Keating said.

"You told them about us." Rungawa's face became somber.

"I told them about *you*."

"That was not wise."

"Don't worry about it," Keating said. "Lyle thinks that either I'm a colossal liar or a crackpot."

The black man almost smiled. "Still, we would prefer that no one knew of our presence. I told you only because my life was at stake."

"Well, it's my life that's at stake now. Lyle's going to terminate me."

"Yes, we know. It will happen tonight."

"How can I . . ."

"You can't. You mustn't. The game must be played to its conclusion."

"Game? It's my *life* we're talking about!"

"It is your faith we are talking about," the black man said solemnly, in his rumbling bass voice. "You believed what I told you that night in front of the Parthenon. You spared my life."

"But you're not going to spare mine," Keating said.

"Have faith, Mr. Keating. Haven't your own prophets told you that faith can carry you beyond death? Christ, Mohammed, Buddha—haven't they all tried to tell you the same thing?"

"Don't talk philosophy to me! I need help!"

"I know you do, Mr. Keating. It will come. Have faith."

Keating started to reply, but found that he could not open his mouth, could not even move his tongue. He no longer had control of his limbs. He sat frozen in the recliner chair, unable to move his legs, his arms. He could not even lift a finger from the padded armrest.

His throat was dry with sudden fear, his innards trembled with a fear that was fast approaching panic. I don't want to die! his mind screamed silently, over and again. I don't want to die!

"I know the terror you feel, Mr. Keating," Rungawa's deep voice said gravely. "It pains me to put you through this. But it must be done. They will never rest until you are dead and can no longer harm or embarrass them. I am truly sorry, but you will not be the first casualty we suffer."

Don't let them kill me! Keating shrieked inside his head.

But Rungawa said only, "Good night, Mr. Keating."

Jeremy's eyes slowly closed, like the curtain going down on the last act of a tragic play. Locked inside his paralyzed body, imprisoned within his own unresponding flesh, Keating saw nothing but darkness as he awaited inevitable death.

Slowly, slowly, the thundering of his heart eased. In the background he could hear the television set's sound again. The eleven o'clock news chattered away, to be followed by a talk show. Still Keating sat, unable to move a voluntary muscle, unable even to open his eyes. He tried to picture Joanna and little Jerry, Jr., tried to tell himself that he would be with them at last, but a cold voice in his mind laughed mockingly and told him that he had never believed in life after death. Get accustomed to the darkness, Jeremy, he told himself. This is all there will ever be.

He wanted to cry, but even that was denied him. You're already as good as dead, the ice-hard voice said. What did you have to live for, anyway?

Time became meaningless. The voices from the television set changed, but Keating paid scant attention to them. They were nothing more than background sound effects; like the muted organ music played in a cathedral before the funeral service begins.

The click of the lock sounded like a pistol shot to him. He heard the front door open and then softly close. They had the key to the apartment, of course. The jailers always have the keys. The floor was carpeted, but Keating clearly heard the soft footfalls approaching him. Like a man who had been blind from birth, Keating's sense of hearing seemed magnified, hypersensitive. He could hear the man's breathing from halfway across the living room.

He knew it was not Lyle himself. The section chief

would never dirty his own hands. With something of a shock Keating realized that he hardly knew anyone else at the agency. Four years of service and he had barely made an acquaintance. The voice inside his head laughed scornfully again. You've been dead for years, old boy. You just didn't realize it.

"Wake up, man. Come on, wake up!"

Jeremy's eyes snapped open.

A swarthy, pinch-faced, dapper little man with a neatly trimmed black mustache was leaning over him.

"Wha . . . who . . .?" Jeremy's tongue felt thick, his eyes gummy. But he could speak. He could move again.

"Never mind who," the man said. "We gotta get you outta here! Fast!"

Feeling almost dizzy with surprise, Jeremy sat up straight in the recliner and planted his feet on the floor. "What's going on?"

"I don't got time to explain, man. We only got a couple minutes before they get here! Come on!"

He looked Hispanic, or maybe Italian. He wore a white suit with a double-breasted jacket; strange outfit for an undercover agent. Or an extraterrestrial. Confused, Jeremy struggled to his feet. Out of the corner of his eye, he saw that the television set was playing an old black-and-white movie now.

"Splash some water on your face, wake yourself up. We gotta move fast."

Jeremy tried to shake the cobwebs out of his head. He lumbered to the bathroom and ran the cold water. The little man watched from the doorway. His suit was rumpled, baggy; it looked as if he had been wearing it for a long time. He pulled a small silver flask from his inside pocket, opened it, and took a long pull from it.

"Take a swig of this; it'll open your eyes for you."

Jeremy took the pint-sized flask and sniffed at its open mouth. Spanish brandy. He took a small, testing sip.

"Where are we . . ."

He never finished the sentence. A searing explosion of pain blasted through him. The flask fell from his spasming fingers, and the last thing he saw was the little man deftly catching it before it hit the floor.

Jeremy lurched to the sink, then collapsed across it and slid to the tile flooring. The pain faded away into darkness. He could feel nothing. He could not hear his heart beating, could not draw a breath.

Vaguely, far off in the darkly vast distance, he heard the electronic bleep of a pocket radio and the little man's voice saying, "Okay, he's had his heart attack. Looks very natural."

He opened his eyes and saw a featureless expanse of white. For what seemed like a measureless eternity he stared blankly at it. Then, at last, realizing that he was breathing slowly, rhythmically, he deliberately blinked his eyes and tried to turn his head.

The expanse of white was nothing more than the ceiling of the room he was in. He was lying in a bed, covered with a sheet and a thin white blanket. It looked like a hospital room, or perhaps a private room in an expensive rest home. Modern furniture, all in white: dresser, desk and chair, night table beside the bed, comfortable-looking upholstered chair beside the window. Sunshine streaming in, but the window blinds were angled so that he could not see outside. And he noticed that there were no mirrors in the room; not one, even over the dresser. Three doors. One of them was slightly ajar and showed the corner of a bathroom sink. The second must be a closet, Keating reasoned.

The third door opened just then and Kabete Rungawa stepped in.

"You have awakened," he said, smiling. Somehow, even when he smiled, his face had the sadness of the ages etched into it.

Keating said nothing.

"You have returned from the dead, Mr. Keating. Welcome back to life."

"I was really dead?"

"Oh, yes. Quite. Your agency is very thorough."

"Then how . . ."

Rungawa asked permission to sit on the edge of the bed by making a slight gesture and raising his snowy eyebrows. Keating nodded and the old man sat beside him. The bed sagged disturbingly under him, even though he looked small and almost frail.

"Your own medical science can bring a man back from clinical death, in certain cases," the Black Saint said gently. "Our science is somewhat more advanced than that."

"And the agency . . . Lyle . . ."

"Mr. Lyle was present at your cremation. He was given your ashes, since you had no next of kin listed in your personnel file."

Keating thought swiftly. "You switched bodies at the crematorium."

"Something like that," said Rungawa.

"Then you really are . . . what you said you were."

Rungawa's smile broadened. "Did you doubt it? Even when you risked your life on it?"

"There's a difference between knowing here," Jeremy tapped his temple, "and believing, here in the guts, where . . ."

He stopped in midsentence and stared at the hand that had moved from his head to his midriff. *It was not his hand.*

"What have you done to me?" Jeremy's voice sounded high, shrill, frightened as a little child's.

"It was necessary," Rungawa's deep voice purred softly, "to give you a new body, Mr. Keating."

"A new . . ."

"Your former body was destroyed. We salvaged your mind—your soul, if you want to use that term."

"Where . . . whose body . . . is this?"

Rungawa blinked slowly once, then replied. "Why, it is your own body, Mr. Keating."

"But before . . . ?"

"Ahh, I understand. We did not steal it from anyone." The black man smiled slightly. "We created it for you especially, just as this body of mine was created for me. You would not expect a being from another world, thousands of light-years from your Earth, to look like a human being, would you?"

Jeremy swallowed once, twice, then managed to say, "No, I guess not."

"It is a very good body, Mr. Keating. A bit younger than your former shell, quite a bit stronger, and with a few special sensitivities added to it."

Jeremy threw back the bedclothes and saw that he was naked. Good strong legs, flat ridged midsection. His hands looked heavier, fingers shorter and somewhat blunter. His skin was pink, like a baby's, new and scrubbed-looking.

Wordlessly, he swung his legs to the floor and stood up. No dizziness, no feeling of weakness at all. He padded to the bathroom, Rungawa a few steps behind him, and confronted himself in the mirror.

The face he saw was squarish, with curly red-blond hair and a light sprinkling of faint freckles across its snub nose and broad cheeks. The eyes were pale blue.

"Christ, I look like a teenager!"

"It is a fully adult body," Rungawa said gravely.

Jeremy turned to the black man, a nervous giggle

bubbling from his throat. "When you say born again, you really mean it!"

"You spared my life, Mr. Keating," said Rungawa. "Now we have spared yours."

"So we're even."

Rungawa nodded solemnly.

"What happens now?" Jeremy asked.

The black man turned away and strode slowly back toward the hospital bed. "What do you mean, Mr. Keating?"

Following him, Jeremy said, "As far as the rest of the world is concerned, Jeremy Keating is dead. But here I am! Where do I go from here?"

Rungawa turned to face him. "Where do you wish to go, Mr. Keating?"

Jeremy felt uncertain, but only for a moment. He was slightly shorter than he had been before, and the Black Saint looked disconcertingly taller.

"I think you know what I want," he said. "I think you've known it all along."

"Really?"

"Yes. This has all been an elaborate form of recruitment, hasn't it?"

Rungawa really smiled now, a dazzling show of pleasure. "You are just as perceptive as we thought, Mr. Keating."

"So it has been a game, all along."

"A game that you played with great skill," Rungawa said. "You began by sparing the life of a man whom you had been instructed to assassinate. Then you quite conspicuously tried to get your employers to murder you."

"I wouldn't put it that way . . ."

"But that is what you did, Mr. Keating. You were *testing* us! You set up a situation in which we would have to save your life."

"Or let me die."

Rungawa shook his head. "You accepted what I had told you in Athens. You believed that we would be morally bound to save your life. Your faith saved you, Mr. Keating."

"And you, on your part, have been testing me to see if I could accept the fact that there's a group of extraterrestrial creatures here on Earth, masquerading as human beings, trying to guide us away from a nuclear holocaust."

Nodding agreement, Rungawa said, "We have been testing each other."

"And we both passed."

"Indeed."

"But why me? Out of five billion human beings, why recruit me?"

Rungawa leaned back and half sat on the edge of the empty hospital bed. "As I told you in Athens, Mr. Keating, you are a test case. If *you* could accept the fact that extraterrestrials were trying to help your race to avoid its own destruction, then we felt sure that our work would meet with eventual success."

Keating stood naked in the middle of the antiseptic white room, feeling strong, vibrant, very much alive.

"So I've been born again," he said. "A new life."

The Black Saint beamed at him. "And a new family, of sorts. Welcome to the ranks of the world saviors, Mr. Keating. There are very few of us, and so many of your fellow humans who seem intent on destroying themselves."

"But we'll save the world despite them."

"That is our task," Rungawa said.

Keating grinned at him. "Then give me some clothes and let's get to work."

Laser Propulsion ===================

High-powered lasers have many more uses than to "merely" shoot down ballistic missiles.

Someday, sooner than most people think, spacecraft will lift off planet Earth propelled by nothing more than a beam of light.

The work described here started at Avco Everett Research Laboratory, when I was still working there. It has been carried on by a group of Avco Everett "alumni," who started their own company—Physical Sciences, Inc.

While I was editing *Analog* magazine, I encouraged Jerry Pournelle to develop the concept of laser propulsion in a cover story he was writing. Kelly Freas painted the cover illustration, which ran in the March 1974 issue. I estimate that thirty years after that story appeared, we will be able to go out to Cape Canaveral and check on the accuracy of Kelly's painting.

The shuttle orbiter opens its big cargo bay doors. Its long manipulator arm lifts a set of six communications satellites, one by one, out of the cargo bay and leaves them floating freely in empty space. Then the orbiter fires its maneuvering jets and departs from the area.

A brilliant pencil-thin beam of light lances up from

the ground, reflects off a mirror orbiting hundreds of miles away, and reaches its dazzling finger to a small rocket nozzle on one of the satellites. The rocket flares to life, propelling the satellite toward its desired final destination in an orbit higher than the shuttle could reach. Within a few minutes, each of the satellites has been sent on its way, propelled by the energy of the laser's beam.

Riding such a beam of light may become the most efficient and economical way to maneuver satellites in space, according to Anthony N. Pirri, a vice-president of Physical Sciences, Inc., a fifty-five-man research company in Andover, Massachusetts.

"We've shown that laser propulsion works in the laboratory," says Pirri. "Now we're investigating the details of the physics so that we can optimize the concept and make it work in the practical world."

Small models of rocket thrusters have been propelled by laser light in laboratory experiments at PSI. The idea of using a laser to provide propulsion energy for a rocket is also being studied at Penn State University, the University of Illinois, the University of Tennessee Space Institute, and at the NASA Marshall Space Flight Center in Huntsville, Alabama.

Like an automobile engine, a rocket needs to deliver power and fuel efficiency. In an auto, power is measured in terms of horsepower, efficiency in terms of miles per gallon. In a rocket engine, power is measured in terms of pounds of thrust, and fuel efficiency is rated by a factor called *specific impulse*, which is usually expressed in units of seconds.

Chemical rockets, such as those used to boost the space shuttle into orbit, can provide thousands of pounds of thrust, but are not very efficient. The shuttle's main engines, for example, have a specific impulse of less than four hundred seconds.

On the other hand, there are electrical rockets,

which are very efficient, but produce very low power. An ion rocket, for example, which uses electrostatic forces to accelerate ionized atoms of cesium to very high velocities, can yield specific impulses of many thousands of seconds. But it produces only micropounds of thrust because it is very small and very little cesium actually flows through the rocket's nozzle. To make electric rockets larger would mean making their electrical power plants too huge to lift off the ground. An ion rocket, therefore, would be highly efficient, but it would take months for it to lift a communications satellite from low orbit to geosynchronous orbit.

A laser-powered rocket can give specific impulses of one thousand to two thousand seconds, and thrust of up to one hundred pounds. It may be ideal for the task of quickly raising a satellite's orbit or otherwise maneuvering satellites once they have been placed in low orbit by the shuttle.

Laser propulsion offers two basic advantages: one, the laser itself does not have to be lifted off the ground; most of the weight of the propulsion system never leaves the earth. Two, the laser beam can heat propellants to far higher temperatures than can be obtained by chemical burning; the higher the propellant's temperature, the faster it flows through the rocket nozzle; the faster it flows, the higher the specific impulse.

A laser-driven rocket would carry hydrogen or possibly argon in its fuel tank, laced with a small amount of water, ammonia, or another compound that absorbs laser energy well.

Hydrogen would make the best propellant, since it is the lightest element and therefore would produce the highest flow velocity per watt of laser power input. High flow velocity is much more important to high specific impulse than the mass of the propellant. But hydrogen tends to link into a two-atom molecule, so some laser energy would be used up in dissociating the molecules. Argon, although nearly forty times heavier than hydrogen, is a monatomic gas and would not have to be dissociated.

Experiments at PSI have included both pulsed and continuous-wave lasers. The pulsed laser beam is fired right into the rocket nozzle itself. Pulsing the beam every few microseconds allows the rocket exhaust gases to clear away from the nozzle before the next burst of laser energy comes in. But this means that fast-acting valves may have to be built into the system to pulse the propellant flow on and off within microseconds. A continuous-wave laser would not require gas valving, but needs a window of some sort and a complicated optical system to allow the beam into the rocket chamber upstream of the nozzle.

There are several practical problems facing laser propulsion. Nelson Kemp, a principal scientist at PSI, points out that the materials of the rocket nozzle must handle "a very large amount of energy in a very small volume of gas." Gas temperatures at the core of the rocket chamber may be as high as 20,000°K and pressures can go up to one hundred atmospheres.

Conventional chemical rockets can run at equally high chamber pressures, but the gas temperature in a chemical rocket is limited to the amount of energy released by the combustion of the rocket's propellants. In a laser-driven rocket, says Kemp, "there's virtually no limit to how high you can heat the gas," because the energy comes from the laser, rather than from the propellants' inherent chemical energy.

The Hungarian recipe for an omelet begins, "First, steal some eggs . . ." Laser propulsion depends on the development of lasers of unprecedented power—ten megawatts or more—and pointing systems of astronomical precision. The low-level research efforts currently funded by NASA and the Air Force Office of Scientific Research are many orders of magnitude too small for such hardware development.

But the White House's Strategic Defense Initiative (i.e., "Star Wars") is aimed at developing lasers powerful and accurate enough to destroy ballistic missiles. Such lasers would be more than adequate for raising a satellite's orbit or otherwise maneuvering it in space. The Star Wars weaponry may have broad peaceful applications.

"There's no reason why laser propulsion can't be a practical system," says Robert F. Weiss, president of PSI. He foresees satellites lifted from the ground by high-flying airplanes or air-breathing ramjet boosters, then propelled into orbit from the upper fringes of the atmosphere by laser energy, by the late 1990s.

Robert L. Forward, of Hughes Research Laboratories in Malibu, California, looks even farther ahead and envisions huge lasers in orbit near the Earth that propel spacecraft through the far reaches of the solar system, and even out toward other stars.

No rocket engine even conceivable today could propel spacecraft across interstellar distances. But Forward believes that laser-pushed lightsail systems using "known laws of physics and fairly reasonable engineering extrapolation of known technologies" could send spacecraft to the stars—riding a beam of light.

The Sightseers

While we are thinking about how best to defend the nation, it is good also to think about the condition of the nation we want to defend. "The Sightseers" is a rather dark vision of some of the disturbing trends that you can see in almost any of our largest cities.

Actually, this short-short story is the result of an embarrassment of riches.

Years ago, when the Milford Science Fiction Writers Conference was actually held in Milford, Pennsylvania, I found myself in a quandary. It was a week before the conference started. To participate in the conference, you had to bring an *unpublished* piece of fiction and submit it to the workshop. I did not have any unpublished fiction on hand. Everything I had written, at that point in time, had been bought.

So I sat down and dashed off this short-short, based on a vague idea that was gestating in the back of my mind.

The idea is this: large cities and large stars exhibit the same kind of life cycle.

As massive stars burn up their energy fuels, they swell gigantically while their cores get hotter and denser and finally become the kind of matter that astronomers call "degenerate." As large cities use up their energy sources (taxpaying citizens and corporations, who eventually leave the city), the city swells into urban sprawl while its core degenerates into ghettos.

For massive stars, the ultimate outcome of this evolutionary track is a catastrophic explosion. We have already seen serious riots in many of our large cities. Will a city-wrecking explosion occur one fine day?

As I recall that Milford workshop twenty-some years ago, most of the participants did not think much of this story. Except for Gordon Dickson, canny pal that he is. "This looks to me like the germ of an idea for a novel," he suggested.

How right he was. The novel is called *City of Darkness*. It attracted a fair amount of attention in Hollywood after it was published, but no firm offers were made. A few years later, somebody produced a film called *Escape from New York*, which bothered me somewhat. It seemed to have certain elements from *City of Darkness*. But plagiarism laws do not protect ideas; if they did, Hollywood would have starved to death long ago. Still, the producers of that film may well have come on their ideas independently.

The film does have one element that "The Sightseers" and *City of Darkness* could only hint at: Adrienne Barbeau's bosom. That is one of the great advantages of film over print.

My heart almost went into fibrillation when I saw the brown cloud off on the horizon that marked New York City. Dad smiled his wiser-than-thou smile as I pressed my nose against the plane's window in an effort to see more. By the time we got out of the stack over LaGuardia Airport and actually landed, my neck hurt.

The city's fantastic! People were crowding all over, selling things, buying, hurrying across the streets, gawking. And the noise, the smells, all those old gasoline-burning taxis rattling around and blasting horns. Not like Sylvan Dell, Michigan!

"It's vacation time," Dad told me as we shouldered our way through the crowds along Broadway. "It's always crowded during vacation time."

And the girls! They looked back at you, right straight at you, and smiled. They knew what it was all about, and they liked it! You could tell, just the way they looked back at you. I guess they really weren't any prettier than the girls at home, but they dressed . . . wow!

"Dad, what's a bedicab?"

He thought it over for a minute as one of them, long and low, with the back windows curtained, edged through traffic right in front of the curb where we were standing.

"You can probably figure it out for yourself," he said uncomfortably. "They're not very sanitary."

Okay, I'm just a kid from the north woods. It took me a couple of minutes. In fact, it wasn't until we crossed the street in front of one—stopped for a red light—and I saw the girl's picture set up on the windshield that I realized what it was all about. Sure enough, there was a meter beside the driver.

But that's just one of the things about the city. There were old movie houses where we saw real murder films. Blood and beatings and low-cut blondes. I think Dad watched me more than the screen. He claims he thinks I'm old enough to be treated like a man, but he acts awfully scared about it.

We had dinner in some really crummy place, down in a cellar under an old hotel. With live people taking our orders and bringing the food!

"It's sanitary," Dad said, laughing when I hesitated about digging into it. "It's all been inspected and approved. They didn't put their feet in it."

Well, it didn't hurt me. It was pretty good, I guess . . . too spicy, though.

We stayed three days altogether. I managed to meet a couple of girls from Maryland at the hotel where we stayed. They were okay, properly dressed and giggly and always whispering to each other. The New York girls were just out of my league, I guess. Dad was pretty careful about keeping me away from them . . . or them away from me. He made sure I was in the hotel room every night, right after dinner. There were plenty of really horrible old movies to watch on the closed-circuit TV; I stayed up past midnight each night. Once I was just drifting off to sleep when Dad came in and flopped on his bed with all his clothes on. By the time I woke up in the morning, though, he was in his pajamas and sound asleep.

Finally we had to go. We rented a sanitary car and decontaminated ourselves on the way out to the airport. I didn't like the lung-cleansing machine. You had to work a tube down one of your nostrils.

"It's just as important as brushing your teeth," Dad said firmly.

If I didn't do it for myself, he was going to do it for me.

"You wouldn't want to bring billions of bacteria and viruses back home, would you?" he asked.

Our plane took off an hour and a half late. The holiday traffic was heavy.

"Dad, is New York open every year . . . just like it is now?"

He nodded. "Yes, all during the vacation months. A lot of the public health doctors think it's very risky to keep a city open for more than two weeks out of the year, but the tourist industry has fought to keep New York going all summer. They shut it down right after Labor Day."

As the plane circled the brown cloud that humped over the city, I made up my mind that I'd come back again next summer. Alone, maybe. That'd be great!

My last glimpse of the city was the big sign painted across what used to be the Bronx:

NEW YORK IS A SUMMER FESTIVAL OF FUN!

Telefuture

This a good-news, bad-news story.

After four years of editing *Omni* magazine, it was fun to be a free-lance writer and be asked to do a story for the magazine.

"What will the phones of the future be like?" the new editor asked me.

The answer is "Telefuture."

That's the good news.

The bad news is that when the article appeared in the magazine, it had been edited much more extensively than I liked. In particular, the editors had chopped the final lines into hash. I know that every writer screams that whatever the editor cuts "are the best lines in the piece."

But in this case I think it's quite true! Here is the original article, as I wrote it. If you have a copy of the February 1985 *Omni*, compare the two and let me know what you think.

It is growing.

Like a living, sentient creature it has spread its tendrils across the land and snaked them along the bottom of the sea. It has even probed upward into space, growing, learning, expanding, becoming more complex, more sophisticated with every passing year.

Like an extraterrestrial invader of superhuman powers, the Creature acquires human workers to serve it, to help it grow, to become more subtle, more pervasive, and so ubiquitous that we barely notice its presence among us. The Creature's proclaimed desire is nothing less than to serve humankind. Its instruments have penetrated virtually every home in the United States, and every office of business and government in the world.

The "Creature" is, of course, the telephone system, that incredibly complex electronic infrastructure that links the people of the world in just the same way that the human nervous system links together the billions of individual cells in our bodies.

When the Creature was born, little more than a century ago, telephones were a curiosity, a luxury. Today they have evolved into a necessity that no one can do without. We proudly proclaim that our human civilization of today is international, global in scope. But it is the telephone system that holds our global civilization together; the Creature's tendrils unite the human world. Without telephones, melons grown in California would never get to supermarkets in New York. Jet airliners would be grounded, or take off empty, without the passengers who book their reservations by phone. Clothes designed in Paris and manufactured in Hong Kong out of materials produced in New Zealand, Mississippi, and Manchester would never get to their retail markets in São Paulo, Pretoria, or Podunk without telephonic signals that cross the oceans and leap out to relay satellites hovering 22,300 miles above the equator.

Most human beings have no idea of how complex the Creature is. We see little more than the instrument that sits on the desk, by the bed, or hangs on the kitchen wall. But that is merely a fingertip, a nerve ending, compared to the Creature's entire body. Beyond that visible, palpable instrument is the Creature's vast, almost-alive nervous system, changing, evolving, humming with electrical signals, flickering with pulses of laser light, learning, growing. Its tendrils hide in our walls, snake out to the streets, run from pole to pole, tunnel beneath the pavement, leap across empty air on microwave links. Like nerve pathways, the Creature's electrical circuits converge to form nodes called *exchanges,* where the messages they carry are routed with the speed of light to their destinations.

When the Creature first came into existence, it carried the babble of human voices over copper wires. Human work crews strung tens of thousands of miles of wire, across continents, through tunnels, along the abyssal beds of the oceans. Probably the richest deposit of copper in the world lies beneath the streets of Manhattan, tons upon tons of purified copper, like the bulging node of a giant nerve ganglion.

Within recent years, though, the Creature has become aware that another kind of voice is using its circuits with rapidly growing frequency. The digital chatter of computers is taking up more and more of the Creature's time and capability. At first, it was merely the computers that served the Creature itself: the computers used by the telephone network to help route messages along the system. But increasingly, computers in homes and offices are speaking to one another over the phone links, threatening to overload the Creature's capacity.

The answer to this is twofold: the Creature is itself becoming a digital entity, a mammoth interlinked computer the size of North America; and it is adding fiber optics *lightguide* circuits to its systems, nerve pathways made of glass rather than copper.

The Creature's heart—no, really, its *brain* —resides in a complex of modernistic buildings in several locations spread over a twenty-five-mile radius of northern New Jersey: the AT&T Bell Telephone Laboratories. Since 1925 the men and women of Bell Labs have faithfully served the Creature, working night and day to help it grow and learn. The transistor was invented here; radio astronomy began here; the basic research that led to the development of the maser and the laser was done here; fiber optics lightguides, which transmit pulses of laser light for many miles, is another BTL development.

The first city-to-city television broadcast, carrying President Herbert Hoover's image from Washington to New York, was accomplished by Bell Labs. High-fidelity and stereo records were developed at Bell Labs. The movies learned to talk with Bell Labs' Vitaphone system. The latest breakthrough made here is *solitons*: single pulses of light that may be able to glide through hundreds of miles of fiber optics cables without losing their strength. Seven Bell Labs scientists have received the Nobel prize.

Never far from the high-speed Jersey Expressway, Bell Labs centers in Holmdel, Murray Hill, Whippany, and Short Hills look rather more like the campuses of very posh universities than industrial research laboratories. The buildings are sleek and new; even the older ones have had their exteriors refaced in reddish brick and sweeping glass facades. The interiors tend to have dual personalities: the lobbies look as if they are sets in the latest Fellini film, while the actual laboratories are like labs everywhere —busy, crowded with people and equipment, metal desks topped with humming computer terminals.

Bell Labs is the one part of American Telephone and Telegraph Corporation that has been allowed to retain the name of Bell, even after AT&T divested itself of its operating telephone companies. It is here that the Creature's future growth and evolution are being planned and developed. Some 25,000 men and women work here, supported by a budget of more than $2 *billion* per year.

Solomon J. Buchsbaum, executive vice-president of AT&T Bell Labs, sees the Creature's future in terms of its usefulness to people. Today, he points out, the average American home contains a telephone, a television receiver, and a computer.

"The key question," he says, "is what kind of integration, or synergy, between these various forms of communications services can we produce? None of them will be obliterated . . . but the telephone of tomorrow will be very different from the telephone of today."

Buchsbaum sees computers and telephones merging into a new instrument, the *telephone terminal*. In essence, today's telephone is evolving into a true computer-communications device capable of linking not only human voices but much denser computer data and video signals as well. To handle the enormous growth in demand for the Creature's time and capacity, the Creature itself is being changed. It is evolving, in Buchsbaum's words, into "one giant interconnected computer."

For more than two decades, computers have been taking over more and more of the Creature's work load. Having human operators handle phone traffic was fine in the early days. But by the 1950s it became obvious that either the phone network would move toward automation or every human being in the United States would be needed to serve the Creature's growing work load. Computers began to take over the tasks of the telephone operator, so much so that in 1983, when some 750,000 operators and repair personnel went on strike against AT&T for several weeks, the Creature was hardly affected at all.

Today, when you speak into a telephone, your voice

is transformed into an electrical current that is carried to a telephone exchange, where the message is routed to your intended listener. The telephone converts the fluctuations in air pressure caused by your voice into fluctuations of the electric current, then converts the current back into audible sound at the receiving end of the transmission. This is called an *analog* system.

At more and more exchanges, though, the electrical signal is converted into digital bits so that it can be processed by the computers that handle the work there. Voice signals are carried at a rate of 64,000 bits (64 kilobits) per second over the Creature's existing copper wires, while lightguide links can carry 90 million bits (90 megabits) per second, and have achieved 2 billion bits (2 gigabits) per second in laboratory tests.

The path of the Creature's evolution is toward digitizing the entire system, from the phone instrument in your hand to the receiver on the other end of your conversation.

A digital system is powerful and flexible. It can handle voice, computer data, or video signals with equal ease. Its performance quality is superior because the digital signal is less likely to be distorted in transmission than a continuously varying electrical current. And digital systems can yield all these benefits at lower cost than the older analog systems, because the cost of the microchips that are the heart of all digital systems is constantly moving downward.

Bell Labs developed its own 256K memory chip, which is the heart of the digitization of the Creature. More than 80 percent of AT&T's urban exchanges are now digital. The growth in long-distance links, the switching systems that transmit calls from one urban center to another, is slower: 10 percent now, growing to some 40 percent over the next ten years.

Digital systems can also use pulses of light in place of electrical signals. "Optical signal processing is the wave of the future," says Ira Jacobs, director of Bell Labs' Wideband Transmission Facilities Laboratory.

Hair-thin glass fibers can transmit laser light pulses, and light waves can carry tremendously more information than can electrical currents.

Today's copper telephone cable, three inches wide, consists of 1,500 pairs of wires. It can carry 20,000 two-way voice signals. It needs repeaters to boost the signal every mile, and it costs thirty dollars per meter. Optical cables are half-inch-wide bundles of 144 fibers. They can carry 80,000 two-way signals today and will handle three times that amount in a few years, and need repeaters only every six to twenty miles. In a test in 1983, Bell Labs transmitted an optical signal through a one-hundred-mile length of lightguide fiber without a repeater to boost the signal: the world record for optical transmission. Optical fibers cost roughly twice as much as copper, meter for meter, but they carry four times the work load and will soon carry twelve times the load.

The light that optical fibers transmit is generated by ultrasmall semiconductor lasers, transistorlike devices that emit pulses of light. Their power output is only a few watts, but this is sufficient to carry thousands of conversations along lightguide cables.

The Creature is also acquiring more and more microwave links, where signals are beamed by ultrashort radio waves from one antenna to another. Neither copper nor optical fiber cables are needed, but microwave transmission is horizon-limited: the radio beams do not bend around the curve of the horizon, so antennas are needed every few miles, at least.

As the Creature's central nervous system begins to flicker with laser pulses carrying digitized voice, computer, and video data, the part of the Creature that we see—the telephone itself—is evolving swiftly.

On Buchsbaum's desk at Bell Labs, next to a symbolic quill pen, sits "the phone of the future": EPIC, which stands for Everyone's Planning and Information Communication system.

EPIC looks like a small computer terminal, which it is, in part. It has a display screen, a keyboard for typing out commands and messages, and a handset for talking and listening, together with a speakerphone feature if you don't want to use the handset. It also includes a touch-screen feature: instead of typing commands on the keyboard, you can tell the terminal what you want it to do merely by touching the cues displayed on its screen.

It is a very smart telephone, an evolutionary step beyond the clever phones available today. Where they have a few chips built into them to remember a short list of often-called numbers, EPIC's built-in computer gives it much more power. No need for phone books with EPIC; the terminal can store your entire personal phone list, and even query the Creature's various information services for phone numbers anywhere in the country. Local telephone companies will not need to print phone directories: the telephone itself will find the numbers you want.

EPIC's screen can show you the number of the phone that is calling you, so that you can decide if you want to take the call, ignore it, or have EPIC's answering service record the caller's message. If you are not at home, EPIC can refer your caller to the phone where you are. It can also be mated to sensors that will detect smoke, or fire, or burglars, and immediately contact the police or fire department. In service for more than two years at Bell Labs, EPIC also handles mail electronically. Phone your letters to other EPIC terminals across town or across the country. They will arrive with the speed of light, instead of the speed of the Postal Service.

You can pay your bills by phone, and EPIC will keep track of your checks. You can shop by phone. Ultimately you will be able to talk to EPIC and have the phone reply to you: the system will include voice recognition and response.

Telephone terminals are becoming clever enough to recognize human voices. Although it is very difficult to program a computer to understand every voice it hears ("We all talk differently," Buchsbaum observes wryly, with the faintest hint of a Middle-European accent), a computer *can* be programmed to understand a few individual voices—the voices of the family that owns the telephone terminal, for example. Family members will be able to talk to their own phone, have it understand them and answer them vocally.

AT&T's marketing plans for EPIC are still unclear. The hardware has been tested for more than two years at Bell Labs, but questions of manufacturing, pricing, and distribution have not yet been settled. Like all new capabilities, however, this flexible, smart telephone terminal is going to change our lives. The nine-to-five working day may well be the first casualty of the Creature's new telephone-cum-computer.

Buchsbaum has found that Bell Labs employees who have terminals in their homes "plug them into our computers here at the laboratories and work all kinds of crazy hours. . . . Our computer centers are busy chugging away at three o'clock Sunday morning. . . . Communication is going to change travel patterns, working mores and modes, in a way that is very difficult to predict."

Arthur C. Clarke, inventor of the communications satellite and author of science fiction classics such as *2001: A Space Odyssey*, foresees the advent of a global communications network that transcends national boundaries and, more important, national politics.

"During the coming decade," he believes, "more and more businessmen, well-heeled tourists, and virtually *all* newspersons will be carrying attaché-case-sized units that will permit direct two-way communications with their homes or offices, via the most convenient satellite. These will provide voice, telex, and video facilities. . . . As these units become cheaper, they will make travelers *totally independent of national communications systems.*" (Clarke's italics.)

The Creature, according to Clarke, can help to unify the world. "It means the end of closed societies." Nations that refuse to allow visitors to bring "such subversive machines across their borders" will face economic suicide, "because very soon they would get no tourists, and no businessmen offering foreign currency. They'd get only spies, who would have no trouble at all concealing the powerful new tools of their ancient trade."

The attaché-case phone terminal is but an intermediate step toward the old science fiction dream of the wrist communicator: a telephone as small as a wristwatch, with enough computer power in it to do everything an EPIC-like phone terminal can do.

Rich Adleman, head of Bell Labs' Transmission Network Architecture Department, says, "There's no reason why we can't make [a communicator] that small. But is there a reason to make it so small?" He points out that until phones become clever enough to respond to voice commands, the size of the human finger limits how small the device can be. And "you give up a little bit in sound quality" when you go to wristwatch-sized speakers.

But just as the Creature's network of electronic linkages is going digital, the telephone at the nerve ends of the Creature's system will become smaller, cheaper, and smarter. Within a decade the technology will bring out a wristwatch-sized communicator that will be a combination of telephone, computer, data service, and even a clock that can tell you the local time for any spot on Earth, as well as a calendar that can remind you of important dates such as birthdays, anniversaries, or when the next income-tax payment is due (no new technology is without its drawbacks).

Ivan Bekey, director of Advanced Programs for NASA, foresees a wrist phone system that can provide 25 million users in seven thousand U.S. cities instant access to each other. While the wrist phones would be small and cheap (less than twenty-five dollars, Bekey believes), they would be linked by a very powerful and sophisticated communications satellite hovering in a geostationary orbit. The satellite would weigh more than fifteen tons, and would require a 220-foot-wide antenna and 280 kilowatts of electrical power—far beyond that of any satellite in operation today.

With millions of simultaneous calls to relay, the wrist phone system will have to use higher frequencies than today's commsats, which operate at the C-band frequencies: between 4 and 6 billion cycles per second (four to six gigahertz). By comparison, the electrical current in your home is sixty hertz. The wrist phone will demand frequencies of twenty to thirty gigahertz, which communications engineers call the Ka-band.

Given that the communications links for wrist phones and other advanced systems will be created, that the Creature will continue to grow and evolve, what happens next?

Clearly, as the Creature grows in complexity and capability, as its tendrils bind all the world together ever more closely and its terminals become so ubiquitous that we carry them on our persons, human society will change drastically. In Arthur Clarke's words, instead of commuting, we will communicate.

Currently, about 11 million Americans work at home: some 7 percent of the labor force works at home full-time, and 6 percent more "moonlights" at part-time jobs from their homes. Alvin Toffler, author of *Future Shock* and *The Third Wave*, predicts that as many as 15 million workers will "telecommute" by the end of this decade.

It will be preposterous for millions of office workers to create traffic jams twice a day merely to get to work in the morning and back home in the evening. The paper shuffling they do in a business office can be done at home—without the paper—with smart-phone terminals. The face-to-face conferences they must attend can also be done at home with videophone services. The gallon of gasoline that will move an automobile twenty-some miles through urban traffic can provide enough electricity for more than one hundred hours of videophone communications.

John Naisbitt, author of *Megatrends*, welcomes the growing decentralization that telecommuting brings. "Decentralization . . . means more opportunities and more choices for individuals. . . . Your home computer [and telephone] . . . will enable you to work at home. . . . On the other hand, the cities that some leave will become less crowded and more pleasant for the others who stay."

But I wonder about the effect of telecommuting on today's large cities. Already most large cities in the United States are suffering from urban sprawl and downtown blight because their taxpayers, both individuals and corporations, have fled to the suburbs or hinterlands.

When it is no longer necessary for any office worker to come downtown for business, the last vestiges of most cities' tax base will dry up. Major cities can become crumbling ghost towns, inhabited only by those who are too poor to get away.

What of the suburban home dweller, with his or her smart-telephone terminal, who never has to leave the house to earn a living? The children need not go to school, school can come to them, electronically, with better teachers and more sophisticated curricula than most schools offer today.

Pundits such as Marshall McLuhan have spoken of "the electronic cottage," but the home of the future will evolve into a self-sufficient electronic castle, guarded from intruders by its smart phone, its heating, electrical, and water systems monitored microsecond by microsecond, and powered by solar cells on the roof that will generate the electricity to run the house.

A new affliction could strike such homes: electronic cabin fever. Every member of a family needs time away from the others, time outside the home. The self-sufficient electronic castle will have a strong impact on family relations, child rearing, and the divorce rate.

As miniaturization keeps shrinking the size of the communications hardware, it seems likely that early in the next century, microminiaturized communicators can be mated directly with the human nervous system.

The marriage of biology and electronics began with the search for better medical devices that can be implanted in the human body to monitor body functions and release medications into the bloodstream in a controlled, continuous manner. *Biosensor* research has been conducted at the University of Pittsburgh Medical School, the University of Lund, in Sweden, the University of Utah, in Salt Lake City, and at several commercial research laboratories.

The development of *molecular electronics*, which is

pointing toward electronic devices made of biological materials such as proteins, is taking place at the University of North Carolina, Chapel Hill, and at EMV Associates, of Rockville, Maryland.

This research can result in biocommunicators wired directly to the human brain or sensory nervous system, a capability so revolutionary, and so far beyond the realm where scientists are willing to even speculate, that only the science fiction writers have contemplated what this may mean to the human spirit.

Let me share a science fiction writer's vision of what the world may be like when we can intimately link molecular electronic devices to the human nervous system.

Sometime in the next century, such implants may be put into babies' skulls at birth. More likely, they will be implanted after the person has reached full growth. Perhaps a twenty-first-century puberty rite will include implantation of a microcommunicator in the skull or some other part of the anatomy—an evolution of today's ritual of giving a teenager his or her own telephone.

If microelectronic communicators can be wired into the nervous system, then eventually the wiring can be connected so intimately with sensory receptors that a person will not merely talk and listen to phone messages, he or she will *experience* the full range of sensory stimuli with every communication: see, hear, feel, taste, and smell each communication.

It will be possible to reproduce, electronically, all the aspects of hallucinations. And then some.

The teenagers of today who saunter through city streets with earphones clamped to their heads, blasting rock music directly into their semicircular canals, will become the catatonics of the twenty-first century, totally immersed in their very private worlds of sensory stimulation.

It may even become possible to wire the stimulating input directly to the brain's pleasure center(s). Today we worry about drug and alcohol addiction. Tomorrow we may have the technology to create "juice heads" who would rather be tuned in to their own pleasure centers than do anything else—including eating, sleeping, and perhaps even breathing.

Even though the Creature's only professed desire is to serve humankind (and make a profit for the various phone companies), it is clear that over the past century, the Creature has become so important to human society that we now live in a symbiotic relationship with it. Our lives could not be the same without telephones.

In tomorrow's society, this symbiosis will be even stronger—for better or for worse.

Indeed, our grandchildren will find it strange, even quaint, to learn that there were once human beings who went through their entire lives without a communicator implanted in their skulls, with nothing up there between the ears except the gray matter they were born with, without the ability to tap into the Library of Congress whenever they wanted to, or to share an experience with a friend halfway across the world.

"How lonely you must have been," they will tell us, "in olden times." And we will hear their words inside our brains, and see their faces, and hold their hands in our own—even though they may be standing on the red sands of Mars as they converse with us.

Foeman ═══════════════════════════════

High-tech warfare may be in our future. Has it existed in our distant past? There is a small but fascinating subgenre of science fiction that is made up of stories dealing with high human civilizations that existed *before* our current "historical" era. This story is part of that group.

This is the only story I ever wrote in response to a picture. Frederik Pohl, who was then editor of the now-gone and much-missed *Galaxy* magazine, showed me a cover sketch for a future issue and asked me to write a novelet based on it. This I did. Fred liked the story, but not the title. (He was always changing titles!) Onto my masterpiece he appended the title "Foeman, Where Do You Flee?" Which I *hated*.

The story used one of the characters and much of the background material from one of my earliest magazine stories, "The Towers of Titan," which graced the cover of the January 1962 issue of *Amazing Stories*. Eventually I combined the two with additional material to produce the novel *As on a Darkling Plain* (Tor Books, 1985).

But this original novelet, by itself, still strikes me as the best part of that longer tale. I have shortened the title to "Foeman," mainly because I cannot remember what my original title was. In those days before word processors, before electric typewriters, when editors never returned manuscripts after they had been published, keeping records was much chancier than it is now. I lost my carbon of the original manuscript somewhere along the line, and with it went the original title.

I

Deep in cryogenic sleep the mind dreams the same frozen dreams, endlessly circuiting through the long empty years. Sidney Lee dreamed of the towers on Titan, over and again, their smooth blank walls of metal that was beyond metal, their throbbing, ceaseless, purposeful machines that ran at tasks that men could not even guess at. The towers loomed in his darkened dreams, standing menacing and alien above the frozen wastes of Titan, utterly unmindful of the tiny men that groveled at their base. He tried to scale those smooth, steep walls and fell back. He tried to penetrate them and failed. He tried to scream. And in his dreams, at least, he succeeded.

He didn't dream of Ruth, or of the stars, or of the future or the past. Only of the towers, of the machines that blindly obeyed a builder who had left Earth's solar system countless millennia ago.

He opened his eyes.

"What happened?"

Carlos Pascual was smiling down at him, his round dark-skinned face relaxed and almost happy. "We are there . . . here, I mean. We are braking, preparing to go into orbit."

Lee blinked and sat up. "We made it?"

"Yes, yes," Pascual answered softly as his eyes shifted to the bank of instruments on the console behind Lee's shoulder. "The panel claims you are alive and well. How do you feel?"

That took a moment's thought. "A little hungry."

"A common reaction." The smile returned. "You can join the others in the galley."

The expedition's medical chief helped Lee to swing his legs over the edge of the couch, then left him and went to the next unit, where a blonde woman lay still sleeping. With an effort, Lee recalled her: Doris McNertny, primary biologist, backup biochemist. Lee pulled a deep breath into his lungs and tried to get himself started. The overhead light panels, on full intensity now, made him want to squint.

Standing was something of an experiment. *No shakes*, Lee thought gratefully. The room was large and circular, with no viewports.

Each of the twenty hibernation couches had been painted a different color by some psychology team back on Earth. Most of them were empty now. The remaining occupied ones had their lids off and the life-system connections removed as Pascual, Tanaka, and May Connearney worked to revive the people. Despite the color scheme, the room looked uninviting, and it smelled clinical.

The galley, Lee focused his thoughts, *is in this globe, one flight up*. The ship was built in globular sections that turned in response to gee-pulls. With the main fusion engines firing to brake their approach to final orbit, "up" was temporarily in the direction of the engines' thrusters. But inside the globes it did not make much difference.

He found the stairwell that ran through the globe. Inside the winding metal ladderway the rumbling vibrations from the ship's engines were echoing strongly enough to hear as actual sound.

"Sid! Good morning!" Aaron Hatfield had stationed himself at the entrance to the galley and was acting as a one-man welcoming committee.

There were only a half-dozen people in the galley. *Of course,* Lee realized. *The crew personnel are at their stations.* Except for Hatfield, the people were bunched at the galley's lone viewport, staring outside and speaking in hushed, subdued whispers.

"Hello, Aaron." Lee didn't feel jubilant, not after a fifteen-year sleep. He tried to picture Ruth in his mind and found that he couldn't.

She must be nearly fifty by now.

Hatfield was the expedition's primary biochemist, a chunky, loud-speaking, overgrown kid whom it was impossible to dislike, no matter how he behaved. Lee knew that Hatfield wouldn't go near the viewport because the sight of empty space terrified him.

"Hey, here's Doris!" Hatfield shouted to no one. He scuttled toward the entrance as she stepped rather uncertainly into the galley.

Lee dialed for coffee. With the hot cup in his hand, he walked slowly toward the viewport.

"Hello, Dr. Lee," Marlene Ettinger said as he came up alongside her. The others at the viewport turned and muttered their greetings.

"How close are we?" Lee asked.

Charnovsky, the geologist, answered positively, "Two days before we enter final orbit."

The stars crowded out the darkness beyond their viewport: spattered against the blackness like droplets from a paint spray. In the faint reflection of the port's plastic, Lee could see six human faces looking lost and awed.

Then the ship swung, ever so slightly, in response to some command from the crew and computers. A single star—close and blazingly powerful—slid into view, lancing painfully brilliant light through the polarizing viewport. Lee snapped his eyes shut, but not before the glare burned its afterimage against his closed eyelids. They all ducked back instinctively.

"Welcome to Sirius," somebody said.

Man's fight to the stars was made not in glory, but in fear.

The buildings on Titan were clearly the work of an alien intelligent race. No man could tell exactly how old they were, how long their baffling machines had been running, what their purpose was. Whoever had built them had left the solar system hundreds of centuries ago.

For the first time, men truly dreaded the stars.

Still, they had to know, had to learn. Robot probes were sent to the nearest dozen stars, the farthest that man's technology could reach. Nearly a generation passed on Earth before the faint signals from the probes returned. Seven of the stars had planets circling them. Of these, five possessed Earthlike worlds. On four of them, some indications of life were found. Life, not intelligence. Long and hot were the debates about what to do next. Finally, manned expeditions were dispatched to the Earthlike ones.

Through it all, the machines on Titan hummed smoothly.

"They should have named this ship *Afterthought*," Lee said to Charnovsky. (The ship's official name was *Carl Sagan*.)

"How so?" the Russian muttered as he pushed a pawn across the board between them. They were sitting in the pastel-lighted rec room. A few others were scattered around the semicircular room, reading, talking, dictating messages that wouldn't get to Earth for more than eight years. Soft music purred in the background.

The Earthlike planet—Sirius A-2—swung past the nearest viewport. The ship had been in orbit for nearly three weeks now and was rotating around its long axis to keep a half-gee feeling of weight for the scientists.

"We were sent here as an afterthought," Lee continued. "Nobody expects us to find anything. Most of the experts back on Earth didn't really believe there could be an Earthlike planet around a blue star."

"They were correct," Charnovsky said. "Your move."

Picture our solar system. Now replace the sun with Sirius A, the Dog Star; a young, blue star, nearly twice as hot and big as the sun. Take away the planet Uranus, nearly 2 billion kilometers from the sun, and replace it with the white dwarf Sirius B, the Pup: just as hot as Sirius A, but collapsed to a hundredth of a star's ordinary size. Now sweep away all the planets between the Dog and the Pup except two: a bald chunk of rock the size of Mercury, orbiting some 100 million kilometers from A, and an Earth-sized planet some seven times farther out.

Give the Earth-sized planet a cloud-sprinkled atmosphere, a few large seas, some worn-down mountain chains, and a thin veneer of simple green life clinging to its dusty surface. Finally, throw in one lone gas giant planet, far beyond the Pup, some 200 billion kilometers from A. Add some meteoroids and comets and you have the Sirius system.

Lehman, the psychiatrist, pulled up a webchair to the kibitzer's position between Lee and Charnovsky.

"Mind if I watch?" He was trim and athletic-looking, kept himself tanned under the UV lights in the ship's gym booth.

Within minutes they were discussing the chances of finding anything on the planet below them.

"You sound terribly pessimistic," the psychiatrist said.

"The planet looks pessimistic," Charnovsky replied. "It was scoured clean when Sirius B exploded, and life has hardly had a chance to get started again on its surface."

"But it *is* Earthlike, isn't it?"

"Hah!" Charnovsky burst. "To a simpleminded robot it may seem Earthlike. The air is breathable. The chemical composition of the rocks is similar. But no man would call that desert an Earthlike world. There are no trees, no grasses, it's too hot, the air is too dry . . ."

"And the planet's too young to have evolved an intelligent species," Lee added, "which makes me the biggest afterthought of all."

"Well, there might be something down there for an anthropologist to puzzle over," Lehman countered. "Things will look better once we get down to the surface. I think we're all getting a touch of cabin fever in here."

Before Lee could reply, Lou D'Orazio—the ship's geophysicist and cartographer—came bounding through the hatchway of the rec room and, taking advantage of the half-gravity, crossed to their chess table in two jumps.

"Look at this!"

He slapped a still-warm photograph on the chess table, scattering pieces over the floor. Charnovsky swore something Slavic, and everyone in the room turned.

It was one of the regular cartographic photos, crisscrossed with grid lines. It showed the shoreline of one of the planet's mini-oceans. A line of steep bluffs followed the shore.

"It looks like an ordinary . . ."

"*Aspetti un momento* . . . wait a minute . . . see here." D'Orazio pulled a magnifier from his coverall pocket. "Look!"

Lee peered through the magnifier. Fuzzy, wavering, gray . . .

"It looks like—"

Lehman said, "Whatever it is, it's standing on two legs."

"It's a man," Charnovsky said flatly.

II

Within minutes the whole scientific staff had piled into the rec room and crowded around the table, together with all the crew members except the two on duty in the command globe. The ship's automatic cameras took twenty more photographs of the area before their orbit carried them over the horizon from the spot.

Five of the pictures showed the shadowy figure of a bipedal creature.

The spot was in darkness by the time their orbit carried them over it again. Infrared and radar sensors showed nothing.

They squinted at the pictures, handed them from person to person, talked and argued and wondered through two entire eight-hour shifts. Crewmen left for duty and returned again. The planet turned beneath them, and once again the shoreline was bathed in Sirius's hot glow. But there was no trace of the humanoid. Neither the cameras, the manned telescopes, nor the other sensors could spot anything.

One by one, men and women left the rec room, sleepy and talked out. Finally, only Lee, Charnovsky, Lehman, and Captain Rassmussen were left sitting at the chess table with the finger-grimed photos spread out before them.

"They're men," Lee murmured. "Erect, bipedal men."

"It's only one creature," the captain said. "And all we know is that it looks like a man."

Rassmussen was tall, ham-fisted, rawboned, with a ruddy face that could look either elfin or Viking but nothing in between. His voice, though, was thin and high. To the everlasting applause of all aboard, he had fought to get a five-year supply of beer brought along. Even now, he had a mug tightly wrapped in one big hand.

"All right, they're humanoids," Lee conceded. "That's close enough."

The captain hiked a shaggy eyebrow. "I don't like jumping at shadows, you know. These pictures—"

"Men or not," Charnovsky said, "we must land and investigate closely."

Lee glanced at Lehman, straddling a turned-around chair and resting his arms tiredly on the back.

"Oh, we'll investigate," Rassmussen agreed, "but not too fast. If they are an intelligent species of some kind, we've got to go gingerly. I'm under orders from the Council, you know."

"They haven't tried to contact us," Lee said. "That means they either don't know we're here, or they're not interested, or—"

"Or what?"

Lee knew how it would sound, but he said it anyway. "Or they're waiting to get their hands on us."

Rassmussen laughed. "That sounds dramatic, sure enough."

"Really?" Lee heard his voice as though it were someone else's. "Suppose the humanoids down there are from the same race that built the machines on Titan?"

"Nonsense," Charnovsky blurted. "There are no cities down there, no sign whatever of an advanced civilization."

The captain took a long swallow of beer; then, "There is no sign of Earth's civilization on the planet either, you know. Yet *we* are here, sure enough."

Lee's insides were fluttering now. "If they are the

ones who built on Titan . . ."

"It is still nonsense!" Charnovsky insisted. "To assume that the first extraterrestrial creature resembling a man is a representative of the race that visited the solar system hundreds of centuries ago . . . ridiculous! The statistics alone put the idea in the realm of fantasy."

"Wait, there's more to it," Lee said. "Why would a visitor from another star go to the trouble to build a machine that works for centuries, without stopping?"

They looked at him, waiting for him to answer his own question: Rassmussen with his Viking's craggy face, Charnovsky trying to puzzle it out in his own mind, Lehman calm and half amused.

"The Titan buildings are more than alien," Lee explained. "They're hostile. That's my belief. Call it an assumption, a hypothesis. But I can't envision an alien race building machinery like that except for an all-important purpose. That purpose was military."

Rassmussen looked truly puzzled now. "Military? But who were they fighting?"

"Us," Lee answered. "A previous civilization on Earth. A culture that arose before the Ice Ages, went into space, met an alien culture, and was smashed in a war so badly that there's no trace of it left."

Charnovsky's face was reddening with the effort of staying quiet.

"I know it's conjecture," Lee went on quietly, "but if there was a war between ancient man and the builders of the Titan machines, then the two cultures must have arisen close enough to each other to make war possible. Widely separated cultures can't make war, they can only contact each other every few centuries or millennia. The aliens had to come from a nearby star . . . like Sirius."

"No, no, no!" Charnovsky slapped a hand on his

thigh. "It's preposterous, unscientific! There is not one shred of evidence to support this, this . . . pipe dream!"

But Rassmussen looked thoughtful.

"Still . . ."

"Still, it is nonsense," Charnovsky repeated. "The planet down there holds no interstellar technology. If there ever was one, it was blasted away when Sirius B exploded. Whoever is down there, he has no cities, no electronic communications, no satellites in orbit, no cultivated fields, no animal herds . . . nothing!"

"Then maybe he's a visitor, too," Lee countered.

"Whatever it is," Rassmussen said, "it won't do for us to go rushing in like berserkers. Suppose there's a civilization down there that's so advanced we simply do not recognize it as such?"

Before Charnovsky could reply, the captain went on, "We have plenty of time. We will get more data about surface conditions from the robot landers and do a good deal more studying and thinking about the entire problem. Then, if conditions warrant it, we can land."

"But we don't have time!" Lee snapped. Surprised at his own vehemence, he continued, "Five years is a grain of sand compared to the job ahead of us. We have to investigate a completely alien culture and determine what its attitude is toward us. Just learning the language might take five years all by itself."

Lehman smiled easily and said, "Sid, suppose you're totally wrong about this, and whoever's down there is simply a harmless savage. What would be the shock to his culture if we suddenly drop in on him?"

"What'll be the shock to our culture if I'm right?"

Rassmussen drained his mug and banged it down on the chess table. "This is getting us nowhere. We have not enough evidence to decide on an intelligent course of action. Personally, I'm in no hurry to go blundering into a nest of unknowns. Not when we can learn safely from orbit. As long as the beer holds out, we go slow."

Lee pushed his chair back and stood up. "We won't learn a damned thing from orbit. Not anything that counts. We've got to go down there and study them close up. And the sooner the better."

He turned and walked out of the rec room. *Rassmussen's spent half his life hauling scientists out to Titan, and he can't understand why we have to make the most of our time here,* he raged to himself.

Halfway down the passageway to his quarters, he heard footsteps padding behind him. He knew who it would be. Turning, he saw Lehman coming along toward him.

"Sacking in?" the psychiatrist asked.

"Aren't you sleepy?"

"Completely bushed, now that you mention it."

"But you want to talk to me," Lee said.

Lehman shrugged. "No hurry."

With a shrug of his own, Lee resumed walking to his room. "Come on. I'm too worked up to sleep anyway."

All the cubicles were more or less the same: a bunk, a desk, a filmspool reader, a sanitary closet. Lee took the webbed desk chair and let Lehman plop on the sighing air mattress of the bunk.

"Do you really believe this hostile-alien theory? Or are you just—"

Lee slouched down in his chair and interrupted. "Let's not fool around, Rich. You know about my breakdown on Titan and you're worried about me."

"It's my job to worry about everybody."

"I take my pills every day . . . to keep the paranoia away."

"That wasn't the diagnosis of your case, as you're perfectly well aware."

"So they called it something else. What're you after, Rich? Want to test my reflexes while I'm sleepy and my guard's down?"

Lehman smiled professionally. "Look, Sid. You had a breakdown on Titan. You got over it. That's finished."

Nodding grimly, Lee added, "Except that I think there might be aliens down there plotting against me."

"That could be nothing more than a subconscious attempt to increase the importance of the Anthropology Department," Lehman countered.

"Crap," Lee said. "I came out here expecting something like this. Why do you think I fought my way onto this expedition? It wasn't easy, after my breakdown. I had to push ahead of a lot of former friends."

"And leave your wife."

"That's right. Ruth divorced me for it. She's getting all my accumulated dividends. She'll die in comfort while we're sleeping our way back home."

"But why?" Lehman asked. "Why should you give up everything—friends, wife, family, position—to get out here?"

Lee knew the answer, hesitated about putting it into words, then realized that Lehman knew it, too. "Because I had to face it . . . had to do what I could to find out about those buildings on Titan."

"And that's why you want to rush down and contact whoever it is down there? Am I right?"

"Right," Lee said. He almost wanted to laugh. "I'm hoping they can tell me if I'm crazy or not."

III

It was three months before they landed.

Rassmussen was thorough, patient, and stubborn. Unmanned landers sampled and tested surface conditions. Observation satellites crisscrossed the planet at the lowest possible altitudes—except for one thing that hung in synchronous orbit in the longitude of the spot where the first humanoid had been found.

That was the only place where humanoid life was seen, along that shoreline for a grand distance of perhaps five kilometers. Nowhere else on the planet.

Lee argued and swore and stormed at the delay. Rassmussen stayed firm. Only when he was satisfied that nothing more could be learned from orbit did he agree to land the ship. And still he sent clear word back toward Earth that he might be landing in a trap.

The great ship settled slowly, almost delicately, on a hot tongue of fusion flame, and touched down on the western edge of a desert some two hundred kilometers from the humanoid site. A range of rugged-looking hills separated them. The staff and crew celebrated that night. The next morning, Lee, Charnovsky, Hatfield, Doris McNertny, Marlene Ettinger, and Alicia Monteverdi moved to the ship's "Sirius globe." They were to be the expedition's "outsiders," the specialists who would eventually live in the planetary environment. They represented anthropology, geology, biochemistry, botany, zoology, and ecology, with backup specialties in archaeology, chemistry, and paleontology.

The Sirius globe held their laboratories, workrooms, equipment, and living quarters. They were quarantined from the rest of the ship's staff and crew, the "insiders," until the captain agreed that the surface conditions on the planet would be no threat to the rest of the expedition members. That would take two years minimum, Lee knew.

Gradually, the "outsiders" began to expose themselves to the local environment. They began to breathe the air, acquire the microbes. Pascual and Tanaka made them sit in the medical examination booths twice a day, and even checked them personally every other day. The two M.D.s wore disposable biosuits and worried expressions when they entered the Sirius globe. The medical computers compiled miles of data tapes on each of the six "outsiders," but still Pascual's normally pleasant face acquired a perpetual frown of anxiety about them.

"I just don't like the idea of this damned armor," Lee grumbled.

He was already encased up to his neck in a gleaming white powersuit, the type that crew members wore when working outside the ship in a vacuum. Aaron Hatfield and Marlene Ettinger were helping to check all the seams and connections. A few feet away, in the cramped "locker room," tiny Alicia Monteverdi looked as though she were being swallowed by an oversized automaton; Charnovsky and Doris McNertny were checking her suit.

"It's for your own protection," Marlene told Lee in a throaty whisper as she applied a test meter to the radio panel on his suit's chest. "You and Alicia won the toss for the first trip outside, but this is the price you must pay. Now be a good boy and don't complain."

Lee had to grin. "*Ja, Fräulein Schulmeisterin.*"

She looked up at him with a rueful smile. "Thank God you never had to carry on a conversation in German."

Finally Lee and Alicia clumped through the double

hatch into the air lock. It took another fifteen minutes
for them to perform the final checkout, but at last they
were ready. The outer hatch slid back, and they
started down the long ladder to the planet's surface.
The armored suits were equipped with muscle-
amplifying power systems, so that even a girl as slim
as Alicia could handle their bulk easily.

Lee went down the ladder first and set foot on the
ground. It was bare and dusty, the sky a reddish haze.
The grand adventure, Lee thought. *All the expected
big moments in life are flops.* A hot breeze hummed in
his earphones. It was early morning. Sirius had not
cleared the barren horizon yet, although the sky was
fully bright. Despite the suit's air-conditioning, Lee
felt the heat.

He reached up a hand as Alicia climbed warily
down the last few steps of the ladder. The plastic
rungs gave under the suit's weight, then slowly
straightened themselves when the weight was removed.

"Well," he said, looking at her wide-eyed face
through the transparent helmet of her suit, "what do
you think of it?"

"It is hardly paradise, is it?"

"Looks like it's leaning the other way," Lee said.

They explored—Lee and Alicia that first day, then
the other outsiders, shuffling ponderously inside their
armor. Lee chafed against the restriction of the
powersuits, but Rassmussen insisted and would brook
no argument. They went timidly at first, never out of
sight of the ship. Charnovsky chipped samples from
the rock outcroppings, while the others took air and
soil samples, dug for water, searched for life.

"The perfect landing site," Doris complained after
a hot, tedious day. "There's no form of life bigger

than a yeast mold within a hundred kilometers of here."

It was a hot world, a dry world, a brick-dust world, where the sky was always red. Sirius was a blowtorch searing down on them, too bright to look at even through the tinted visors of their suits. At night there was no moon to see, but the Pup bathed this world in a deathly bluish glow far brighter yet colder than moonlight. The night sky was never truly dark, and only a few strong stars could be seen from the ground.

Through it all, the robot satellites relayed more pictures of the humanoids along the seacoast. They appeared almost every day, usually only briefly. Sometimes there were a few of them, sometimes only one, once there were nearly a dozen. The highest-resolution photographs showed them to be human in size and build. But what their faces looked like, what they wore, what they were *doing*—all escaped the drone cameras.

The robot landers, spotted in a dozen scattered locations within a thousand kilometers of the ship, faithfully recorded and transmitted everything they were programmed to look for. They sent pictures and chemical analyses of plant life and insects. But no higher animals.

Alicia's dark-eyed face took on a perpetually puzzled frown, Lee saw. "It makes no sense," she would say. "There is nothing on this planet more advanced than insects . . . yet there are men. It's as though humans suddenly sprang up in the Silurian period on Earth. They *can't* be here. I wish we could examine the life in the seas . . . perhaps that would tell us more."

"You mean those humanoids didn't originate on this planet?" Lee said to her.

She shook her head. "I don't know. I don't see how they could have . . . ."

IV

Gradually they pushed their explorations farther afield, beyond the ship's limited horizon. In the motorized powersuits a man could cover more than a hundred kilometers a day, if he pushed it. Lee always headed toward the grizzled hills that separated them from the seacoast. He helped the others to dig, to collect samples, but he always pointed them toward the sea.

"The satellite pictures show some decent greenery on the seaward side of the hills," he told Doris. "That's where he should go."

Rassmussen wouldn't move the ship. He wanted his base of operations, his link homeward, at least a hundred kilometers from the nearest possible threat. But finally he relaxed enough to allow the scientists to go out overnight and take a look at the hills.

And maybe the coast, Lee added silently to the captain's orders.

Rassmussen decided to let them use one of the ship's two air-cushion vehicles. He assigned Jerry Grote, the chief engineer, and Chien Shu Li, electronics specialist, to handle the skimmer and take command of the trip. They would live in biosuits and remain inside the skimmer at all times. Lee, Marlene, Doris, and Charnovsky made the trip: Grote did the driving and navigating, Chien handled communications and the computer.

It took a full day's drive to get to the hills. Grote, a lanky, lantern-jawed New Zealander, decided to camp at their base as night came on.

"I thought you'd be a born mountaineer," Lee poked at him.

Grote leaned back in his padded chair and planted

a large sandaled foot on the skimmer's control panel.

"I could climb those wrinkles out there in my sleep," he said pleasantly. "But we've got to be careful of this nice, shiny vehicle."

From the driver's compartment, Lee could see Marlene pushing forward toward them, squeezing between the racks of electronics gear that separated the forward compartment from the living and working quarters. Even in the drab coveralls, she showed a nice profile.

"I would like to go outside," she said to Grote. "We've been sitting all day like tourists in a shuttle."

Grote nodded. "Got to wear a hard suit, though."

"But—"

"Orders."

She glanced at Lee, then shrugged. "Very well."

"I'll come with you," Lee said.

Squirming into the armored suits in the aft hatchway was exasperating, but at last they were ready and Lee opened the hatch. They stepped out across the tail fender of the skimmer and jumped to the dusty ground.

"Being inside this is almost worse than being in the car," Marlene said.

They walked around the skimmer. Lee watched his shadow lengthen as he placed the setting Sirius at his back.

"Look . . . *look*!"

He saw Marlene pointing and turned to follow her gaze. The hills rising before them were dazzling with a million sparkling lights: red and blue and white and dazzling, shimmering lights as though a cascade of precious jewels were pouring down the hillside.

"What is it?" Marlene's voice sounded excited, thrilled, not the least afraid.

Lee stared at the shifting multicolored lights, it was like playing a lamp on cut crystal. He took a step toward the hills, then looked down to the ground. From inside the cumbersome suit, it was hard to see the ground close to your feet and harder still to bend down and pick up anything. But he squatted slowly and reached for a small stone. Getting up again, Lee held the stone high enough for it to catch the fading rays of daylight.

The rock glittered with a shower of varicolored sparkles.

"They're made of glass," Lee said.

Within minutes Charnovsky and the other "outsiders" were out of the ship to marvel at it. The Russian collected as many rocks as he could stuff into his suit's thigh pouches. Lee and Grote helped him; the women merely stood by the skimmer and watched the hills blaze with lights.

Sirius disappeared below the horizon at last, and the show ended. The hills returned to being brownish, erosion-worn clumps of rock.

"Glass mountains," Marlene marveled as they returned to the skimmer.

"Not glass," Charnovsky corrected. "Glazed rock. Granitic, no doubt. Probably was melted when the Pup exploded. Atmosphere might have been blown away, and rock cooled very rapidly."

Lee could see Marlene's chin rise stubbornly inside the transparent dome of her suit. "I name them the Glass Mountains," she said firmly.

Grote had smuggled a bottle along with them, part of his personal stock. "My most precious possession," he rightfully called it. But for the Glass Mountains he dug it out of its hiding place, and they toasted both the discovery and the name. Marlene smiled and insisted that Lee also be toasted, as codiscoverer.

Hours later, Lee grew tired of staring at the metal ceiling of the sleeping quarters a few inches above his top-tier bunk. Even Grote's drinks didn't help him to sleep. He kept wondering about the humanoids, what they were doing, where they were from, how he would get to learn their secrets. As quietly as he could, he slipped down from the bunk. The two men beneath him were breathing deeply and evenly. Lee headed for the rear hatch, past the women's bunks.

The hard suits were standing at stiff attention, flanking both sides of the rear hatch. Lee was in his coveralls. He strapped on a pair of boots, slid the hatch open as quietly as he could, and stepped out onto the fender.

The air was cool and clean, the sky bright enough for him to make out the worn old hills. There were a few stars in the sky, but the hills didn't reflect them.

He heard a movement behind him. Turning, he saw Marlene.

"Did I wake you?"

"I'm a very light sleeper," she said.

"Sorry, I didn't mean—"

"No, I'm glad you did." She shook her head slightly, and for the first time Lee noticed the sweep and softness of her hair. The light was too dim to make out its color, but he remembered it as chestnut.

"Besides," she whispered, "I've been longing to get outside without being in one of those damned suits."

He helped her down from the fender, and they walked a little way from the skimmer.

"Can we see the sun?" she asked, looking skyward.

"I'm not sure, I think maybe . . . there . . ." He pointed to a second-magnitude star, shining alone in the grayish sky.

"Where, which one?"

He took her by the shoulder with one hand so that she could see where he was pointing.

"Oh, yes, I see it."

She turned, and she was in his arms, and he kissed her. He held on to her as though there were nothing else in the universe.

If any of the others suspected that Lee and Marlene had spent the night outside, they didn't mention it. All six of them took their regular prebreakfast checks in the medical booth, and by the time they were finished eating in the cramped galley, the computer had registered a safe green for each of them.

Lee slid out from the galley's folding table and made his way forward. Grote was slouched in the driver's seat, his lanky frame a geometry of knees and elbows. He was studying the viewscreen map.

"Looking for a pass through these hills for our vehicle," he said absently, his eyes on the slowly moving photomap.

"Why take the skimmer?" Lee asked, sitting on the chair beside him. "We came across these hills in the powersuits."

Grote cocked an eye at him. "You're really set on getting to the coast, aren't you?"

"Aren't you?"

That brought a grin. "How much do you think we ought to carry with us?"

V

They split the team into three groups. Chien and Charnovsky stayed with the car; Marlene and Doris would go with Lee and Grote to look at the flora and fauna (if any) on the shore side of the hills. Lee and the engineer carried a pair of TV camera packs with them, to set up close to the shoreline.

"Beware of the natives," Charnovsky's voice grated in Lee's earphones as they walked away from the skimmer. "They might swoop down on you with bows and arrows!" His laughter showed what he thought of Lee's worries.

Climbing the hills wasn't as bad as Lee had thought it would be. The powersuit did most of the work, and the glassy rock was not smooth enough to cause real troubles with footing. It was hot, though, even with the suit's cooling equipment turned up full bore. Sirius blazed overhead, and the rocks beat glare and heat back into their faces as they climbed.

It took most of the day to get over the crest of the hills. But finally, with Sirius edging toward the horizon behind them, Lee saw the water.

The sea spread to the farther horizon, cool and blue, with long gentle swells that steepened into surf as they ran up toward the land. And the land was green here: shrubs and mossy-looking plants were patchily sprinkled around.

"Look! Right here!" Doris's voice.

Lee swiveled his head and saw her clumsily sinking to her knees, like an armor-plated elephant getting down ponderously from a circus trick. She knelt beside a fernlike plant. They all walked over and helped her to photograph it, snip a leaf from it, probe its root system.

"Might as well sleep here tonight," Grote said. "I'll take the first watch."

"Can't we set the scanners to give an alarm if anything approaches?" Marlene asked. "There's nothing here dangerous enough to——"

"I want one of us awake at all times," Grote said firmly. "And nobody outside of his suit."

"There's no place like home," Doris muttered. "But after a while even your own smell gets to you."

The women lay down, locking the suits into roughly reclining positions. To Lee they looked like oversized beetles that had gotten stuck on their backs. It didn't look possible for them to ever get up again. Then another thought struck him, and he chuckled to himself. *Super chastity belts.*

He sat down, cranked the suit's torso section back to a comfortable reclining angle, and tried to doze off. He was dreaming of the towers on Titan again when Grote's voice in his earphones woke him.

"Is it my turn?" he asked groggily.

"Not yet. But turn off your transmitter. You were groaning in your sleep. Don't want to wake up the girls, do you?"

Lee took the second watch and simply stayed awake until daybreak without bothering any of the others. They began marching toward the sea.

The hills descended only slightly into a rolling plateau that went on until they reached the bluffs that overlooked the sea. A few hundred feet down was a narrow strip of beach, with the breakers surging in.

"This is as far as we go," Grote said.

The women spent the morning collecting plant samples. Marlene found a few insects and grew more excited over them than Doris had been about the shrubbery. Lee and Grote walked along the edge of the cliffs looking for a good place to set up their cameras.

"You're sure this is the area where they were seen?" Lee asked.

The engineer, walking alongside him, turned his head inside the plastic helmet. Lee could see he was edgy, too.

"I know how to read a map."

"Sorry, I'm just anxious—"

"So am I."

They walked until Sirius was almost directly overhead, without seeing anything except the tireless sea, the beach, and the spongy-looking plants that huddled close to the ground.

"Not even a damned tree," Grote grumbled.

They turned back and headed for the spot where they had left the women. Far up the beach, Lee saw a tiny dark spot.

"What's that?"

Grote stared for a few moments. "Probably a rock." But he touched a button on the chest of his suit.

Lee did the same, and an electro-optical viewpiece slid down in front of his eyes. Turning a dial on the suit's control panel, he tried to focus on the spot. It wavered in the heat currents of the early afternoon, blurred and uncertain. Then it seemed to jump out of view.

Lee punched the button, and the lens slid away from his eyes. "It's moving!" he shouted, and started to run.

He heard Grote's heavy breathing as the engineer followed him, and they both nearly flew in their powersuits along the edge of the cliffs.

It was a man! No, not one, Lee saw, but two of them walking along the beach, their feet in the foaming water.

"Get down, you bloody fool," he heard Grote shrilling at him.

He dove headlong, bounced, cracked the back of his head against the helmet's plastic, then banged his chin on the soft inner lining of the collar.

"Don't want them to see us, do you?" Grote was whispering now.

"They can't hear us, for God's sake," Lee said into his suit radiophone.

They wormed their way to the cliff's edge again and watched. The two men seemed to be dressed in black. *Or are they black-skinned and naked?* Lee wondered.

After a hurried council, they unslung one of the video cameras and its power unit, set it up right there, turned it on, and then backed away from the edge of the cliff. Then they ran as hard as they could, staying out of sight of the beach, with the remaining camera. They passed the startled women and breathlessly shouted out their find. The women dropped their work and started running after them.

About a kilometer or so farther on they dropped to all fours again and painfully crawled to the edge once more. Grote hissed the women into silence as they hunched up beside him.

The beach was empty now.

"Do you think they saw us?" Lee asked.

"Don't know."

Lee used the electro-optics again and scanned the beach. "No sign of them."

"Their footprints," Grote snapped. "Look there."

The trails of two very human-looking sets of footprints marched straight into the water. All four of them searched the sea for hours, but saw nothing. Finally, they decided to set up the other camera. It was turning dark by the time they finished.

"We've got to get back to the car," Grote said wearily, when they finished. "There's not enough food in the suits for another day."

"I'll stay here," Lee replied. "You can bring me more supplies tomorrow."

"No. If there's anything to see, the cameras will pick it up. Chien is monitoring them back at the car, and the whole crew of the ship must be watching the view."

Lee saw there was no sense arguing. Besides, he was bone-tired. But he knew he'd be back again as soon as he could get there.

VI

"Well, it settles a three-hundred-year-old argument," Aaron Hatfield said as he watched the viewscreen.

The biochemist and Lee were sitting in the main workroom of the ship's Sirius globe, watching the humanoids as televised by the cameras on the cliffs. Charnovsky was on the other side of the room, at a workbench, flashing rock chips with a laser so that a spectrometer could analyze their chemical composition. The other "outsiders" were traveling in the skimmer again, collecting more floral and insect specimens.

"What argument?" Lee asked.

Hatfield shifted in his chair, making the webbing creak. "About the human form . . . whether it's an accident or a result of evolutionary selection. From *them*," he nodded toward the screen, "I'd say it's no accident."

One camera was on wide-field focus and showed a group of three of the men. They were wading hip-deep in the surf, carrying slender rods high above their heads to keep them free of the surging waves. The other camera was fixed on a close-up view of three women standing on the beach, watching their men. Like the men, they were completely naked and black-skinned. They looked human in every detail.

Every morning they appeared on the beach, often carrying the rods, but sometimes not. Lee concluded that they must live in caves cut into the cliffs. The rods looked like simple bone spears but even under the closest focus of the cameras he couldn't be sure.

"They're not Negroid," he muttered, more to himself than anyone listening.

"It's hard to tell, isn't it?" Hatfield asked.

Nodding, Lee said, "They just don't look like terrestrial Negroes . . . except for their skin coloring. And that's an adaptation to Sirius's brightness. Plenty of ultraviolet, too."

Charnovsky came over and pulled up a chair. "So. Have they caught any fish this morning?"

"Not yet," Lee answered.

Jabbing a stubby finger toward the screen, the Russian asked, "Are these the geniuses who built the machines on Titan? Fishing with bone spears? They don't make much of an enemy, Lee."

"They could have been our enemy," Lee answered, forcing a thin smile. He was getting accustomed to Charnovsky's needling, but not reconciled to it.

The geologist shook his head sadly. "Take the advice of an older man, dear friend, and disabuse yourself of this idea. Statistics are a powerful tool, Lee. The chances against this particular race being the one that built on Titan are fantastically high. And the chances . . ."

"What're the chances that two intelligent races will both evolve along the same physical lines?" Lee snapped.

Charnovsky shrugged. "We have two known races. They are both human in form. The chances must be excellent."

Lee turned back to watch the viewscreen, then asked Hatfield, "Aaron, the biochemistry is very similar to Earth's, isn't it?"

"Very close."

"I mean . . . I could eat local food and be nourished by it? I wouldn't be poisoned or anything like that?"

"Well," Hatfield said, visibly thinking it out as he spoke, "as far as the structure of the proteins and other foodstuffs is concerned . . . yes, I guess you could get away with eating it. The biochemistry is basically the same as ours, as nearly as I've been able to tell. But so are terrestrial shellfish, and they make me deathly ill. You see, there're all sorts of enzymes, and microbial parasites, and viruses . . ."

"We've been living with the local bugs for months now," Lee said. "We're adapted to them, aren't we?"

"You know what they say about visiting strange places: don't drink the water."

One of the natives struck into the water with his spear, and instantly the water began to boil with the thrashing of some sea creature. The other two men drove their spears home, and the thrashing died. They lifted a four-foot-long fish out of the water and started back for the beach, carrying it triumphantly over their heads. The camera's autotracker kept the picture on them. The women on the beach were jumping and clapping with joy.

"Damn," Lee said softly. "They're as human as we are."

"And obviously representative of a high technical civilization," Charnovsky said.

"Survivors of one, maybe," Lee answered. "Their culture might have been wiped out by the Pup's explosion . . . or by war."

"Ah, now it gets even more dramatic: two cultures destroyed, ours *and* theirs."

"All right, go ahead and laugh," Lee said. "I won't be able to prove anything until I get to live with them."

"Until what?" Hatfield said.

"Until I go out there and meet them face-to-face, learn their language, their culture, live with them."

"Live with them?" Rassmussen looked startled; the first time Lee had seen him jarred. The captain's monomolecular biosuit gave his craggy face a faint sheen, like the beginnings of a sweat.

They were sitting around a circular table in the

conference room of the Sirius globe: the six "outsiders," Grote, Chien, Captain Rassmussen, Pascual, and Lehman.

"Aren't you afraid they might put you in a pot and boil you?" Grote asked, grinning.

"I don't think they have pots. Or fire, for that matter," Lee countered.

The laugh turned on Grote.

Lee went on quietly, "I've checked it out with Aaron, here. There's no biochemical reason why I couldn't survive in the native environment. Doris and Marlene have agreed to gather the same types of food we've seen the humanoids carrying, and I'll go on a strictly native diet for a few weeks before I go to live with them."

Lehman hunched forward, from across the table, and asked Lee, "About the dynamics of having a representative of our relatively advanced culture step into their primitive—"

"I won't be representing an advanced culture to them," Lee said. "I intend to be just as naked and toolless as they are. And just as black. Aaron can inject me with the proper enzymes to turn my skin black."

"That would be necessary in any event if you don't want to be sunburned to death," Pascual said.

Hatfield added, "You'll also need contact lenses that'll screen out the UV and protect your eyes."

They spent an hour discussing all the physical precautions he would have to take. Lee kept glancing at Rassmussen. *The idea's slipping out from under his control.* The captain watched each speaker in turn, squinting with concentration and sinking deeper and deeper into his Viking scowl. Then, when Lee was certain that the captain could no longer object, Rassmussen spoke up: "One more question. Are you willing to give up an eye for this mission of yours?"

"What do you mean?"

The captain's hands seemed to wander loosely without a mug of beer to tie them down. "Well . . . you seem to be willing to run a good deal of personal risk to live with these . . . eh, people. From the expedition's viewpoint, you will also be risking our only anthropologist, you know. I think the wise thing to do, in that case, would be to have a running record of everything you see and hear."

Lee nodded.

"So we can swap one of your eyes for a TV camera and plant a transmitter somewhere in your skull. I'm sure there's enough empty space in your head to accommodate it." The captain chuckled toothily at his joke.

"We can't do an eye procedure here," Pascual argued. "It's too risky."

"I understand that Dr. Tanaka is quite expert in that field," the captain said. "And naturally we would preserve the eye to restore it afterward. Unless, of course, Professor Lee—" He let the suggestion dangle.

Lee looked at them sitting around the big table; Rassmussen, trying to look noncommittal; Pascual, upset and nearly angry; Lehman, staring intently right back into Lee's eyes.

You're just trying to force me to back down, Lee thought of Rassmussen. Then, of Lehman, *And if I don't back down, you'll be convinced that I'm crazy*.

For a long moment there was no sound in the crowded conference room except the faint whir of the air blower.

"All right," Lee said. "If Tanaka is willing to tackle the surgery, so am I."

VII

When Lee returned to his cubicle, the message light under the phone screen was blinking red. He flopped on the bunk, propped a pillow under his head, and asked the computer, "What's the phone message?"

The screen lit up: PLS CALL DR. LEHMAN.

My son, the psychiatrist. "Okay," he said aloud, "get him."

A moment later Lehman's tanned face filled the screen.

"I was expecting you to call," Lee said.

The psychiatrist nodded. "You agreed to pay a big price just to get loose among the natives."

"Tanaka can handle the surgery," he answered evenly.

"It'll take a month before you are fit to leave the ship again."

"You know what our Viking captain says . . . we'll stay here as long as the beer holds out."

Lehman smiled. *Professional technique,* Lee thought.

"Sid, do you really think you can mingle with these people without causing any cultural impact? Without changing them?"

Shrugging, he answered, "I don't know. I hope so. As far as we know, they're the only humanoid group on the planet. They may have never seen a stranger before."

"That's what I mean," Lehman said. "Don't you feel that—"

"Let's cut the circling, Rich. You know why I want to see them firsthand. If we had the time I'd study them remotely for a good long while before trying any contact. But it gets back to the beer supply. We've got to squeeze everything we can out of them in a little more than four years."

"There will be other expeditions, after we return to Earth and tell them about these people."

"Probably so. But they may be too late."

"Too late for what?"

His neck was starting to hurt; Lee hunched up to a sitting position on the bunk. "Figure it out. There can't be more than about fifty people in the group we've been watching. I've only seen a couple of children. And there aren't any other humanoid groups on the planet. That means they're dying out. This gang is the last of their kind. By the time another expedition gets here, there might not be any of them left."

For once, Lehman looked surprised. "Do you really think so?"

"Yes. And before they die, we have to get some information out of them."

"What do you mean?"

"They might not be natives of this planet," Lee said, forcing himself to speak calmly, keeping his face a mask, freezing any emotion inside him. "They probably came from somewhere else. That elsewhere is the home of the people who built the Titan machine . . . their real home. We have got to find out where it is." *Flawless logic.*

Lehman tried to smile again. "That's assuming your theory about an ancient war is right."

"Yes. Assuming I'm right."

"Assume you *are*," Lehman said. "And assume you find what you're looking for. Then what? Do you just take off and go back to Earth? What happens to the people here?"

"I don't know," Lee said, ice-cold inside. "The main problem will be how to deal with the home world of their people."

"But the people here, do we just let them die out?"

"Maybe. I guess so."

Lehman's smile was completely gone now; his face didn't look pleasant at all.

It took much more than a month. The surgery was difficult. And beneath all the pain was Lee's rooted fear that he might never have his sight fully restored again. While he was recovering, before he was allowed out of his infirmary bed, Hatfield turned his skin black with a series of enzyme injections. He was also fitted for a single quartz contact lens.

Once he was up and around, Marlene followed him constantly. Finally she said, "You're even better looking with black skin; it makes you more mysterious. And the prosthetic eye looks exactly like your own. It even moves like the natural one."

Rassmussen still plodded. Long after he felt strong enough to get going again, he was still confined to the ship. When his complaints grew loud enough, they let him start on a diet of native foods. The medics and Hatfield hovered around him while he spent a miserable week with dysentery. Then it passed. But it took a while to build up his strength again; all he had to eat now were fish, insects, and pulpy greens.

After more tests, conferences, a two-week trial run out by the Glass Mountains, and then still more exhaustive physical exams, Rassmussen at last agreed to let Lee go.

Grote took him out in the skimmer, skirting the long way around the Glass Mountains, through the surf and out onto the gently billowing sea. They kept far enough out at sea for the beach to be constantly beyond their horizon.

When night fell, Grote nosed the skimmer landward. They came ashore around midnight, with the engines clamped down to near silence, a few kilometers up the beach from the humanoids' site. Grote, encased in a powersuit, walked with him partway and buried a relay transceiver in the sand, to pick up the signals from the camera and radio embedded in Lee's skull.

"Good luck." His voice was muffled by the helmet.

Lee watched him plod mechanically back into the darkness. He strained to hear the skimmer as it turned and slipped back into the sea, but he could neither see nor hear it.

He was alone on the beach.

Clouds were drifting landward, riding smoothly overhead. The breeze on the beach, though, was blowing warmly out of the desert, spilling over the bluffs and across the beach, out to sea. The sky was bright with the all-night twilight glow, even though the clouds blotted out most of the stars. Along the foot of the cliffs, though, it was deep black. Except for the wind, there wasn't a sound: not a bird nor a nocturnal cat, not even an insect's chirrup.

Lee stayed near the water's edge. He wasn't cold, even though naked. Still, he could feel himself trembling.

Grote's out there, he told himself. *If you need him, he can come rolling up the beach in ten minutes.*

But he knew he was alone.

The clouds thickened and began to sprinkle rain, a warm, soft shower. Lee blinked the drops away from his eyes and walked slowly, a hundred paces one direction, then a hundred paces back again.

The rain stopped as the sea horizon started turning bright. The clouds wafted away. The sky lightened, first gray, then almost milky white. Lee looked toward the base of the cliffs. Dark shadows dotted the rugged cliff face. Caves. Some of them were ten feet or more above the sand.

Sirius edged a limb above the horizon, and Lee,

squinting, turned away from its brilliance. He looked back at the caves again, feeling the warmth of the hot star's might on his back.

The first ones out of the cave were two children. They tumbled out of the same cave, off to Lee's left, giggling and running.

When they saw Lee, they stopped dead. As though someone had turned them off. Lee could feel his heart beating as they stared at him. He stood just as still as they did, perhaps a hundred meters from them. They looked about five and ten years old, he judged. *If their life spans are the same as ours.*

The taller of the two boys took a step toward Lee, then turned and ran back into the cave. The younger boy followed him.

For several minutes nothing happened. Then Lee heard voices echoing from inside the cave. Angry? Frightened? *They are not laughing.*

Four men appeared at the mouth of the cave. Their hands were empty. They simply stood there and gaped at him, from the shadows of the cave's mouth.

Now we'll start learning their customs about strangers, Lee said to himself.

Very deliberately, he turned away from them and took a few steps up the beach. Then he stopped, turned again, and walked back to his original spot.

Two of the men disappeared inside the cave. The other two stood there. Lee couldn't tell what the expressions on their faces meant. Suddenly other people appeared at a few of the other cave entrances. *They're interconnected.*

Lee tried a smile and waved. There were women among the onlookers now, and a few children. One of the boys who saw him first—at least, it looked like him—started chattering to an adult. The man silenced him with a brusque gesture.

It was getting hot. Lee could feel perspiration

dripping along his ribs as Sirius climbed above the horizon and shone straight at the cliffs. Slowly, he squatted down on the sand.

A few of the men from the first cave stepped out onto the beach. Two of them were carrying bone spears. Others edged out from their caves. They slowly drew together, keeping close to the rocky cliff wall, and started talking in low, earnest tones.

They're puzzled, all right. Just play it cool. Don't make any sudden moves.

He leaned forward slightly and traced a triangle on the sand with one finger.

When he looked up again, a grizzled, white-haired man had taken a step or two away from the conference group. Lee smiled at him, and the elder froze in his tracks. With a shrug, Lee looked back at the first cave. The boy was still there, with a woman standing beside him, gripping his shoulder. Lee waved and smiled. The boy's hand fluttered momentarily.

The old man said something to the group, and one of the younger men stepped out to join him. Neither held a weapon. They walked to within a few meters of Lee, and the old man said something, as loudly and bravely as he could.

Lee bowed his head. "Good morning. I am Professor Sidney Lee of the University of Ottawa, which is one hell of a long way from here."

They squatted down and started talking, both of them at once, pointing to the caves and then all around the beach and finally out to the sea.

Lee held up his hands and said, "It ought to be clear to you that I'm from someplace else, and I don't speak your language. Now if you want to start teaching me—"

They shook their heads, talked to each other, said something else to Lee.

Lee smiled at them and waited for them to stop

talking. When they did, he pointed to himself and said very clearly, "Lee."

He spent an hour at it, repeating only that one syllable, no matter what they said to him or to each other. The heat was getting fierce; Sirius was a blue flame searing his skin, baking the juices out of him.

The younger man got up and, with a shake of his head, spoke a few final words to the elder and walked back to the group that still stood knotted by the base of the cliff. The old man rose, slowly and stiffly. He beckoned to Lee to do the same.

As Lee got to his feet he saw the other men start to head out for the surf. A few boys followed behind, carrying several bone spears for their—what? Fathers? Older brothers?

As long as the spears are for the fish and not me, Lee thought.

The old man was saying something to him. Pointing toward the caves. He took a step in that direction, then motioned for Lee to come along. Lee hesitated. The old man smiled a toothless smile and repeated his invitation.

Grinning back at him in realization, Lee said aloud, "Okay. If you're not scared of me, I guess I don't have to be scared of you."

VIII

It took more than a year before Lee learned their language well enough to understand roughly what they were saying. It was an odd language, sparse and practically devoid of pronouns.

His speaking of their words made the adults smile, when they thought he couldn't see them doing it. The children still giggled at his speech, but the old man —Ardraka—always scolded them when they did.

They called the planet Makta, and Lee saw to it that Rassmussen entered that as its official name in the expedition's log. He made a point of walking the beach alone one night each week, to talk with the others at the ship and make a personal report. He quickly found that most of what he saw, heard, and said inside the caves never got out to the relay transceiver buried up the beach; the cliff's rock walls were too much of a barrier.

Ardraka was the oldest of the clan and the nominal chief. His son, Ardra, was the younger man who had also come out to talk with Lee that first day. Ardra actually gave most of the orders. Ardraka could overrule him whenever he chose to, but he seldom exercised the right.

There were only forty-three people in the clan, nearly half of them elderly looking. Eleven were preadolescent children; two of them infants. There were no obvious pregnancies. Ardraka must have been about fifty, judging by his oldest son's apparent age. But the old man had the wrinkled, sunken look of an eighty-year-old. The people themselves had very little idea of time beyond the basic rhythm of night and day.

They came out of the caves only during the early morning and evening hours. The blazing midday heat of Sirius was too much for them to face. They ate crustaceans and the small fish that dwelt in the shallows along the beach, insects, and the grubby vegetation that clung to the base of the cliffs. Occasionally they found a large fish that had blundered into the shallows; then they feasted.

They had no wood, no metal, no fire. Their only tools were from the precious bones of the rare big fish, and hand-worked rock.

They died of disease and injury, and aged prema-

turely from poor diet and overwork. They had to
search constantly for food, especially since half their
day was taken away from them by Sirius's blowtorch
heat. They were more apt to be prowling the beach at
night, hunting seaworms and crabs, than by daylight.
Grote and I damn near barged right into them, Lee
realized after watching a few of the night gathering
sessions.

There were some dangers. One morning he was
watching one of the teenaged boys, a good swimmer,
venture out past the shallows in search of fish. A
sharklike creature found him first.

When he screamed, half a dozen men grabbed
spears and dove into the surf. Lee found himself
dashing into the water alongside them, empty-
handed. He swam out to the youngster, already dead,
sprawled facedown in the water, half of him gone,
blood staining the swells. Lee helped to pull the
remains back to shore.

There wasn't anything definite, no one said a word
to him about it, but their attitude toward him
changed. He was fully accepted now. He hadn't saved
the boy's life, hadn't shown uncommon bravery. But
he had shared a danger with them, and a sorrow.

Wheel the horse inside the gates of Troy, Lee found
himself thinking. *Nobody ever told you to beware of
men bearing gifts.*

After he got to really understand their language, Lee
found that Ardraka often singled him out for long
talks. It was almost funny. There was something that
the old man was fishing for, just as Lee was trying to
learn where these people *really* came from.

They were sitting in the cool darkness of the central
cave, deep inside the cliff. All the outer caves chan-
neled back to this single large chamber, high-roofed
and moss-floored, its rocks faintly phosphorescent. It

was big enough to hold four or five times the clan's present number. It was midday. Most of the people were sleeping. A few of the children, off to the rear of the cave, were scratching pictures on the packed bare earth with pointed, fist-sized rocks.

Lee sat with his back resting against a cool stone wall. The sleepers were paired off, man and mate, for the most part. The unmated teenagers slept apart, with the older couples between them. As far as Lee could judge, the couples paired permanently, although the teens played the game about as freely as they could.

Ardraka was dozing beside him. Lee settled back and tried to turn off his thoughts, but the old man said: "Lee is not asleep?"

"No, Lee is not," he answered.

"Ardraka has seen that Lee seldom sleeps," Ardraka said.

"That is true."

"Is it that Lee does not need to sleep as Ardraka does?"

Lee shook his head. "No, Lee needs sleep as much as Ardraka or any man."

"This . . . place . . . that Lee comes from. Lee says it is beyond the sea?"

"Yes, far beyond."

In the faint light from the gleaming rocks, the old man's face looked troubled, deep in difficult thought.

"And there are men and women living in Lee's place, men and women like the people here?"

Lee nodded.

"And how did Lee come here? Did Lee swim across the sea?"

They had been through this many times. "Lee came across the edge of the sea, walking on land just as Ardraka would."

Laughing softly, the old man said, "Ardraka is too feeble now for such a walk. Ardra could make such a walk."

"Yes, Ardra can."

"Ardraka has tried to dream of Lee's place, and Lee's people. But such dreams do not come."

"Dreams are hard to command," Lee said.

"Yes, truly."

"And what of Ardraka and the people here?" Lee asked. "Is this the only place where such men and women live?"

"Yes. It is the best place to live. All other places are death."

"There are no men and women such as Ardraka and the people here living in another place?"

The old man thought hard a moment, then smiled a wrinkled toothless smile. "Surely Lee jokes. Lee knows that Lee's people live in another place."

We've been around that bush before. Trying another tack, he asked, "Have Ardraka's people *always* lived in this place? Did Ardraka's father live here?"

"Yes, of course."

"And his father?"

A nod.

"And all the fathers, from the beginning of the people? All lived here, always?"

A shrug. "No man knows."

"Have there always been this many people living here?" Lee asked. "Did Ardraka's people ever fill this cave when they slept here?"

"Oh, yes . . . When Ardraka was a boy, many men and women slept in the outer caves, since there was no room for them here. And when Ardraka's father was young, men and women even slept in the lower caves."

"Lower caves?"

Ardraka nodded. "Below this one, deeper inside the ground. No man or woman has been in them since Ardraka became chief."

"Why is that?"

The old man evaded Lee's eyes. "They are not needed."

"May Lee visit these lower caves?"

"Perhaps," Ardraka said. After a moment's thought, he added, "Children have been born and grown to manhood and died since any man set foot in those caves. Perhaps they are gone now. Perhaps Ardraka does not remember how to find them."

"Lee would like to visit the lower caves."

Late that night he walked the beach alone, under the glowing star-poor sky, giving his weekly report back to the ship.

"He's been cagey about the lower caves," Lee said as the outstretched fingers of surf curled around his ankles.

"Why should he be so cautious?" It was Marlene's voice. She was taking the report this night.

"Because he's no fool, that's why. These people have never seen a stranger before . . . not for generations, at least. Therefore their behavior toward me is original, not instinctive. If he's leery of showing me the caves, it's for some reason that's fresh in his mind, not some hoary tribal taboo."

"Then what do you intend to do?"

"I'm not sure yet—" Lee turned to head back down the beach and saw Ardra standing twenty paces behind him.

"Company," he snapped. "Talk to you later. Keep listening."

Advancing toward him, Ardra said, "Many nights, Ardra has seen Lee leave the cave and walk on the beach. Tonight Lee was talking, but Lee was alone.

Does Lee speak to a man or woman that Ardra cannot see?"

His tone was flat, factual, neither frightened nor puzzled. It was too dark to really make out the expression on his face, but he sounded almost casual.

"Lee is alone," he answered as calmly as he could. "There is no man or woman here with Lee. Except Ardra."

"But Lee speaks and then is silent. And then Lee speaks again."

He knows a conversation when he hears one, even if it's only one side of it and in a strange language.

Ardra suggested, "Perhaps Lee speaks to men and women from Lee's place, which is far from the sea?"

"Does Ardra believe that Lee can speak to men and women far away from this place?"

"Ardra believes that is what Lee does at night on the beach. Lee speaks with the *karta*."

"*Karta*? What is the meaning of *karta*?"

"It is an ancient word. It means men and women who live in another place."

Others, Lee translated to himself. "Yes," he said to Ardra, "Lee speaks to the others."

Ardra's breath seemed to catch momentarily, then he said with deliberate care, "Lee speaks with the Others." His voice had an edge of steel to it now.

What have I stepped into?

"It is time to be sleeping, not walking the beach," Ardra said in a tone that Lee knew was a command. And he started walking toward the caves.

Lee outweighed the chief's son by a good twenty pounds and was some ten centimeters taller. But he had seen the speed and strength in Ardra's wiry frame and knew the difference in reaction times that the fifteen years between them made. So he didn't run or fight; he followed Ardra back to the caves and obediently went to sleep. And all the night Ardra stayed awake and watched over him.

IX

The next morning, when the men went out to fish and the women to gather greens, Ardra took Lee's arm and led him toward the back of the central cave. Ardraka and five other elders were waiting for them. They all looked very grim. Only then did Lee realize that Ardra was carrying a spear in his other hand.

They were sitting in a ragged semicircle, their backs to what looked like a tunnel entrance, their eyes hard on Lee. He sat at their focus, with Ardra squatting beside him.

"Lee," Ardraka began without preliminaries, "why is it that Lee wishes to see the lower caves?"

The question caught him by surprise. "Because . . . Lee wishes to learn more about Ardraka's people. Lee comes from far away, and knows little of Ardraka's people."

"Is it true," one of the elders asked, "that Lee speaks at night with the Others?" His inflection made the word sound special, fearful, ominous.

"Lee speaks to the men and women of the place where Lee came from. It is like the way Ardraka speaks to Ardraka's grandfather . . . in a dream."

"But Ardraka sleeps when doing this. Lee is awake."

Ardra broke in, "Lee says Lee's people live beyond the sea. Beyond the sea is the sky. Do Lee's people live in the sky?"

Off the edge of the world, just like Columbus. "Yes," he admitted. "Lee's people live in the sky—"

"*See!*" Ardra shouted. "Lee is of the Others!"

The councilmen physically backed away from him. Even Ardraka seemed shaken.

"Lee is of the Others," Ardra repeated. "Lee must be killed, before he kills Ardraka's people!"

"Kill?" Lee felt stunned. He had never heard any of them speak of violence before.

"Why should Lee kill the people here?"

They were all babbling at once. Ardraka raised his hand for silence.

"To kill a man is very serious," he said painfully. "It is not certain that Lee is of the Others."

"Lee says it with Lee's own mouth!" Ardra insisted. "Why else did Lee come here? Why does Lee want to see the lower caves?"

Ardraka glowered at his son, and the younger man stopped. "The council must be certain before it acts."

Struggling to keep his voice calm, Ardra ticked off on his fingers, "Lee says Lee's people live in the sky . . . the Others live in the sky. Lee wishes to see the lower caves. Why? To see if more of Ardraka's people are living there, so that he can kill *all* the people!"

The council members murmured and glanced at him fearfully. *Starting to look like a lynch jury.*

"Wait," Lee said. "There is more to the truth than what Ardra says. Lee's people live in the sky . . . that is true. But that does not mean that Lee's people are the Others. The sky is wide and larger . . . wider than the sea, by far. Many different peoples can live in the sky."

Ardraka nodded, his brows knitted in concentration. "But, Lee, if both Lee's people and the Others live in the sky, why have not the Others destroyed Lee's people as they destroyed Ardraka's ancestors?"

Lee felt his stomach drop out of him. *So that's it!*

"Yes," one of the councilmen said. "The Others live far from this land, yet the Others came here and destroyed Ardraka's forefathers and all the works of such men and women."

"Tell Lee what happened," he said, stalling for time to work out answers. "Lee knows nothing about the Others." *Not from your side of the war, anyway.*

Ardraka glanced around at the council members sitting on both sides of him. They looked uncertain, wary, still afraid. Ardra, beside Lee, had the fixed glare of a born prosecutor.

"Lee is not of Ardraka's people," the younger man said, barely controlling the fury in his voice. "Lee must be of the Others. There are no people except Ardraka's people and the Others!"

"Perhaps that is not so," Ardraka said. "True, Ardraka has always thought it to be this way, but Lee looks like an ordinary man, not like the Others."

Ardra huffed. "No living man has seen the Others. How can Ardraka say . . ."

"Because Ardraka has seen pictures of the Others," the chief said quietly.

"Pictures?" They were startled.

"Yes. In the deepest cave, where only the chief can go . . . and the chief's son. Ardraka has thought for a long time that soon Ardra should see the deepest cave. But no longer. Ardra must see the cave now."

The old man got up, stiffly, to his feet. His son was visibly trembling with eagerness.

"May Lee also see the pictures?" Lee asked.

They all began to protest, but Ardraka said firmly, "Lee has been accused of being of the Others. Lee stands in peril of death. It is right that Lee should see the pictures."

The council members muttered among themselves. Ardra glowered, then bent down and reached for the spear he had left at his feet. Lee smiled to himself. *If those pictures give you the slightest excuse, you're going to ram that thing through me. You'd make a good sheriff, kill first, then ask questions.*

* * *

Far from having forgotten his way to the deeper caves, Ardraka threaded through a honeycomb of tunnels and chambers, always picking the path that slanted downward. Lee sensed that they were spiraling deeper and deeper into the solid rock of the cliffs, far below the sea level. The walls were crusted, and a thick mat of dust clung to the ground. But everything shone with the same faint luminosity as the upper caves, and beneath the dust the footing felt more like pitted metal than rock.

Finally Ardraka stopped. They were standing in the entryway to a fairly small chamber. The lighting was very dim. Lee stood behind Ardraka and felt Ardra's breath on his back.

"This is the place," Ardraka said solemnly. His voice echoed slightly.

They slowly entered the chamber. Ardraka walked to the farthest wall and wordlessly pointed to a jumble of lines scrawled at about eye level. The cave was dark, but the lines of the drawing glowed slightly brighter than the wall itself.

Gradually, Lee pieced the picture together. It was crude, so crude that it was hard to understand. But there were stick figures of men that seemed to be running, and rough outlines of what might be buildings, with curls of smoke rising up from them. Above them all were circular things, ships, with dots for ports. Harsh jagged lines were streaking out of them and toward the stick figures.

"Men and women," Ardraka said, in a reverent whisper as he pointed to the stick drawings. "The men and women of the time of Ardraka's farthest ancestors. And *here*"—his hand flashed to the circles —"are the Others."

Even in the dim light, Lee could see Ardra's face gaping at the picture. "The Others," he said, his voice barely audible.

"Look at Lee," Ardraka commanded his son. "Does Lee look like the Others, or like a man?"

Ardra seemed about to crumble. He said shakily, "Lee . . . Ardra has misjudged Lee . . . Ardra is ashamed."

"There is no shame," Lee said. "Ardra has done no harm. Ardra was trying to protect Ardraka's people." *And besides, you were right.*

Turning to Ardraka, Lee asked, "Is this all that you know of the Others?"

"Ardraka knows that the Others killed the people of Ardraka's forefathers. Before the Others came, Ardraka's ancestors lived in splendor; their living places covered the land everywhere; they swam the seas without fear of any creature of the deep; they leaped through the sky and laughed at the winds and storms; every day was bright and good and there was no night. Then the Others came and destroyed everything. The Others turned the sky to fire and brought night. Only the people in the deepest cave survived. This was the deepest cave. Only the people of Ardraka escaped the Others."

We destroyed this world, Lee told himself. *An interstellar war, eons ago. We destroyed each other, old man. Only you've been destroyed for good, and we climbed back.*

"One more thing remains," Ardraka said. He walked into the shadows on the other end of the room and pushed open a door. *A door!* It was metal, Lee could feel as he went past it. There was another chamber, larger.

A storeroom! Shelves lined the walls. Most of them empty, but here and there were boxes, containers, machinery with strange writing on it.

"These belonged to Ardraka's oldest ancestors," the chief said. "No man today knows why these things were saved here in the deepest cave. They have no purpose. They are dead. As dead as the people who put them here."

It was Lee who was trembling as they made their way up to the dwelling caves.

X

It was a week before he dared stroll the beach at night again, a week of torment, even though Ardra never gave him the slightest reason to think that he was still under suspicion.

They were just as stunned as he was when he told them about it.

"We killed them," he whispered savagely at them, back in the comfort of the ship. "We destroyed them. Maybe we even made the Pup explode, to wipe them out completely."

"That's . . . farfetched," Rassmussen answered. But his voice sounded lame.

"What do we do now?"

"I want to see those artifacts."

"Yes, but how?"

Lee said, "I can take you down to the cave, if we can put the whole clan to sleep for a few hours. Maybe gas . . ."

"That could work," Rassmussen agreed.

"A soporific gas?" Pascual's soft tenor rang incredulously in Lee's ears. "But we haven't the faintest idea of how it might affect them."

"It's the only way," Lee said. "You can't dig your way into the cave . . . even if you could, they would hear it, and you'd be discovered."

"But gas . . . it could kill them all."

"They're all dead right now," Lee snapped. "Those artifacts are the only possible clue to their early history."

Rassmussen decided. "We'll do it."

Lee slept less than ever the next few nights, and when he did he dreamed, but no longer about the buildings on Titan. Now he dreamed of the ships of an ancient Earth, huge round ships that spat fire on the cities and people of Makta. He dreamed of the Pup exploding and showering the planet with fire, blowing off the atmosphere, boiling the oceans, turning mountains into glass slag, killing every living thing on the surface of the world, leaving the planet bathed in a steam cloud, its ground ruptured with angry new volcanoes.

It was a rainy dark night when you could hardly see ten meters beyond the cave's mouth that they came. Lee heard their voices in his head as they drove the skimmer up onto the beach and clambered down from it and headed for the caves. Inside the caves, the people were asleep, sprawled innocently on the damp musty ground.

Out of the rain a huge, bulky metal shape materialized, walking with exaggerated caution.

"Hello, Sid," Jerry Grote's voice said in his head, and the white metal shape raised a hand in greeting.

The Others, Lee thought as he watched four more powersuited figures appear in the dark rain.

He stepped out of the cave, the rain a cold shock to his body. "Bring the stuff?"

Grote hitched a gauntleted thumb at one of the others. "Pascual's got it. He's insisting on administering the gas himself."

"Okay, but let's get it done quickly, before somebody wakes up and spots you. Who else is with you?"

"Chien, Tanaka, and Stek. Tanaka can help Carlos with the anesthetic. Chien and Stek can look over the artifacts."

Lee nodded agreement.

Pascual and Tanaka spent more than an hour seeping the mildest soporific they knew of through the sleeping cave. Lee fidgeted outside on the beach, in the rain, waiting for them to finish. When Tanaka finally told them it was safe to go through, he hurried past the sprawled bodies, scarcely seeing Pascual —still inside his cumbersome suit—patiently recording medical analyses of each individual.

Even with the suit lamps to light the corridors, it was hard to retrace his steps down to the lowest level of the ancient shelter. But when he got to the storeroom, Lee heard Stek break into a long string of Polish exultation at the sight of the artifacts.

The three suited figures holographed, X-rayed, took radiation counts, measured, weighed, every piece on the ancient shelves. They touched nothing directly, but lifted each piece with loving tenderness in a portable magnetic grapple.

"This one," Stek told Lee, holding a hand-sized, oddly angular instrument in midair with the grapple, "we must take with us."

"Why?"

"Look at it," the physicist said. "If it's not an astronautical sextant or something close to it, I'll eat Charnovsky's rocks for a month."

The instrument didn't look impressive to Lee. It had a lens at one end, a few dials at the other. Most of it was just an angular metal box, with strange printing on it.

"You want to know where these people originally came from?" Stek asked. "If they came from somewhere other than this planet, the information could be inside this instrument."

Lee snapped his gaze from the instrument to Stek's helmeted face.

"If it is a sextant, it must have a reference frame built into it. A tape, perhaps, that lists the stars that these people wanted to go to."

"Okay," Lee said. "Take it."

By the time they got back up to the main sleeping cave and out to the beach again, it was full daylight.

"We'll have to keep them sleeping until almost dawn tomorrow," Lee told Pascual. "Otherwise they might suspect that something unusual's happened."

The doctor's face looked concerned but not worried. "We can do that without harming them, I think. But Sid, they'll be very hungry when they awake."

Lee turned to Grote. "How about taking the skimmer out and stunning a couple of big fish and towing them back here to the shallows?"

Grinning, Grote replied, "Hardly fair sport with the equipment I've got." He turned and headed for the car.

"Wait," Stek called to him. "Give me a chance to get this safely packed in a magnetic casing." And the physicist took the instrument off toward the skimmer.

"Sid," Pascual said gently, "I want you to come back with us. You need a thorough medical check."

"Medical?" Lee flashed. "Or are you fronting for Lehman?"

Pascual's eyes widened with surprise. "If you had a mirror, you would see why I want to check you. You're breaking out in skin cancers."

Instinctively, Lee looked at his hands and forearms. There were a few tiny blisters on them. And more on his belly and legs.

"It's from overexposure to the ultraviolet. Hatfield's skin-darkening didn't fully protect you."

"Is it serious?"

"I can't tell without a full examination."

Just like a doctor. "I can't leave now," Lee said. "I've got to be here when they wake up and make sure that they don't suspect they've been visited by the . . . by us."

"And if they do suspect?"

Lee shrugged. "That's something we ought to know, even if we can't do anything about it."

"Won't it be dangerous for you?"

"Maybe."

Pascual shook his head. "You mustn't stay out in the open any longer. I won't be responsible for it."

"Fine. Do you want me to sign a release form?"

Grote brought the skimmer back around sundown, with two good-sized fish aboard. The others got aboard around midnight, and with a few final radioed words of parting, they drove off the beach and out to sea.

At dawn the people woke up. They looked and acted completely normal, as far as Lee could tell. It was one of the children who noticed the still-sluggish fish that Grote had left in a shallow pool just outside the line of breakers. Every man in the clan splashed out, spear in hand, to get them. They feasted happily that day.

The dream was confusing. Somehow the towers on Titan and the exploding star got mixed together. Lee saw himself driving a bone spear into the sleeping form of one of the natives. The man turned on the ground, with the spear run through his body, and smiled bloodily at him. It was Ardraka.

"Sid!"

He snapped awake. It was dark, and the people were sleeping, full-bellied. He was slouched near one of the entryways to the main sleeping cave, at the mouth of a tunnel leading to the openings in the cliff wall.

"Sid, can you hear me?"

"Yes," he whispered so low that he could only feel the vibration in his throat.

"I'm up the beach about three kilometers from the relay unit. You've got to come back to the ship. Stek thinks he's figured out the instrument."

Wordlessly, silently, Lee got up and padded through the tunnel and out onto the beach. The night was clear and bright. Dawn would be coming in another hour, he judged. The sea was calm, the wind a gentle crooning as it swept down from the cliffs.

"Sid, did you hear what I said? Stek thinks he knows what the instrument is for. It's part of a pointing system for a communications setup."

"I'm on my way." He still whispered and turned to see if anyone was following him.

Grote was in a biosuit, and no one else was aboard the skimmer. The engineer jabbered about Stek's work on the instrument all the way back to the ship.

Just before they arrived, Grote suggested, "Uh, Sid, you do want to put on some coveralls, don't you?"

*   *   *

Two biosuited men were setting up some electronics equipment at the base of the ship's largest telescope, dangling in a hoist sling overhead, the fierce glow of Sirius glinting off its metal barrel.

"Stek's setting up an experiment," Grote explained.

Lee was bundled into a biosuit and ushered into the physicist's workroom as soon as he set foot inside the ship. Stek was a large, round, florid man with thinning red hair. Lee had hardly spoken to him at all, except for the few hours at the cave, when the physicist had been encased in a powersuit.

"It's a tracker, built to find a star in the sky and lock onto it as long as it's above the horizon," Stek said, gesturing to the instrument hovering in a magnetic grapple a few inches above his work table.

"You're sure of that?" Lee asked.

The physicist glanced at him as though he had been insulted. "There's no doubt about it. It's a tracker, and it probably was used to aim a communications antenna at their home star."

"And where is that?"

"I don't know yet. That's why I'm setting up the experiment with the telescope."

Lee walked over to the work table and stared at the instrument. "How can you be certain that it's what you say it is?"

Stek flushed, then controlled himself. With obvious patience, he explained, "X-ray probes showed that the instrument contained a magnetic memory tape. The tape was in binary code, and it was fairly simple to transliterate the code, electronically, into the ship's main computers. We didn't even have to touch the instrument physically . . . except with photons."

Lee made an expression that showed he was duly impressed.

Looking happier, Stek went on, "The computer cross-checked the instrument's coding and came up with correlations: altitude references were on the instrument's tape, and astronomical ephemerides, timing data, and so forth. Exactly what we'd put into a communications tracker."

"But this was made by a different race of people—"

"It makes no difference," Stek said sharply. "The physics are the same. The universe is the same. The instrument can only do the job it was designed to do, and that job was to track a single star."

"Only one star?"

"Yes, that's why I'm certain it was for communicating with their home star."

"So we can find their home star after all." Lee felt the old dread returning, but with it something new, something deeper. *Those people in the caves were our enemy. And maybe their brothers, the ones who built the machines on Titan, are still out there somewhere looking for them—and for us.*

XI

Lee ate back at the Sirius globe, but Pascual insisted on his remaining in a biosuit until they had thoroughly checked him out. And they wouldn't let him eat Earth food, although there was as much local food as he wanted. He didn't want much.

"You've thinned out too much," Marlene said. She was sitting next to him at the galley table.

"Ever see a fat Sirian?" He meant it as a joke; it came out waspish. Marlene dropped the subject.

The whole ship's company gathered around the telescope and the viewscreen that would show an amplified picture of the telescope's field of view. Stek bustled around, making last-minute checks and adjustments of the equipment. Rassmussen stood taller than everyone else, looking alternately worried and excited. Everyone, including Lee, was in a biosuit.

Lehman showed up at Lee's elbow. "Do you think it will work?"

"Driving the telescope from the ship's computer's version of the instrument's tape? Stek seems to think it'll go all right."

"And you?"

Lee shrugged. "The people in the caves told me what I wanted to know. Now this instrument will tell us where they came from originally."

"The home world of our ancient enemies?"

"Yes."

For once, Lehman didn't seem to be amused. "And what happens then?"

"I don't know," Lee said. "Maybe we go out and see if they are still there. Maybe we reopen the war."

"If there was a war."

"There was. It might still be going on, for all we know. Maybe we're just a small part of it, a skirmish."

"A skirmish that wiped out the life on this planet," Lehman said.

"And almost wiped out Earth, too."

"But what about the people on this planet, Sid? What about the people in the caves?"

Lee couldn't answer.

"Do we let them die out, just because they might have been our enemies a few millennia ago?"

"They would still be our enemies if they knew who we are," Lee said tightly.

"So we let them die?"

Lee tried to blot their faces out of his mind, to erase the memory of Ardraka and the children, and Ardra apologizing shamefully and the people fishing in the morning . . .

"No," he heard himself say. "We've got to help them. They can't hurt us anymore, and we ought to help them."

Now Lehman smiled.

"It's ready," Stek said, his voice pitched high with excitement.

Sitting at the desk-sized console that stood beside the telescope, he thumbed the power switch and punched a series of buttons.

The viewscreen atop the desk glowed into life, and a swarm of stars appeared. With a low hum of power, the telescope turned slowly to the left. The scene in the viewscreen shifted. Beside the screen was a smaller display, an astronomical map with a bright luminous dot showing where the telescope was aiming.

The telescope stopped turning, hesitated, edged slightly more to the left, and then made a final, barely discernible correction upward.

"It's locked on."

The viewscreen showed a meager field of stars, with a single bright pinpoint centered exactly in the middle of the screen.

"What is it, what star?"

Lee pushed forward, through the crowd that clustered around the console.

"My God," Stek said, his voice sounding hollow. "That's . . . the sun."

Lee felt his knees wobble. "They're from Earth!"

"It can't be," someone said.

Lee shoved past the people in front of him and stared at the map. The bright dot was fixed on the sun's location.

"They're from Earth!" he shouted. "They're part of us!"

"But how could . . ."

"They were a colony of *ours*," Lee realized. "The Others were an enemy . . . an enemy that nearly wiped them out and smashed Earth's civilization back into a stone age. The Others built those damned machines on Titan, but Ardraka's people did not. And we didn't destroy the people here . . . we're the same people!"

"But that's—"

"How can you be sure?"

"He is right," Charnovsky said, his heavy bass rumbling above the other voices. They all stopped to hear him. "There are too many coincidences any other way. These people are completely human because they came from Earth. Any other explanation is extraneous."

Lee grabbed the Russian by the shoulders. "Nick, we've got work to do! We've got to help them. We've got to introduce them to fire and metals and cereal grains—"

Charnovsky laughed. "Yes, yes, of course. But not tonight, eh? Tonight we celebrate."

"No," Lee said, realizing where he belonged. "Tonight I go back to them."

"Go back?" Marlene asked.

"Tonight I go back with a gift," Lee went on. "A gift from my people to Ardraka's. A plastic boat from the skimmer. That's a gift they'll be able to understand and use."

Lehman said, "You still don't know who built the machinery on Titan."

"We'll find out one of these days."

Rassmussen broke in, "You realize that we will have to return Earthward before the next expedition could possibly get anywhere near here."

"Some of us can wait here for the next expedition. I will, anyway."

The captain nodded and a slow grin spread across his face. "I knew you would even before we found out that your friends are really our brothers."

Lee looked around for Grote. "Come on, Jerry. Let's get moving. I want to see Ardraka's face when he sees the boat."

Symbolism in Science Fiction

This is one of the pieces I write occasionally for *The Writer* magazine. It is also an example of the frustrations of working for magazine editors.

When I edited *Analog* and, later, *Omni*, I made it my policy to buy only what I wanted to print—and then to print what I had bought. I did not believe it to be the editor's job, or right, to mangle the author's prose. If I wanted changes made in a manuscript, I asked the author to make them. It's up to the author to decide if he or she wants to rewrite to suit editorial whim, or take the manuscript to another market.

Maybe it was just laziness on my part. I didn't want to rewrite pieces before publishing them. Maybe it was because I am fundamentally a writer, and I resent having editors muck up my prose—especially after they have bought the piece and I no longer have any control over what they are doing to it.

The editorial changes made in "Symbolism in Science Fiction" were not serious. It is unfair, really, for me to complain about them here. But since this was originally written for writers, especially new writers, perhaps this is the best place to post the warning: Beware of editors editing!

Having posted that notice, I now invite you to read what

I had to say about the uses of symbolism in science fiction.

Nobody writes about the future.

Even in the farthest-out science fiction stories, set millions of years from now on weird exotic alien planets, the science fiction writer is really writing about the world and people of today. The far-future settings, the alien creatures and strange worlds are all *symbols* that replace everyday realities with fantastic inventions.

One of the great strengths of science fiction is to combine symbolism with extrapolative power, thereby producing the ability to examine the world of today by creating a set of symbols that sketch out a future world which is a reflection of here-and-now. Such stories usually are based on a simple question: "If this goes on . . . how will it change the world and the people in it?" The writer takes a trend from today's world—transplant surgery, for example —and exaggerates the situation, stretches it as far as the imagination can reach, then builds a story around that extrapolated society. In this manner, science fiction can produce powerful social commentary. Jonathan Swift, George Orwell, Jules Verne, H. G. Wells, Robert A. Heinlein, Ray Bradbury, and many other writers have held up mirrors to their own societies by writing incisive stories based on that question, "If this goes on . . . then what?"

In such stories the setting, the background, the gadgetry, even the characters themselves, become symbols that stand for the things and people of today's world. For example, Swift's *Gulliver's Travels* is a savage satire of the English society in which he lived. Knowing that a direct attack on his "betters" would get him thrown in prison, or worse, Swift created a series of fantasy worlds in which he could lampoon the people and social customs he saw all around him—while keeping his neck from the chopping block.

Many Russian science fiction writers use that tactic today. It is not healthy to criticize the government in Moscow, or the "progressive" society of the Soviet Union. But a story set on the planet Mars, a hundred years in the future, can satirize government red tape and bungling with virtual impunity. Mars (the Red Planet, you know) becomes a thinly veiled symbol for the USSR. Even though the Soviet authorities see through the disguise, they usually leave the writer in peace.

"The government keeps one eye closed," a Russian writer told me. Even in a society as tightly controlled as the Soviets', there have to be some ways to let off steam, to ease the pressures of oppression; in its way, science fiction serves that purpose in Russia.

It has served similar purposes here. In the McCarthy era, where almost any criticism of American society was pounced upon as evidence of communist subversion, science fiction writers were among the few who fought back. Ray Bradbury's *Fahrenheit 451* was a powerful warning that witch-hunting and book-burning destroy not only freedom and democracy, but the human spirit as well.

By creating future worlds and scenarios, science fiction writers can also reaffirm the values of today's society in ways that ordinary fiction cannot. Much of Robert A. Heinlein's work throughout the 1950s and well into the 1960s, for example, was nothing less than an affirmation of the traditional American values of individual freedom over the threatening dangers of foreign invasion, collectivism, and oppression. The true villains of *The Puppet Masters* are not alien invaders from a moon of Saturn, but the hostile hordes of Russian and Chinese communists whom many Americans saw as a threat to the United States in the 1950s.

But not all of science fiction has a political slant to it, nor are all science fiction stories written specifically to be social commentary. Certainly the field has its share of sheer adventure tales, out-and-out "space operas" that make no pretense of social importance.

Yet, if we look deeper into such stories, we see that even here, symbolism is at work on every page. The symbols are no longer politically inspired. Nor are they symbols in the psychological sense, necessarily, where objects or characters represent hidden thoughts from the writer's subconscious mind. Certainly the psychological symbolism is present; no human being can create a work of fiction without the subtle guidance of the subconscious, and such psychosymbolism is sure to leave an imprint that a trained observer can detect. But the symbolism that is specific to science fiction is of a more conscious, rational, deliberate type.

Take a look at a space opera—even one as shallow as the motion picture *Star Wars*. Inevitably, such stories deal with a young man leaving his home and parents (often they are adoptive parents) to seek his way in the large world beyond the limits of his youthful environment. Frequently the young man is actually a prince, or some other potentially powerful figure, yet does not know it. The story becomes, then, a tale of his discovery of himself and his own abilities. This is an old, old tale: the voyage of self-discovery, the fictional (or mythological) treatment of the transition from adolescence into adulthood. Every culture on Earth has such tales. They tell the youngsters two things: one, that the turmoil of adolescence happens to everyone; and two, that at the end of the turmoil lies the new world of the successful adult.

In recent years science fiction and its companion field of fantasy have seen the growth of tales of young women's transition from adolescence into adulthood. Written mainly by women, this trend reflects the growing power of the women's movement in modern society.

While the underlying psychological symbols of such tales are very much the same, whether they are science fictional space operas or the mystical spirit-haunted ordeals of a primitive tribe, in science fiction the trimmings and trappings of the tale deal quite consciously with modern technological society. Spaceships replace spirit-voyages. Laser guns replace magic amulets. And the hero's challenge usually requires him to learn how to use science and high technology for the purposes of good, against an enemy who would use such knowledge for the purposes of evil. In the less technological and more fantasy-oriented women's stories, dragons, unicorns, and even bloody swordplay are very much in evidence. But often they are "explained" in terms of the physical, biological, or social sciences.

Vonda N. McIntyre's novel *Dreamsnake*, for instance, utilizes biochemistry and anthropology where a typical space opera would use astrophysics and electronic engineering.

One of the major reasons for the tremendous popularity of science fiction among teenagers is that it speaks powerfully to the young reader in terms that today's adolescents instinctively react to, mainly because the symbols it uses are symbols that the teenagers recognize and respond to, even though the recognition may be unconscious. Science fiction is not the "escapist" literature that some critics believe it to be, a genre which allows the reader to forget about the trials and troubles of today's world. Just the opposite. Science fiction examines today's world much more closely than any other form of fiction. Only those critics who fail to understand that the settings and gadgetry in science fiction are symbols of today's reality see the field as "escapist."

It's powerful stuff, symbolism. Like a whisper that can be heard only inside one's own mind, it speaks directly to the reader. It cuts through the visible lines of the story and evokes an unconscious, emotional response deep inside the reader's psyche.

To write science fiction (or any fiction) effectively, the writer must be aware of the symbolic: how to create it, how to recognize it, how to use it.

Symbolism need not be so subtle that only a trained analyst can spot it. In Frank Herbert's classic *Dune*, it is obvious to even the most casual reader that Paul Atreides symbolizes all the messiahs that human societies have longed for since the beginning of time. As he metamorphoses into the godlike Maud'Dib, he transforms the society around him. Herbert is clearly telling us the message of the messiah, that the only way to save the world is to change it, that we cannot become godlike without the pains and turmoils of basic, wrenching change. The planet Arrakis, the desert world called Dune, becomes a world-sized symbol of change; by altering it from a wasteland to a new Eden—a change that we instinctively feel is good and beneficial—Maud'Dib destroys the society and the people that we have come to admire.

Symbols can be used in many ways. In my own novel *Colony*, the very idea of a huge, man-made habitat floating in space equidistant between the Earth and the Moon became a symbol of the vast gulf between the extremely rich and the desperately poor. The symbolism was quite conscious and deliberate.

Hanging there in space, built by a consortium of the wealthiest multinational corporations on Earth, the space colony is so far away from our world that only the very richest people can afford to go to it. In fact, it was built by the leaders of the powerful corporations specifically to be a haven for themselves and their families, a place where they can live in comfort, safety, even splendor—without being threatened by the masses of billions of unruly poor people on Earth.

The space colony becomes a symbol within a symbol, because terrorists—who claim to be fighting to help the poor people—decide to destroy the colony as a symbolic act of their hostility to the very rich and all their privileges.

Another form of symbolism runs through *Colony*. The hero of the novel is a "perfect man," a genetically engineered test-tube baby who has never been on Earth. Born in the space colony, he has never left its comforts. Physically as strong and healthy as it is possible for a human being to be, David Adams carries within his head a miniature implanted electronic communications device which puts him in direct contact with the colony's computerized library. In other words, here we have an Adam in Eden, physically perfect and secure, possessed of all the knowledge he wants.

Except for knowledge of Earth. Naturally he leaves the colony, escapes to Earth, and learns of how the rest of humankind lives.

Like the space colony itself, David Adams is a symbol of the best that modern science can achieve. The colony, though, because it is a lifeless structure of metals and minerals, symbolizes what technology can achieve. David, a living example of human perfection, symbolizes what *we* must be if we are to use our technology for the betterment of the human condition.

In a more recent novel of mine, *Test of Fire*, a slightly different form of symbolism showed itself. In this story, much of the Earth has been destroyed by a gigantic solar flare which set the sunlit half of our world afire. While civilization on Earth has sunk to almost a medieval level, the small human outpost on the Moon was virtually untouched by the solar flare, because it was dug deep underground. The lunar outpost is *almost* self-sufficient; not quite, it still needs certain critical supplies from Earth. And the pitiful remains of civilization on Earth need the technology and scientific knowledge of the lunar pioneers.

The novel deals with this dichotomy and its resolution. But there is a powerful message in this novel, one that I did not really recognize until the book was nearly finished. Underlying the obvious point that humankind needs both the natural environment of Earth and the technological knowledge of science in order to survive, is a deeper point: once the human race has established self-sufficient colonies in space, then the continued survival of humankind no longer depends on what we do on Earth.

Many life forms have appeared on Earth, lived their allotted eons, and then perished into extinction. We human beings now have the power to destroy ourselves with nuclear war or ecological catastrophe. The Sun might one day explode, or some other natural calamity could wipe the Earth clean of human life. But if we have established self-sufficient colonies elsewhere in space, the human race will endure. That is the ultimate justification for space exploration. By expanding into space, humankind can escape the fate of the dinosaurs. A race that has space flight has racial immortality.

Those are powerful ideas. To deal with them directly, in an essay or some other nonfiction form, is less satisfying than dealing with them in fiction—mainly because fiction allows (requires!) the writer to employ the human dimension. In fiction it is not enough merely to expostulate upon the ideas; the writer must show how these concepts affect human beings, how human lives are altered for the better or the worse.

To do this, the writer must employ symbolism. Just as the markings we call an alphabet are actually code symbols for sounds of language, the symbols within a story form a code that speaks directly to the human heart. Without symbolism, fiction is lifeless. With the special richness of symbolism that science fiction allows, the complex and sometimes frightening world of today can be examined and understood by studying it in the mirror world of the future.